# DENIED

EVELYN FLOOD

**Denied**

**Evelyn Flood**

First published by Evelyn Flood in 2023

ASIN B0BJBZ4FCN
Copyright 2023 by Evelyn Flood
All rights reserved. This book or any portion thereof may not be reproduced or used in any manner whatsoever without the express written permission of the publisher, except for the use of brief quotations in a book review.
Formatting by Diana TC@ TriumphBookCovers
Cover by Penn Cassidy @ PC Designs

TRIGGER WARNING

This book includes references of physical harm, forced medication and severe neglect/heat trauma.

# ABOUT THIS BOOK

This book is an **omegaverse**. That means that the characters have some of the characteristics often seen in wolves, but they **do not shift.**

## IN LOVING DEDICATION

This one is for my little bean, and his uncanny knack of converting mom's book sales into Fortnite money.

# 1
# SIENNA

"It's here! Sienna!"

My best friend looks up at me sharply. The nail polish she's been using to paint my toes a bright silver dangles precariously from her fingers, threatening to tip over my cream rug.

"Jessalyn!" I make a grab for it, but she pulls away, waving me off with her eyes wide.

"You don't think...," she breathes. "The Hub?"

Excitement unfurls in my belly as my mother bursts in through my bedroom door, waving a gold, official-looking envelope in her hands. Jessalyn squeals, abandoning my half-painted toenails to dance around the room.

"*Sienna Michaels*! Didn't you hear me calling you?"

Helena Michaels is a beautiful woman. My father likes to say that she's the most beautiful omega in Navarre, and it's hard to disagree, even if he is blinded by his Soul Bond. But despite her infamous beauty, my mother's voice can hit levels only heard by dogs when she's pissed... like now.

She plants her hands on her hips, glancing between me and Jessalyn with a frown. "It's rude to ignore your mother, Sienna."

"Sorry, mama." Jumping up, I plant a kiss on her cheek in

apology, seizing the opportunity to snag the golden envelope. Turning it over, my chest tightens at the sight of the familiar Omega Hub emblem etched into the thick card, the 'O' split open by a curved line on either side at the bottom.

"Holy shit," I wheeze. Jessalyn crows as my mother lights up all over again.

"Language, Sienna! If Ollena heard you, that invite would disappear faster than I could snap my fingers." My mother sniffs indignantly.

"Sorry," I mutter again, still turning the envelope over. Nerves start to twist in my stomach.

I've been waiting for this envelope for years. Well, it feels like years, although I only reached my majority three months ago. Omegas aren't eligible for the Bonding Trials until they turn eighteen.

Right on cue, my mother sniffles, daintily whipping out a handkerchief from her elegant blue dress and dabbing at her cheeks. "I'm sorry," she hiccups, when Jess and I turn to her. "You're just growing up too quickly, Sienna."

Not quickly enough.

"You still have Elise, Mama," I say, and she nods, although her face crumples a little as she comes to sit next to me on the bed. Her arm wraps around my shoulders, a familiar support, and I lean into her embrace.

"You will be perfect," she whispers to me. "I know it, sweetheart. I'm so proud of you."

My throat closes up as I blink back unexpected tears.

*Everything is going to change now.*

The Bonding Trials are the culmination of everything we omegas work towards. All of us are sent to the Omega Hub for tutoring as soon as we reach thirteen. We're taught every possible skill that an omega might need in her arsenal to please her future pack. When we've been assessed as suitable, we're matched to packs through the Trials.

I speak four languages, know every possible form of etiquette there is, can identify every type of fork in existence from a good ten meters away. My painting is passable, and my music speaks for itself. Plus, my nesting skills are on *point*.

I'm *ready* for this.

Even if the idea of standing up in front of dozens of the most important people in Navarre to pledge myself to a group of unknown alphas is making me break out in hives.

Taking a deep breath, I slide my finger under the envelope, lifting the flap and pulling out a letter written on thick, cream paper. Jessalyn settles on my other side, my mother and best friend peering over my shoulder as I scan the flowery script.

"Read it aloud," Mama urges, and I clear my throat.

> *Dear Sienna,*
>
> *Congratulations! I am delighted to offer you the opportunity to participate in the Bonding Trials.*
>
> *You have been matched with the Cohen pack.*
>
> *In order to be accepted as a pack omega, you must progress through the four stages of the Bonding Trials and win the formal approval of your alpha pack.*
>
> *1. Scent marking*
>
> *2. Nesting*
>
> *3. Heats*
>
> *4. Mating ceremony*
>
> *Please note that alpha packs can decide to end the process at any time, and you will be able to repeat the process with a different pack. If a Trial is failed, you will be removed from the Bonding Trials effective immediately, and unable to participate in future Trials.*
>
> *In exceptional circumstances, a pack may decide to Deny an omega.*
>
> *This means that you will no longer be permitted to come into contact with alpha packs. You will be stripped of your omega status and must leave the city to live amongst the beta population.*

*Please be reassured that no omega has been Denied in the history of the Omega Hub.*

*We're delighted to welcome you to the Bonding Trials and wish you the best of luck with your mating process.*

*Kind regards,*
*Ollena Hayward*
*Head of the Omega Hub*

My voice trails off, and we all sit for a moment. My head feels a little dizzy.

"It's happening," Jessalyn whispers. "Sienna! And it's the Cohen pack!"

My mama and I both turn to her. My head feels too slow to keep up with her excitement.

"The Cohen pack?" I push out through the lump in my throat.

Jessalyn squeals. "I *said* you needed to keep up more! The Cohen pack is *the* pack. Jax Cohen is this seriously hot singer, and Tristan Cohen is going to be the next Council leader!"

She hugs me. "I'm so happy for you, bitch face," she mumbles into my shoulder. Her voice shakes a little as I hug her back.

"I'm not going anywhere," I reassure her.

"You're going to be the mate of the next Council leader," Mama repeats numbly. "Oh, Sienna."

I chew on my lip, but don't bother pointing out that I'm likely to be absolutely terrible at being a Council leader's mate. I'm not exactly the best at managing social situations.

"What if they're your Soul Bonded?" Mama gasps, her hands to her chest. My heart jumps a little, but reality soon steps in.

"I doubt it," I remind her gently. "Once in a lifetime, remember? You and Dad were lucky to find each other."

Soul Bonded. That incredibly rare moment of connection, of meeting the eyes of an alpha – or *alphas* – and just… knowing. That you're meant to be theirs. The way my parents describe it, the heavens open up and the angels sing. But we have to take their word for it, since my parents have been the only Soul Bonded pairing to appear in Navarre in more than a hundred years.

There's not much point in waiting around for something none of us are guaranteed.

Clearing my throat, I turn back to Jess. "So, tell me about my future mates," I tease her. "Who else is in the Cohen pack?"

Jessalyn shakes her wild bronze curls away from her shoulders, holding up her fingers in the air. "We covered Jax and Tristan. Then you have Logan. He's an amazing artist. His paintings and sculptures are incredible – he has a gallery in the Artist's Quarter. Then there's Gray Cohen. He's an architect. He designed the Opera House when he was fourteen!"

A bottomless pit of inadequacy opens up in my chest.

She flops back dramatically on the bed. "You lucky bitch," she breathes. "They're all super-hot, Si."

My mother yelps as I tug her back and we all sprawl out on the bed. "Looks aren't everything, Jessalyn," she says primly. I turn my head to her.

"They don't hurt, though, right?"

"Well… no." My staid mother actually giggles. "Certainly not."

I can't help but join in her laughter, a heaviness lifting from my shoulders as the worry I've been carrying around for weeks evaporates.

*The Cohen Pack.*
*Sienna Cohen.*

I'm on the verge of pulling out a notepad to practice my future signature when my little sister bursts through my bedroom door.

"Sienna!" Elise gasps, her blonde hair dancing around her face. "Is it true?"

I sit up, opening my arms, and she dives into them as I drop my head to breathe in her soft, flowery scent. "I don't want you to leave," she mumbles. Stroking her hair, I lift up her face to look into her blue eyes, the exact mirror of my own.

"I'll still be around, 'Lise. And it means you get to have my room."

She shakes her head stubbornly. "Don't care."

"Now, Elise," Mama scolds. "Be happy for your sister. It'll be your turn soon enough, miss."

Elise retches dramatically into my stomach. "Eurgh. No, thank you."

A grin tugs at the edges of my lips. All we have to get through is the Bonding Trials, and they're only a formality, a stupid process set up by the Council when Navarre first separated from the mainland more than a hundred years ago. I've been preparing for *years*.

What could possibly go wrong?

2

# TRISTAN

"Out of the question. To bring down the wall would be to destroy more than a century of building Navarre to the crowning jewel that it is today. It would be heresy."

I fail to muffle my yawn, and Council Justice Milo swings to me, his finger pointing accusingly.

"Sacrilege," he hisses. "How easily you dismiss our long and prosperous history, Tristan!"

My father sighs, pinching the bridge of his nose as he closes his eyes. "Milo, please. We're not dismissing anything. We are merely presenting the opportunities that may come from opening a relationship between Navarre and Herrith."

Milo postures, throwing up his hands. "Have you forgotten the reason the wall was built in the first place, David? To protect us. We were significantly outnumbered against the beta population. To bring down the wall that keeps our people safe is nothing but foolishness."

"It kept us safe a century ago, Justice. Now, it only holds us back."

My father turns to me as Milo's face suffuses with color, his cheeks darkening. "You are not part of this Council, Tristan," he reminds me, his voice gentle but firm. "Not yet."

Milo sniffs. "Your boy needs to learn his place, David."

Dad's voice is calm, but the thread of steel underpinning his words is unmistakable. "Tristan is more than aware of his place, Milo. That is why he is here, observing this Council session." He emphasizes his final words, his eyes landing on me as I nod. The ball of frustration in my gut simmers as the Council members continue to argue, my fists clenching as I bite back from opening my mouth.

One day. One day I'll be able to make a real difference.

As the Council session concludes, Justice Milo sweeps past me with a huff. Health Elio winks at me as he follows, the other Councilors trailing behind. Ollena Hayward, leader of the Omega Hub and omega representative on the Council, stops when she passes my chair.

Impeccably dressed, the older omega still retains an air of elegance as she draws an envelope from the folds of her silver dress. My mouth goes dry at the unmistakable gold shimmer, and her mouth tips up as she hands me the envelope.

"Congratulations, Mr. Cohen," Ollena says, her green eyes sweeping over me. Her expression remains carefully blank, the omega leader always careful to keep her true thoughts well away from her face.

"I look forward to seeing you and your pack at your Bonding ceremony."

My hand reaches out, my fingers trembling slightly as I take the envelope. "Thank you."

Clutching the envelope, I stare down at it, debating whether or not to rip it open right now. The urge to know, to see the name of my mate for the first time, is nearly overwhelming.

But my pack will kill me if I open it without them.

Sighing, I slide the envelope carefully into my briefcase. A shadow casts across the counter, and my shoulders stiffen as an oily voice drawls.

"Congratulations, boy."

"Councilor Erikkson," I acknowledge, not bothering to thank him. Condescension is clear in his tone, the beta representative's disdain for the alpha and omega mating process well known.

"I admired your position today," he comments, and I keep my face blank, hiding my surprise.

"I only propose what I think would be best for our people."

"Of course, of course. From my own position, naturally, I would support any movement that creates a stronger relationship with the beta population."

I barely hold back my snort. Of course, Erikkson would support anything that improved his own position. Whilst I'm all for self-advancement, something about the man just irritates my instincts. His daughter's just as bad.

"I'll keep that in mind." Snapping my briefcase shut, I offer him a perfunctory nod as I move to exit the Council chamber. "Good afternoon, Councilor."

His eyes follow me as I leave, retracing my earlier steps throughout the high-ceilinged Council building as I head to my father's office. I've barely rapped my knuckles on the door before he calls out to me.

"Tristan." He waves me to a seat. My father looks tired, dark bags under his eyes and lines etched into his skin that weren't there just a few months ago. He waves away my concern.

"I'm fine," he grumbles. "I want to talk about you."

I straighten my jacket. "I won't apologize for highlighting what they all refuse to see. Navarre needs to bring down the wall, Dad. You know that."

"I do." My dad leans forward. "But tradition is important to them, Tristan. And you overstepped."

"More important than the security of the people they're supposed to serve, apparently."

"It's not that black and white and you know it." He reaches across to grab my hand. "You'll be an excellent Council leader one day, son. Far, far better than I am or could ever hope to be. I have no doubts about that. But you're still learning. Today shows that you still have more to learn about understanding people."

The jab hits home, my head pulling back as though he's thrown a fist. "So I don't have enough empathy? Have you met Milo?"

"Milo is not Council Leader. There is a reason we have different personalities, different views. It allows us to challenge each other, to make sure each decision is carefully weighted, and the pros and cons thought through. You have empathy, but you don't care enough about others' opinions. A Council leader needs more than logic to succeed, Tristan."

My hand runs through my hair. "I hate it when you get all wise on me," I grumble.

He smirks. "Look and learn, kid."

The tension disappearing, at least for the moment, I reach into my briefcase and produce the letter Ollena gave me. Dad whistles as he leans back in his chair. "The Bonding Trials. How are you feeling?"

"Excited," I admit. "You know we've been waiting a long time."

Six years, to be precise. We graduated from the Alpha compound as a fully-fledged pack six years ago, and we've been waiting to be matched to an omega ever since.

My father smiles. "I'm pleased for you. And I'm looking forward to meeting her, whoever she is."

Curiosity tugs me again, and he laughs.

"Get home, Tristan. Saving the world can wait for a day. Go home and enjoy this moment with the pack."

Grinning, I swipe the envelope from the desk and reach out, each of us grabbing the other's wrist.

"I'm proud of you, you know," he murmurs.

"*Dad.*"

"What? It's true. Now get going. And come and see your mother soon before she hunts you down. She's worried you're not eating properly."

My laugh is genuine. "Tell her she doesn't need to worry anymore," I tease. "We'll have our own omega soon."

My dad grins. "If I tell her that, she'll be banging down your door within an hour. I'll let you break the news."

This is true. My mom is a force to be reckoned with on her best day.

My mind is already on the night ahead as I stride through the marble antechamber, heading for the wide doors and home. Someone collides with me with a thud, my briefcase dropping and splitting open as I'm engulfed in a cloud of red hair and sickly-sweet perfume, a poor imitation of an omega's scent.

"Oh, Tristan! I'm so sorry! Are you all right?"

Alicia's overly girlish tones make my eardrums itch on a normal day, but today I've got especially little patience for Councilor Erikkson's daughter.

"My apologies, Alicia," I mutter, trying to grab my scattered paperwork. Alicia gets there first, her fingers immediately closing on the envelope from the Omega Hub. My fingers itch to snatch it back from her bright red, pointed fingernails as she holds it out like it's poisonous, the vapid smile sliding from her face.

"What's this?" she demands. Sighing, I straighten.

"It's our invite to the Bonding Trials, Alicia. We've been matched with an omega." Her green eyes immediately fill with tears, and I fight back a groan.

"Tristan," she whimpers. "You can't do that to us."

My brows draw down in frustration. "There is no us, Alicia," I say pointedly, reaching over and removing the envelope from her grip. "I have told you this over and over again."

*Unless stalking counts as a relationship nowadays.*

She inhales sharply, and I brace myself for a round of dramatics. Instead, she throws her hair back. "We'll see."

I stare at her in disbelief.

"Alicia," I say as gently as I can manage. "I'm sorry that I can't give you what you want. But I'm very happy to be mated. The Trials are just a formality."

She nods vacantly. "I'll see you soon, Tristan."

She stalks off in the direction of her father's office, her stilettos tapping on the floor as I stand there, my mouth agape.

*What just happened?*

# 3
# GRAYSON

My pen taps against the blank page as I grapple desperately for something. Anything.

Just a hint of inspiration.

When nothing magically appears, I snarl, flinging my pen across the room. The door opens just as Logan sticks his head in, his head jerking back as the pen shatters against the wall next to his head.

"Fucking hell, Gray. What's wrong?"

My head hits the desk with a thump. Even the sight of Logan, standing there with his blonde waves deliciously mussed and his shirt loose and unbuttoned doesn't pull me out of my funk. He circles the desk, his fingers digging into my neck, working out the knots until I groan and tilt my head back against his stomach.

His chestnut eyes blink down at me. "Better?"

"Much," I admit. "Thank you."

My hand closes over his as I draw him around, encasing him between my thighs as my hand slides around to his ass. A low growl rumbles through my chest as he leans into me.

"Now this," I murmur, "feels like a much better use of my time."

He sighs, his hands finding their way into my hair and

pushing back the red strands dangling over my face. "Same, since I'm having precisely zero luck in creating anything new for the gallery."

"You too?" I ask. There's just a hint of relief that I'm not the only one trying to take from an empty pot, entwined with a large dose of guilt.

He nods unhappily, leaning down to rest his forehead against mine. Our breaths mingle together, both of us enjoying the moment. "I need a muse," he blurts. Amusement turns up the corners of my mouth, and I wiggle my brows at him.

He snorts. "Not you. I have plenty of paintings of you, and I can't exactly show them. I need something for the new showing, or I'm toast. They won't renew my lease in the Artist's Quarter unless I can prove I deserve to be there."

"You do deserve it," I tell him, and it's true. Logan is a phenomenal artist.

His mouth tightens. "I'm worried I'm dried up, Gray. Maybe this is all I can do, and there's nothing else to show."

"We'll get there, Logan," I tell him as a door slams in the distance. Someone's home. Sighing, I roll my chair back, putting some distance between us. Logan's face drops.

"Gray... maybe we should tell them."

My headshake is firm. "No, Lo. We've talked about this."

Logan's face falls as he turns away. I reach for his hand, but he pulls it back. "Logan."

"Don't," he shoots back. "What, I'm not allowed to have feelings now? I'm not just here for convenience, Gray. I'm not ashamed of us. Why are you?"

A lump appears in my throat. "I'm not ashamed," I whisper. "But you know, Logan. If the Council finds out – if Navarre finds out…"

Homosexuality is non-existent in Navarre. As in, we would be completely ostracized from society if Logan and I ever went public with our relationship. Alphas mate with omegas. Betas with betas. But two alphas, together? My mouth dries at the thought.

"This is bigger than us. The whole pack would be affected."

Logan takes a step towards the door. "We don't know that, Gray. Just because it doesn't happen doesn't mean it never could."

"One day," I insist. "But we need to be more established, Logan. We need to be strong enough to ride out the fallout. When Tristan is Council leader, we'll be in a much better position."

He stops, turning to stare at me. "That could be years," he says softly. "You want me to wait that long?"

My heart twists. "You won't?"

Logan throws up his hands. "I don't know, Gray. But I don't think I can carry on like this, sneaking around in our own home. Maybe we should just tell Tristan and Jax."

I push myself up from my chair, grabbing his hand and drawing him to me as my hands land on either side of his face. "We will," I promise. "We will, Lo. Just not yet. Give me a little more time. Okay?"

His mouth turns down as he tries to pull away, but I hold him firmly, my heart beating wildly against my chest. I can't lose him. Logan is my best friend, my partner.

"I'm sorry," I press, staring into his eyes. "Soon, Lo. I swear it."

Finally, he nods, relief loosening the knot in my chest. We break apart as footsteps thump up the corridor, Tristan poking his head in and looking between us.

"Pack meeting," he demands. "Jax is on his way. I have news."

"What's going on?" Logan asks. He takes another step away from me, and I withdraw behind my desk. Tristan grins, his normally deadpan expression the most carefree I've seen in a long time.

"I'll tell you when he gets here."

# 4
# JAX

Blowing a kiss at the cluster of beta girls outside the club, I smirk as they giggle. My eyes slide over them, lingering on a pretty little brunette who tosses her hair back, her smile a touch nervous. As I open my mouth to call out to her, my cell buzzes in my pocket. Her face falls when I break eye contact to pull it from my jeans, the summons from Tristan making my heart thump. With a wink, I hit the throttle on my bike.

"Maybe next time, sweetness."

The wind runs cool fingers through my hair as I weave in and out of the city traffic. Dozens of beat-up, second-hand vehicles with the odd flashy model thrown in zoom past me, blurring as I increase the speed and lean over my handlebars, my heart racing as I feel the speed gradually ticking up.

*I could ride like this forever.*

The turn-off for our pack house comes up much sooner than I'd like, and I shove back the curling dissatisfaction in my chest as I take the turning, my wheels spinning as I push my bike to the max. Guilt tickles the back of my neck, and I blow out a breath as the mansion comes into view.

*It's not my pack's fault that I feel so fucking restless.*

Day after day of doing the same thing, singing the same songs, playing to the same crowds. Navarre is a small place. There're only so many times you can play before the anticipation becomes a little less, the buzz dropping just a little until your pre-gig high becomes... nothing at all. Just a job.

I hate feeling like that about my music. Restricted. Like I'm playing in a box, and every time I open my mouth, the box squeezes just a little tighter until I'm clawing at the walls, gasping for breath.

Tristan lights up my phone again, and I silence the call, jogging up the steps and pushing open the main door to the marble entrance hall.

*Look at what you've got, Jax. No point pining over things you can't have.*

Tristan calls out from the study. He turns his eyes to me as I wander in, grabbing a glass from the side and helping myself to some of his liquor. He frowns at me, his future Council leaders' hat firmly in place.

"Jax," he says, a frown lining his forehead. "It's a bit early, isn't it?"

Slouching into my chair, I raise the crystal tumbler to him mockingly, squinting at his warped reflection in the glass. His eyes stare back at me disapprovingly, the green and blue combining into one.

"Come on, brother," I grin lazily. "Live a little. Besides, you're the one that called me back here and away from a delightful little beta bit. What's up?"

The disapproval slides from his face, replaced by a hint of excitement that has me sitting up in my seat. Tris is just as jaded – if not more so – than I am.

"Did the Council discuss the wall coming down?" I ask, a thread of hope in my voice.

The fucking wall separating Navarre from the mainland, Herrith. The wall preventing me from being anything more than a pretend star, playing to the same couple of hundred adoring fans until I'm old and gray and my balls shrivel up like dates.

Tristan shakes his head. "Sorry, Jax," he apologizes. "I couldn't get anywhere with it. I tried."

I shrug away my disappointment, looking over to the door. "No harm, no foul. Only a matter of time before you're in the hot seat, right?"

His face tightens, but he nods. "Right."

Logan stalks into the room, closely followed by Gray. They both nod at me before collapsing into chairs, Logan snatching the tumbler and downing half my drink before I can blink.

"Don't," he grouses at me when I open my mouth to complain. "I need it more than you do."

"Still no muse?" Tristan asks, and Logan grunts. "At this point, I'd be happy to paint a basket of fruit. A brick. A fucking flower. The well has well and truly dried the fuck up."

Sympathy fills me. Writing the music isn't my issue. It's the audience that doesn't change.

Tristan turns to Gray next, his eyes sliding over his rumpled suit. "Rough day?"

Gray shrugs. "Looks like all the muses have packed up and fucked off to Herrith. They want a new design for the Council chamber, and they won't even look at the designs I put in for new housing in the sticks."

Gray's been pushing for better quality housing in the beta area of the city for years. It's little more than a slum, the glamor and beauty of Navarre ending abruptly at the city limits where poverty takes over. Wages are low and the beta population barely has enough to scrape by. Tristan's dad has been trying to persuade the Council to implement minimum wages and better conditions for years, but they won't have it. Even the Beta representative, Erikkson, is more concerned about lining his own fucking pockets than the people he's supposed to represent.

Tristan frowns. "Did you show Dad?"

"Yeah. We both know it won't make it past the rest of them, though."

"Why are we here, Tristan?" I interrupt them, done with the

pity party. We sit here most nights moaning about our shitty luck unless I'm out on a gig, so I'm not keen to do the same thing again.

Tristan brightens again, that weird expression coming over his face. He leans down to his leather briefcase, fiddling with the buckle before he brandishes an envelope triumphantly in the air.

"We finally got in," he announces.

I lean closer, the churning in my stomach changing to fucking swoops.

Holy shit.

*Holy shit.*

"Is that…," I breathe. Tristan nods, looking around at us, his fractured eyes glittering.

"We finally got into the Bonding Trials," he laughs. "We're getting a mate!"

We stare at the gold envelope in his hand, the unmistakable seal of the Omega Hub glittering in the low light. "Yes!" I whoop, jumping up and grabbing the letter.

Tristan leans back in his chair, a smirk on his perfect face. "Feeling a little happier now, are we?"

"Fuck, yes." Fuck the betas hanging around the club. Fuck every groupie with wide eyes and wider legs.

I've been waiting for a mate for six years.

An omega. A mate to cherish, to spoil, to love. Someone who'll be ours. Someone to fill the fucking empty gap in my heart.

I spin, turning to Logan and Gray. They're frozen in their seats, Logan's face leeching of color. Gray looks over to him slowly, his mouth opening.

"Why do you look like someone's died?" I demand. "We've been waiting for this!"

Gray nods hesitantly, his eyes still on Logan as I follow his gaze. "Lo?" I ask impatiently. "Come on, brother. This could be the muse you've been waiting for."

My teasing note draws out a smile, even if it does look like he's chewing a wasp. "I'm just shocked," he murmurs. "An omega. After all this time…"

"I'm opening the envelope." I slide my finger underneath and glance up just in time to catch Tristan's look of disappointment before he smooths it away, the political mask dropping into place.

Eyeing it longingly, I hold it out to him as he looks at me, his eyes moving from the envelope to my face.

"Go on," I insist, shaking the envelope at him. "Before I freaking explode."

Tristan's long fingers grip the golden card, barely hesitating as he slides his finger under the flap and lifts it, pulling out a matching gold letter with a curling, calligraphic script.

*For the attention of Alpha Tristan Cohen,*

*Congratulations! I am delighted to inform you that the Cohen pack has been chosen to participate in the Bonding Trials.*

*You have been matched with Sienna Michaels.*

*Your omega must progress through the four stages of the Bonding Trials and win the formal approval of your alpha pack in order for the final mating ceremony to take place. Further information on these trials is enclosed with this letter.*

*Scent marking*

*Nesting*

*Heats*

*Mating ceremony*

*During the trials, your pack is responsible for the safety and wellbeing of your omega match. This will be assessed by the Head of the Omega Hub, and should the omega be deemed 'at risk' at any time, they will be given an opportunity to withdraw from the Trials.*

*Please note that alpha packs can decide to end the process at any time, and the omega will be able to repeat the process in future with a different pack. If a Trial is failed, the omega will be removed from the Bonding Trials effective immediately, and unable to participate in future Trials.*

*In exceptional circumstances, a pack may decide to Deny an omega at the conclusion of the Bonding Trials.*

*Denial should only be considered in extreme circumstances. Should an omega be Denied, they will no longer be permitted to come into contact with alpha packs. They will be banished from Navarre and must cross the wall into Herrith. All contact with Navarre will be banned.*

*Please note that no omega has been Denied in the history of the Omega Hub.*

*We're delighted to welcome you to the Bonding Trials and wish you the best of luck with your mating process.*

*Kind regards,*
*Ollena Hayward*
*Head of the Omega Hub*

Tristan falls back into his seat, the letter held tightly in his hand. "Fucking finally."

This is everything we've talked about. Excitement tingles in my spine.

*Sienna Michaels.*

"I wonder what she's like?" Tristan muses, running his hand through his hair.

Logan glances between us, a tic in his jaw. "Sienna Michaels? Is she related to Helena Michaels?"

My brow furrows. "Who?"

Gray stirs. "Helena Michaels. That's that omega, right?"

Tristan nods, his spine stiffening. "She was Soul Bonded."

My eyes widen. *Soul Bonded.*

It's described as a type of ecstasy. A moment of euphoria, of souls connecting for the first time. Soul Bonding is almost unheard of. I remember the name now, although I've never met her. The only Soul Bonded for a hundred years.

I lick my lips. "Think it runs in the family?" I ask hoarsely.

Fuck, I hope so. To have that connection with someone, to be their everything... I can't think of any better feeling than that.

My hands already itch for my pencil, words flowing to my fingers like a fucking waterfall.

Bonding Trials? Bring it the fuck on.

## 5
## SIENNA

"I like the feathers," my mother says defiantly.

Behind her, Jessalyn pulls a face, and my lips purse as I fight back a grin. We've been here for hours, and Jess has had a little too much of the free champagne.

Sighing dramatically, she throws herself down onto a purple chaise lounge, spreading her arms out pleadingly. "Helena, she looks like an ostrich."

We all turn to peer into the mirror as Madame Dumas huffs. "Nobody leaves my premises looking like an ostrich, Ms Rogers."

"I think it's the amount," I murmur quietly. "Maybe the corset *and* the skirt being covered in feathers is a little too much?"

I do feel like a giant bird. That's not the impression I want to give my new pack.

Madame Dumas frowns, but nods reluctantly. "I think the skirt looks lovely, Miss. Perhaps some beading on the bodice?"

I tilt my head towards Mama, who nods. As Madam Dumas bustles over to her assistant, I stroke my hand gently down the softness of the white feathers that make up the skirt.

White. For purity.

It's tradition for any omega entering the Bonding Trials to

wear white to the opening ceremony. White for innocence. White for virginity.

My stomach clenches again as Jessalyn hiccups loudly, staring at my dress.

"Why don't the alphas have to wear white?" she points out loudly, earning a disapproving look from my mother. "Why is it just the omega?"

I scoff lightly. "Alphas aren't expected to remain chaste, Jess," I point out. "That's all on me."

The nerves churn, a hint of nausea threatening as Jess grumbles. "That's insane. Fuck the patriarchy!"

She punctuates her *extremely loud* statement with a punch to the air. Madam Dumas and her assistant turn to look over, their mouths agape.

"*Jessalyn!*" My mother's face flushes bright red as she looks around, scandalized. I clamp my mouth shut to try and force back the laughter, but my shaking shoulders give me away as I cover my face.

The crystal chandelier above my head clinks lightly as the door to the boutique pushes open, the afternoon sunshine glinting off the mirrors lining the room.

I squint as the sun hits my eyes, moving my hand up to block the rays. Blinking rapidly, I turn back to Jess, catching her pouring herself yet another glass of champagne.

"Jess," I mutter under my breath. "I need you sober."

"I am – *hic* – sober. Sober as a judge. Sober as the Justice Milo."

My mother whips out a hand and grabs the perilously full glass. "No more for you, sweetheart."

"Hey!"

The click of heels echoes on the floor behind me as I turn to take in the newcomer.

She's a freaking goddess. Tall, curves in all the right places, and long scarlet hair falling dramatically down her back with just the right amount of curl. Green eyes glitter as she glances at me, and I offer a smile. It slips away as she takes a long look at my dress, her lip curling in unmistakable derision.

"*Bitch.* I thought people only curled their lip in books," Jess whisper-shouts. My face feels like it's about to burst into flames.

"*You're* the Cohen omega?" the girl says, her tone high and cutting. "*You?*"

I feel myself shrink.

"What did you just say to my daughter?" my mother asks, outraged. "You need to leave. This is a private appointment."

Doesn't she have a point, though? If this pack is as important as everyone says…, what am I doing matching with them?

Madam Dumas splits from her assistant, holding her hands up apologetically as Jessalyn pulls herself up and advances threateningly toward our intruder.

"Ms Erikkson. We're not open today unless you have an appointment."

Erikkson. There's only one Erikkson in Navarre, and that's the Council Beta liaison.

Jessalyn clearly reaches the same conclusion as she puts her hand on her hip and smiles sweetly.

Oh, this is not good.

"You know, green really isn't a good look for you." She gestures dismissively at the beta. "I thought your daddy was all about better relations between the designations? You're really not helping his case here."

The beta sniffs. "I was just offering some helpful advice."

Leaning forward, she stares me straight in the eye.

"You're really not the right match for the Cohen pack, you know," she whispers. Her words are almost soft in their poison, aiming straight for my insecurities.

"They need someone who fits. And you, Sienna Michaels… don't."

"Enough of this." Pale-faced, my mother reaches forward and grabs the Erikkson girl by the arm as she squawks in outrage. Jessalyn cheers as Mama drags her to the door, pulling it open and throwing her through it. Slamming it behind her, she turns back to us with a huff, her eyes on me.

Dismissing Madame Dumas with an impatient wave, Mama walks up to me and cups my cheek. "You," she pushes out, her words shaky but determined, "are worth a hundred of that little jumped-up bitch."

Jess gasps. "Helena, you swore!"

My mother sniffs. "There's a time and a place, Jessalyn. One day, you'll learn. This was definitely the time and place." She turns back to me, her eyes soft. "Do you understand me, sweetheart? They are privileged to have you."

My throat tightens, my chest fighting to push out a full breath. "You have to say that," I say, trying to stop my voice from wobbling. "You're my mother."

She kisses my forehead. "And I am privileged to be your mother, just as much as they are to have you as a mate, Sienna."

6
# SIENNA

Jess bounces eagerly up and down in her seat next to me as I try my best to hide in the corner of the backseat.

"I'm so excited!" she yelps, her curls flying everywhere. In the front seat, my dad laughs.

"You be careful tonight, girls," he says, an edge of sternness in his voice as he catches Jessalyn's eye in the rear-view mirror before he moves over to me. "And make sure you stay well away from the stage, sweetheart."

Nodding, I gnaw at my fingernails. When Jess told me she'd gotten my parents' approval to go and see Haven's End at the Waterhole, I hadn't honestly believed her.

I've never been a big fan of crowds or noise, and truthfully, just the idea of standing right in the middle of a shouting, screaming horde makes me feel ill.

But this is my chance to see one of my alphas in the flesh for the first time, even if we have to be sneaky about it. It's not permitted to meet your mates ahead of the ceremony.

Jax Cohen is the lead guitarist for Haven's End. And whilst I might not have had the courage to go and see them live before, I know every single one of their songs, thanks to my own unusual skill.

My fingers tap out the beat to *Touch* before Jess grabs me, squeezing my hand in hers.

"This is going to be epic," she promises, a familiar feral gleam in her eye that settles as she looks at me properly. "Hey," she nudges, her tone quietening. "Just the two of us, right?"

I nod hesitantly. As enthusiastic and full of *life* as Jessalyn is, I'd trust her to the end of the earth and back. She's been my best friend for as long as I can remember – nobody else has even come close to joining our friendship group.

"Here we go," my dad calls, pulling the car up to the end of a very long line of leggy, pretty girls.

Great. More reasons to feel inadequate. Jax Cohen certainly can't be hurting for female company.

The crowd, mostly beta girls from the edges of town by the looks, give us dirty looks as Jess and I exit the car and she pulls me to the front of the line.

"Hey, Jimmy." She nods to one of the bouncers and he grins, his teeth flashing in the echoes of the strobe lighting cutting through the open doorway.

"Well, if it isn't little Jessalyn. Who's your pretty friend?"

Giving him a hesitant smile, I see him frown as he looks at Jess. "Watch out in there. It's looking rowdy."

*Fantastic.*

Jess barely stops to nod her head as she pulls me through the doorway, Jimmy lifting a red rope and winking as I slide past him. "Have a good evening, ladies."

I tug on Jess's hand to stop her, sucking in a deep breath as a wave of heat slams into my face. "Maybe this isn't such a great idea," I start. "I probably won't even be able to see him."

Jess spins, her hands settling on my arms as she rubs them up and down briskly, giving the stink-eye to a girl who huffs as she pushes past us.

"You're getting Bonded, Si. That means alphas, and babies, and a whole new life for you. And I am so freaking pleased for you – but it means that our lives are going to change. You're my best friend, and I want us to have one night of celebration before I have to hand you over to a bunch of Neanderthals and watch you go all googly-eyed for them."

Her voice wobbles at the end, and she glances away. Shame curls in my stomach. I've been so caught up in my own anxiety, I haven't even thought about how this'll affect Jess.

"You'll always be my best friend, Jess. Always."

"I know," she mumbles, but her face is still turned away as her breath hitches.

"The PB to my jelly."

A small huff of laughter.

"The cheese to my macaroni."

A snort slips out.

"The verruca to my foot."

"Ew!" Jess wrinkles her nose, but she's grinning.

"Come on." Threading her arm through mine, I sigh dramatically. "Let's get this over with. He's probably a troll."

Jess pinches the underside of my arm gently. "He is not a troll. You're going to eat your words and I can't wait."

We push into the swarming, sweating crowd, clasping each other's hand tightly as Jess tows us to the bar, ordering two sodas with a flick of her fingers to the bartender. He looks her over as he slides the drinks over, a clear invitation in his eyes that fades in disappointment as Jess turns away from him to hand over my lemonade.

I sip at the cool drink, letting the coldness slide down my throat as I turn to look around.

This place is *packed*.

Heads bounce up and down on a dancefloor just ahead of us, already full despite the early hour. A pulsing beat sounds underneath my foot and I tap my feet in response, a melody weaving itself in my mind despite the bass pounding from the speakers attached to every wall.

This… isn't so bad.

Jess leans in to bellow in my ear over the music. "See?"

I nod, a smile lifting the corners of my lips as the music trails off, replaced by a low swell of chanting and stomping feet. Frowning, I lean in to try to pick it up.

Is that—

Oh my god. It *is*.

*Co-hen.*

*Co-hen.*

*Co-hen.*

A pulse of noise draws my attention to the stage, still cloaked in darkness. A burst of static sounds from a microphone and I wince, but the crowd goes *wild*.

*Co-hen!*

*Co-hen!*

*Co-hen!*

Jess tugs at my sleeve, but something is tugging me towards the stage. I take a step away from her. My heartbeat pulses in my ear, the beat quickening above the sound of the screaming chant.

A spotlight appears, a silhouette framed against the lights as everyone screams in unison. I suck in a breath as Jax Cohen raises impossibly violet eyes to the crowd, a cocky smirk pulling at his full lips.

"Well, good evening, Navarre."

His voice rasps, the sensation akin to a nail sliding down my back. My whole body shivers.

*Is this normal?*

Jess's face pops up in front of me, breaking my one-way stare-off with my future alpha.

"What did I say?" she laughs. "Bitch, I can see you eating those words."

I can't even respond as I duck around her, moving closer to the stage as Jax's fingers strum effortlessly over a stunning, ebony guitar, his other hand pulling the mic stand closer.

There's a slight breeze behind me as more people push through the door, and his fingers still as a frown plays over his perfect face. Glancing up, he shades his face to look out across the room, and girls everywhere scream with their hands outstretched.

He pauses as his eyes scan over us and my body locks into place, straining for something I don't understand. He's too far away to possibly be able to see us properly amongst the crowd.

Shaking his shoulders back, he strums again before the band launches into one of my favorite songs.

Jess begins to dance. People around me move, some of them bumping into me with their enthusiasm, but my feet are locked to the floor. All I can do is watch Jax Cohen – and listen.

A lock of hair falls over his forehead as he leans forward, his espresso-colored hair gleaming under the lights as he sings, his mouth brushing the mic as his eyes close with the strength of his voice.

And what a freaking voice.

*In the shadows we dance*
*Two souls longing for their chance*
*Bound by chains of circumstance*
*We're caught in this romance*
*But the fire within us burns so bright*
*Igniting desires we cannot fight*
*Touch*
*Our hearts collide, we can't deny*
*In a world that's tearing us apart…*

I remain staring at the stage for the rest of the first song. The second. The third. Each just as good, each getting underneath my skin as I watch Jax Cohen curl the crowd around his little finger.

Jess is smug as only a best friend can be, and I nudge her when the band finally takes a break, raising my voice so she can hear me. "Stop gloating."

"Gloating? Me? Never." She smirks. "I'm going to the bathroom. You wanna come?"

Shaking my head, I motion to my drink. "I'll wait here."

I'm not ready to exchange this feeling for the bright, pushing constraints of dozens of girls competing for a very small amount of bathroom space just yet.

Leaning against the bar, I'm lost in my own world when there's a bump from behind me, the last of my lemonade spilling out down my silver satin top and making me jump back, hitting a hard body.

"Oh, I'm sor—"

My words break off as textured hands gently grasp the top of my arms. A warm huff of breath lands on my head. A choked sound follows.

My feet root to the floor even as I lean into the heat of a total stranger. What is wrong with me tonight?

I can't help but take deep, gulping breaths of his scent. Whoever this is, he's clearly an alpha.

An alpha who smells freaking amazing, like the earth after rainfall. Petrichor.

I suck it down like oxygen, even as my breathing speeds up and I feel lightheaded. The hands resting on my arms rub up and down, gently soothing me, the alpha curving himself over me as whispered words brush my ear.

"Turn around, sweetheart. I need to see your face."

There's a familiar rasping undertone to his words, but I'm still lost in his scent. Spinning, I press myself into a broad chest, my nose seeking the touch of bare skin left open at the top of his dark shirt. My hands slide up, gripping the collar of his shirt as I breathe deeply, and his head drops to the crook of my neck as he breathes in.

"Fuck."

His growl reverberates through my bones, settling deep in my chest with a harsh tug.

It's want, it's longing, it's straight-up lust like I've never felt before in my life.

And as he moves back, for the first time in my life I let out a long, needy whine.

*Holy shit.*

*Is this—no.*
*It can't be.*

But as my head clears and I yank myself back to stare into impossibly familiar, widened violet eyes, I know there's no mistake.

Jax Cohen isn't just my future alpha.

He's my damn Soul Bonded.

# 7
# JAX

The omega lifts her nose from my skin, her cheeks flushed as a low, drawn-out whine reverberates against my chest.

A sense of rightness settles over me as I slide my hand behind her back, my thumb stroking her skin through the satin of her top. Leaning in, I brush my nose along her neck, pulling her closer as she shudders. She's mouthwatering, the waves coming from her skin reminding me of raspberry ripple ice cream, my favorite.

"Mate." My voice is hoarse, the shock of the evening finally hitting home.

I came out for another standard gig, another night of playing to the same crowds at the same place. But this... I didn't expect this.

She's my Soul Bonded.

My hand clenches possessively against her as I pull her against me, drawing a startled mew from her throat. Turquoise eyes scan my face hesitantly as I take her in, from her short frame, barely reaching my chest, to her gloriously pink hair, loose curls tumbling to her waist.

And those *curves*.

Stunning.

*Mine.*

We explore each other in silence, our eyes roving over the other. As I open my mouth, a high-pitched squeal cuts through our moment.

"Oh my *God! Jax Cohen*?"

The glazed look in her eyes evaporates, a hint of fear entering them. When I move to pull her in to me, I'm stopped by a hand on my arm. Looking around, I realize that there's a small crowd forming, girls starting to push at each other to try and get closer.

Fuck. Clearly, my old baseball cap only covered me for so long. But I had to come out here, had to find out what was drawing my attention like a damn homing beacon.

And I sure as hell found it.

Looking around, I make sure to keep a firm grip on my mate, not wanting her to get pushed around by the swell of people around us. She draws in a shuddering gasp that I pick up even over the noise – and then she's gone, my hand grasping on empty air.

*No.*

The growl that erupts has more than a few of my fans stopping and backing away nervously. Beta they might be, but anybody knows to keep well back from a furious alpha – and I am livid.

I try to go after her, to follow her through the crowd, but despite the hesitancy of the people around me, the ones behind them have no issue pushing forward.

Belatedly, I realize the possible danger of a crowd crush, and my heart thuds in panic as I dart my head from side to side. Where the fuck has my Soul Bonded gone?

I catch a glimpse of pink hair by the exit, and my heart clenches.

"Stop!"

The bellow is furious, and she darts a look back at me, her eyes filled with... guilt?

Then she ducks outside, and just like that, I've lost her.

"Back the hell off," I bark. "You're causing a crush!"

Pushing my way to the bar, I haul myself over with help from

Alex, the bartender, and grab the megaphone. A few clipped orders gets everyone to settle down with the promise of another song, but by the time I'm able to push my way outside, my Bonded is long gone.

"Fucking hell!" Cursing, I kick the side of the door and Jimmy gives me a funny look. "Everything alright, man?"

Hesitating, I wonder if he knows her, but dismiss it. I've never seen that girl before in my life, and I spend more time here than he does.

Shaking my head, I storm back inside, tugging the guitar angrily over my head as my bandmates look on in amusement.

"Er – Jax?" Mal, my drummer, asks slowly. "You okay?"

Gritting my teeth, I force a nod and head for the stage. "Let's get this over with. I need to get home."

And hunt down my missing Bonded.

8
# SIENNA

I finally pause for breath, Jessalyn's panicked voice ringing in my ears as she demands to know what's wrong. She caught me by the doors, following me without a word of complaint as I ran past Jimmy and down the street.

Holding up a hand, I force my words out between my pants.

"I'm – *heh* – okay – *ngh* – just – second – *heh*."

*I am not built for running.*

I collapse onto the ground, leaning back against the wall of a building as I try desperately to catch my breath. Jess eases herself down beside me, giving me the stink-eye as I get myself under control.

It's not just my flight from the club.

I'm Soul Bonded. To Jax Cohen.

And if the rumor holds true, it means I'm probably Soul Bonded to the rest of his pack too.

"Holy fucking shit!" I blurt out. Jess slaps her hands down on her legs.

"That's it! Tell me what's going on, Si. Do you know how worried your dad is gonna be when we're not there? We're going to have to run back!"

"Can't," I force out. The pounding in my chest is only

growing, and I pull my legs up to my chest, recognizing the signs of a panic attack. Dropping my forehead to my knees, I try to slow my breathing. Jess sets her hand on my shoulder, counting softly in our familiar routine.

"Do not pass out on me here," she scolds me lightly but worry filters through. "I will not be able to drag your ass back to your dad's car."

I laugh weakly, the worst of the anxiety dissipating.

"You'll be relieved to know that no dragging is required."

Relief sags Jess's shoulders. "Thank fuck for that. Now tell me – what happened in there? You looked as though you'd seen a ghost!"

Swallowing, I train my eyes on the wall opposite us, counting the pale gold bricks to try and get my head under control. A hand slips into mine, and I return the squeeze Jess gives me.

"Jax Cohen is my Soul Bonded."

My words drop like a stone in the sudden silence. Jess gapes at me, her mouth open.

"Your…Soul Bonded? Are you serious? How do you know?"

"I know."

Now I know what my parents meant. There is no denying your Soul Bonded. It's as though every atom that makes up Jax calls to every atom of mine – like a yearning.

Even now, I have to fight the urge to run straight back to the Waterhole, to rub myself against Jax like a damned cat in heat.

Jess bursts into laughter. When I stare at her, she collapses against me, her whole body shaking.

"Sienna… this is the best news ever! You're Soul Bonded to your pack before the Trials even begin!"

I start to gnaw at my fingers again until Jess slaps my hands away. "Stop that," she scolds. "This is nothing to worry about. We should be celebrating!"

At her words, mortification overwhelms me. Oh my God. I *ran away* from my Soul Bonded.

Fled. Like a thief in the night. Who does that?

Groaning, I lean my head back against the cold brick. "I'm an idiot, Jess."

Sighing, my best friend climbs to her feet, brushing off her hands and holding one out to me.

"Yeah, but you're my idiot. Come on. We need to get back."

"What if he's still there?"

Jess frowns. "Wouldn't that be a good thing? He's your Soul Bonded. Your forever mate."

A wash of heat warms my chest. Mine. But it's closely followed by another dip in my stomach.

Shaking my head, I grab her hand and pull myself up. "I know. I just...need some time to process. And we can't tell anyone, either. You know we're not supposed to meet them before the Trials begin."

We begin making our way back to the club, my fingers twisting restlessly. As we turn the corner, I see my dad pull up in his sleek black car and make a rapid dash for the backseat. Turning, he frowns as we scramble in.

"Are you okay, honey? Was it too much?"

"No, it was… good. I'm just tired."

Dad pulls away from the curb. "Was it busy?"

Thank god he has no idea Jax Cohen was there tonight.

"Very."

He humphs, making a left and heading towards Jess's home. "Well, I'm glad you enjoyed it, sweetheart. Your mother was worried it would be too much, on top of the Trials starting."

My breathing threatens to come a little faster. "She worries too much."

"Mother's prerogative, I'm afraid."

He pulls up to a set of familiar gates, and Jess slides a look at me as she unbuckles her belt. "I'll see you tomorrow?"

Tomorrow. My last day of prep before the Trials begin on Monday. I have a full day of people poking and prodding at me, making sure I look my absolute best to be presented to my alphas in front of most of Navarre. I can barely force out my nod.

But Jax will be there. A hint of excitement unfurls as I bite my lip.

*Soul Bonded.*

At this stage, the Trials are really just a formality.

After all, nobody is going to reject their Soul Bonded.

## 9
# TRISTAN

My fingers drum on the edge of my desk as I try to focus on the reports in front of me. But the latest economic report on agricultural expenditure isn't keeping my attention this evening.

My mind keeps spinning and turning. The start of the Bonding Trials is just two days away, and we're ready. Our suits are arranged, the house has been scoured to within an inch of its life, our mate's room for the duration of the trials prepared along with her nesting space.

Our pack is completely prepared to welcome our very own omega.

So why do I feel so on edge?

Rocking to my feet, I walk over to the tiny window that lets a little light into my office. Tucked away in the corner of the Council Building, I'm normally in and out too much to pay attention to the view. But tonight, I take a moment to look out at the glittering lights that cover our city. An expanse of wealth, of privilege, a view marred only by the ramshackle sight of the dilapidated buildings that make up the beta area of Navarre.

I wonder where she is. Is she down there, in one of those

windows? Is she wondering about us as much as we are about her? Is she scared?

There's a clenching in my chest, a warm surge of protectiveness.

*I won't let anything happen to you.*

We've waited far too long for our mate to let her slip through our fingers now.

There's a *rat-tat-tat* sound at the door, and my eyes flick to the brass clock overlooking my desk, highlighting the lateness of the hour. I should have left earlier, but Jax is playing in the city tonight and Logan and Gray are wrapped up in their own projects, so I figured my restlessness could be put to work at the office instead. But it's late for anyone else to be hanging around.

When I call out, the door slides open, and I bite back a groan at the oily face that appears.

"Councilor Erikkson." I force a smile. "I'm surprised to see you here this late."

"The Council's work is never done, Tristan. Something you'll learn in time, I'm sure."

I wave him to a seat, trying not to grind my teeth at his condescending tone. The Councilor stares down his nose as he looks around my poky office, settling into a chair with a file propped on his lap.

"It's fortuitous you were here this evening, Tristan. I have something to discuss with you, and I felt it would be best done in private." The Councilor's voice is low, but his tone sends the hairs at the back of my neck prickling.

"Oh? I'm curious as to what would warrant a chat at this hour."

I watch him carefully, noting the way his gaze shifts to the door.

"How are you feeling about your Bonding ceremony?" he asks abruptly. "I cannot imagine that such an archaic practice sits well with your... modern approach."

My brows draw down. "I'm very pleased to be taking part in

the Trials, Councilor. Whilst I would agree that the overall methods of matching alphas and omegas are in need of review, I do appreciate the important work of the Omega Hub in finding appropriate matches. I'm looking forward to meeting Sienna formally at the ceremony."

Erikkson smirks at me. "I'm sure. In any case, what I have to discuss relates to your Bonding."

Surprise fills me, but I remain steady, my eyes on his as I lean back in my chair, affecting a casual pose despite the tension locking up my spine at his words. "Oh?"

"Indeed." Leaning forward, Erikkson slides a manila file across the desk. I leave it where it is for a moment, watching the spark of temper on his face when I don't immediately jump to open it.

Scanning his face, I lean in and pick up the folder, turning it over in my hands. "A late-night visit, an anonymous folder – all very cloak and dagger, Councilor. Should I be concerned?"

Erikkson tilts his head. "Why not open it and see?"

Keeping a bored look on my face, I flip the folder over, sliding out the contents. As I thumb through them nonchalantly, my focus sharpens, my hands tightening on the paper until my knuckles turn white.

"This is untrue, Councilor. I don't know where these doctored invoices have come from—"

"Keep going, boy." Vicious delight glints in Erikkson's pale green gaze. "I assure you; the evidence is there."

A weight appears in my stomach, growing heavier as I continue to look through the documents and reach a selection of photos. My eyes flicker from one to the other.

"As you can see," Erikkson points out smoothly, "These photographs clearly show your father meeting with some… rather unsavory individuals."

And the invoices showing large sums of missing funds from Council coffers tell another side to the story.

EVELYN FLOOD

My throat tightens. I refuse to believe that my father is involved in embezzling Council funds. I don't believe it.

I clear my throat.

"This is all very… interesting, Councilor. What I don't understand is why you have brought this to me."

When the obvious response is to go straight to my father with it, even if Erikkson thought I wasn't involved. Or even the main Council, if he's so damn concerned.

The Councilor stands up, moving to the small corner bar and pouring us both a glass of whisky without asking. My hands curl around the glass when he hands it to me, but I don't drink, keeping my eyes on him as he settles back in his seat, looking perfectly at ease.

"These are difficult times for us all, boy. There is much discussion around the future of Navarre, of your alpha and omega population. Whilst the beta population tends to drop off the list of priorities at every stage."

Swirling my drink in my hand, I motion at him to continue.

"As much as I disagree with many of your ideas, I have never disagreed with your views on the beta population. And as much as the evidence in your hand has shocked me, I find myself reluctant to hand them over, given the certainty of that outcome."

Realization hits. If my father is removed as Council Leader, I'll lose my place as the future Leader – the shadow of the controversy will make it impossible for me to ascend.

The sudden implications of what's in my hand hit me hard. Everyone we know will be affected. My pack will be ruined. My mother and family disgraced, stripped of our assets.

The law in Navarre is harsh, but it is the law.

We will lose *everything*.

Anger tightens my throat, but I look over to Erikkson. "Tell me what you want, Erikkson."

He picks at something on the sleeve of his black Council robe. "It's rather simple, really. I wish to improve the relationship with the beta population. And that's where you come in."

Rising, he walks to the door and pulls it open. A sick feeling invades my stomach as Alicia stalks into the room, her vapid smile wide in the dim lighting.

"Good evening, Tristan," she purrs. "Isn't this all very exciting?"

Anger tenses my muscles as I move my gaze to Erikkson. "Explain, Councilor."

"It's quite simple, really. You will publically select Alicia as the mate of the Cohen pack, forgoing your relationship with the omega girl. Your relationship will demonstrate the potential for the beta population to ascend to the dizzying heights of the Council – particularly once you become Council Leader with my daughter at your side. And in grateful thanks for your partnership, the evidence in your hands will simply… disappear."

I'm speechless as I stare from one to the other. Erikkson clasps his hands together, watching my face as Alicia claps her hands with delight. "I told you we'd find a way to be together, darling!"

My fingers tighten on the arms of the chair until a crack sounds. Alicia's smile dims.

"No."

My voice is resolute. Take Alicia as our mate? Fake a relationship in public for the rest of my life?

Not a fucking chance.

"As much as I admire your aspiration, Councilor, there are better ways to ensure stronger relationships with the betas. I'm afraid that I will have to decline your offer – *kind* as it is."

The smile slides from Alicia's face completely as she turns to her father. "Daddy?"

Ignoring her, Erikkson simply reaches forward, a second folder in his hands. Gritting my teeth, I wave it off.

"I don't need further evidence, Erikkson. We'll manage the allegations through the Justice system, along with any repercussions. Now, take your daughter, and get the *fuck* out of my office."

Erikkson simply snorts. "Don't be dramatic, boy. Take the damned folder. You'll want to see it."

Dread breaks out in cold sweat along my hairline as I snatch it from him, expecting more incriminating photographs.

My breathing stops when I open the contents.

And just like that, my dreams, my future mate, the memories we could make – it all disappears like smoke.

"You see," Erikkson adds into the silence. "There is more riding on your participation than you thought, Tristan."

Alicia strains to see the images in my hand, and I pull them closer to my chest.

"I will withdraw my pack from the Trials immediately." My voice is rough, the anger underlying each word clear. Alicia flinches back and then barks a sharp laugh.

"Oh, no, Tristan. The Trials will be proceeding as normal. Right, Daddy?"

I blink as Erikkson turns to her. "That's right, sweetheart."

He turns back to me with a curled lip. "It seems that Alicia and one Sienna Michaels are already acquainted. Alicia wishes to add an additional layer to your story by publically rejecting Ms Michaels at the conclusion of the Trials."

The images in front of me blur together as I think through the implications. "You want us to participate in the trials – and Deny her?"

An omega has never been Denied in Navarre. Ever.

Alicia sniffs. "It'll serve the little stuck-up bitch right."

My head spins as I try and think around this, to come up with an alternative that doesn't put my family – or the omega we're supposed to be mating – at risk.

"I need to think," I say abruptly. "Get out."

Alicia huffs, but Erikkson pulls her up. "I expect your answer within twenty-four hours, Tristan. Think carefully. How much is your family worth to you? How much is your pack worth?"

He points at the folder in my hands. "You can keep that. I have copies."

I don't respond, my fury a tight knot inside me as they leave. Gripping the glass of whiskey, I down it in one before I hurl it with all my strength.

It smashes against the wall.

## 10

# LOGAN

Scratching absently at the stubble lining my jaw, I stare despondently at the mess in front of me.

"What is that?"

Groaning, I drop my head into my hands as Gray touches his hand to my shoulder, his smoky scent wrapping around us. "It's supposed to be a tree."

"Huh. I can see it."

"Liar." It's a disaster, the white plaster setting into more of a weird bush than anything resembling the majestic oak tree I had in mind when I started.

Sighing, I lean back against Gray's warmth. "Maybe I'm not cut out for this anymore, Gray."

Six years of creating, of using every possible medium – oils, clay, marble, wood – to create art. Awe-inspiring, jaw-dropping art. But the well is dry now. Reaching over to my desk, I pull out a letter and hand it to Gray, watching his electric blue eyes scan the contents before he looks up at me, his brows drawing into a deep frown. "Lo, you're not a teacher."

"A lecturer," I correct him with a hint of embarrassment. When I first received the invite from the college in Navarre to join their

Creative department, I nearly threw it away. But that was before I lost sight of everything that inspires me.

Gray moves in front of me, setting his hands on my shoulders as I watch the letter fall lazily to the floor. "You are not dried up, Logan. And that's not a reason to teach. You should do it because you're passionate, not because you feel you don't have another choice. Look at me."

A low growl vibrates in my chest as he tugs my face to him, my hand pushing him away as I meet his eyes with a hint of challenge. "I'm not some little omega you can manage, Gray."

And maybe I've hit the end of my tether. I'm tired of living a double life – one where Gray and I are just members of the same Pack, considered closer than brothers but not good enough to stand at his side.

Gray's hand drops as he maintains eye contact. "And I'm not your whipping boy for every time you feel a little lost, Lo."

His words hit home, the apology in his eyes reaching his mouth a little too late. "Logan, I—"

"Enough." Cutting him off, I stand and move to the door. My hand lingers on the handle for just a second, enough to see Gray's reflection in the polished brass as he runs a hand over his face.

"It's enough, Gray." My words are quiet, but I know he can hear me. "We need to take a break. I can't live like this anymore."

"Logan."

Shaking my head, I turn to face him. Gray stares back at me, his face pale, his copper hair in tousled disarray.

"Don't do this," he says firmly. "Don't give up on us."

My laugh is rusty. "There has never been an us, Gray. Not really."

When the door closes behind me, I take a second. Just one second of giving in to the jagged shard carved into my chest. No footsteps follow me. No voice calling out for me to wait.

Pushing myself back, I walk away from my studio. And I don't look back.

Entering the kitchen, I nearly turn around when Tristan raises his head and spots me.

"Lo. Have you seen Gray? Jax is on his way home and he wants to talk to us."

Tristan looks awful. His face is almost gray, his hair all over the place. His eyes flick away from me as he stares down at the table.

"What's the matter?" I ask him as Jax's bike revs out in the courtyard, announcing his imminent arrival. Tristan has been the one most excited about the Bonding Trials. But his normally impeccable suit is crumpled, his tie askew as he drinks deeply from a full glass of whiskey.

"Nothing." His eyes move to the door. "Sit down, Lo. Have a drink."

Eyeing him as concern fills me, I move to the fridge and grab some beers, setting them out on the table. Gray walks in, his eyes moving straight to me before he breaks contact and takes a seat. Tristan watches us closely, a look on his face that I can't decipher.

We sit in awkward silence for a few minutes until the door crashes open, Jax throwing himself through it with a wild grin on his face. "Pack, I have news."

"As do I," says Tristan tiredly. "Sit down, Jax."

Jax ignores him, pacing up and down the length of the kitchen.

"I found her," he announces suddenly, spinning towards us.

"Who?" Gray asks.

"Our Soul Bonded. That's who."

Everyone stills as Jax swings his head between us with a shit-eating grin.

"I'm serious! She's fucking beautiful. Short, pretty shy. Amazing pink hair."

I'm first to break the silence as I blink rapidly. "What do you mean, you found our Soul Bonded?"

It's a myth. Apart from that one alpha and omega, Soul Bonding only exists in books.

As Jax explains his encounter with the pink-haired omega, Tristan sinks his head into his hands.

"Tris!" Jax says, settling beside him and clapping his hand to his shoulder. "This is incredible! I thought you'd be pleased. I mean, we'll have to explain to the Council and the Hub, but we've found her."

Tristan shoves his hand off, reaching for the whiskey. Jax hesitates, finally picking up on the atmosphere. "Tris?"

He sounds bewildered, and I don't blame him. I catch Gray's eye and he frowns at me in question. None of us have ever seen Tristan like this.

"Are you nervous?" I offer quietly. "About Monday?"

Tristan snorts. "I wish it was that simple."

Leaning back, he cradles his glass in his hand. "I had a visit at my office tonight. From Erikkson."

Revulsion fills me. I can't stand the beta Council representative, and his daughter's a psychopath.

"What happened?" Gray presses.

Tristan rubs at his eyes tiredly, before he launches into the story. As he speaks, I can see my growing anger reflected in the faces of my pack.

"What the actual fuck?" Jax shouts, standing up. "You need to speak to David, Tristan."

Tris shakes his head. "I can't," he says flatly. "Erikkson will expose him the moment he thinks I've said anything. He wouldn't want to lose his advantage."

And even if David is guilty, it's likely he'd hand himself in as soon as Tristan raised it.

"But you said no, right?" Jax presses.

"I tried." Tristan's mouth is a thin line as he looks at us. "I tried to say no, but he had something else."

"What could he possibly have that would make you agree to Alicia becoming our mate?" Gray demands, anger lacing his tone.

Tristan looks away as he slides the folder down until I grasp it, tugging out the photos.

It takes me a moment to understand.

Gray swears a blue streak over my shoulder.

Us. Erikkson has us.

Gray has me pressed up against the car door, his mouth on my neck and his hands down my jeans. My head is thrown back, my face clearly visible to the camera watching us.

"How long?" Tristan asks hoarsely as Jax makes his way down to us. "How long have you been lying to us?"

"It wasn't a lie." I shake my head in staunch refusal. "We knew, if anyone found out – what they would say, what it would mean—"

"It was a fucking lie." Jax snarls, betrayal in his face as he looks between us. "We're a goddamned pack! You didn't think you could trust us with this?"

"Years." Gray cuts everyone off abruptly. "Four years."

Silence reigns in the kitchen until Tristan laughs abruptly.

"Well. Better be punished for something real than just a fling. I need to tell Erikkson we'll do it."

I stare desperately around the room, searching for an idea, something. The idea that Gray and I could cost Tristan and Jax – fuck, all of us – our mate, our happy fucking ending. I can't cope with it.

"There must be something we can do," I say desperately. "We need to think."

"We need to go along with it," Gray says quietly. Jax and I stare at him in dismay, but I catch Tristan nodding, obviously having reached the same conclusion.

"For now. Until we find something to take him down." Tristan drains his glass.

Jax glares at us all. "And the Michaels girl? We're just going to go through with this and destroy her fucking life? I don't think so!"

"It won't get that far." Gray moves around the table, pouring his own glass of liquor. "We go through with the ceremony. We make it so clear she's not wanted that she withdraws herself before the final mating ceremony. She doesn't get Denied. She gets a chance to meet another pack, one who'll treat her right. And if we get rid of Alicia and Erikkson, we're free to look for our Soul Bonded."

A muscle tics in Jax's jaw. "Soul Bonded or not, I'm not happy with this. You think you can treat an omega so badly that she withdraws?"

Gray straightens. "When the alternative is Denial?"

Tristan nods, slowly, but I can see the frustration I feel mirrored on his face. She'll be here for weeks, and we'll need to do everything we can to put her off. It goes against everything – every instinct we have that says omegas are to be cherished, protected.

"Maybe we could tell her," I offer. "If she seems decent—"

"You want to take that risk?" It's Tristan who poses the question, the answer in his eyes. "When there's so much at stake?"

Staring down at the table, I shake my head.

"I'm sorry," I offer. That's all I can say. Next to me, Gray is silent.

Jax swipes the bottle from the table, making his way out of the kitchen. "Sorry you didn't trust us, or sorry you got found out?"

The door slams shut before I can respond.

"He's not angry," Tristan says. "He's hurt."

"And you?" Gray asks, his fist curling.

"I never thought we were the kind of pack to keep secrets from each other. I thought we were a team." Tristan sighs. "I understand why you hid it. But I wish you hadn't."

My hand lifts to my chest as if I can rub away the pain. Gray glances at me before looking away.

The door closes again behind Tristan, more quietly this time.

"This is proof, Gray," I whisper. "It shouldn't have happened."

But when I turn around, I'm the only one left.

## 11
# TRISTAN

I straighten my tie as I head up the steps to the Erikkson household. Their mansion is bigger than ours and ostentatious to the extreme, a towering piece of black brickwork that makes Gray shudder and call it an abomination every time we go past it.

Alicia pulls open the door before I can reach for the doorbell, her make-up flawless as ever, but not hiding the manic gleam in her eyes as she leans forward for a kiss.

I push past her, ignoring her pouting as I turn. "Where is your father?"

"Here." Erikkson emerges. "How wonderful to see you, Tristan." He holds out his hand to shake. When I ignore him, he tuts in disapproval. "Not a pleasant greeting for your father-in-law, I must say."

"I haven't agreed to anything yet."

My reminder is pointed, my snarl barely hidden. The urge to leap for his throat is almost more than I can cope with, but we'll have bigger issues if I kill the Beta Council representative.

"Of course. Let's go into my office."

I move to shut the door but Alicia prances in after us, her hand trailing up my arm as she brushes against me.

Taking a step back, I remain standing, pushing out what I've come to say through gritted teeth.

"I agree to your proposal on behalf of the pack."

Erikkson leans forward as Alicia settles into a chair, crossing her bare legs. Biting back a grimace, I don't look at her as she primps in the corner of my eye line.

"Excellent news. I'm delighted to have you as a future son-in-law, Tristan."

I give him a hard stare. "Let's not pretend this is anything more than a farce in private, Erikkson."

He waves a hand dismissively. "Who knows. Love can grow in the most unforeseen places."

Alicia giggles to herself, and even her father glances at her askance.

"In any case." He reaches for some papers. "I have taken the liberty of having Alicia's belongings packed."

My breathing threatens to stop. "Packed?"

"For her to move in." He raises his eyes to mine. "She will be moving in with you ahead of the Trials beginning tomorrow."

Alicia bursts from her seat, wrapping her arms around my neck. "Isn't it wonderful, baby?"

I wrench her arms from me and move her backward. "Do not," I force out, my words icy, "touch me or any member of my pack without my consent. Do you understand?"

Alicia only bats her eyelashes. "I love it when you're so masterful, Tristan."

*How the fuck am I going to do this?*

"Alicia will be able to... keep an eye on you throughout the Trials. And of course, it will help your position with your omega when she sees Alicia as the dominant female in the household."

Alicia smirks. "I have so many ideas. We're going to have a lot of fun together, her and I."

*I'm going to be sick.*

"I have some conditions."

"Naturally." Erikkson steeples his fingers. "Name them."

"Alicia is not to physically harm Sienna Michaels in any way."

Alicia pouts, and my gut clenches. *What the fuck was she planning?*

"Agreed." Erikkson rolls his eyes when Alicia starts to protest. "Anything else?"

"She is not to enter any of our private spaces, including bedrooms, and bathrooms when someone is in there."

"Also agreed."

"We will control the manner in which we engage with Alicia in public. The approach needs to be believable – not just to the Council and the Omega Hub, but to family members too."

"No." Alicia stamps her foot. "I have a plan for the Bonding ceremony."

My temper rises as she talks about how she intends to humiliate our omega at the ceremony.

*Not your omega. Not anymore.*

The reminder hits hard.

"Enough. I'll agree to the first part only."

God knows it'll get the message through to Sienna quickly that this isn't going to be a straightforward Bonding Trials, and she deserves as much of a warning as she can get. She might even withdraw immediately. Alicia is enough of a trial on her own, without any of the other elements.

"Very well, then. Alicia, get ready to leave."

Alicia gives me a final once-over before she exits, a gleeful grin on her lips.

"I'm sorry it's come to this, Tristan." Erikkson purses his lips. "We all only want the best for the ones we love."

"Spare me," I scoff. "You've got what you wanted. I don't need the little sob story to go along with it."

"Fine." He waves his hand at me. "Look after my daughter, Tristan. Or it'll be your head on the block, so to speak."

Fucking hell. My pack is not going to be happy about this.

## 12
## SIENNA

"Rise and shine, sleeping beauty. Today is the day!"

My mother's shrill voice batters against the pain in my head. I turn away from the window, my eyes gritty with lack of sleep as she bursts in, her eyes scanning the bed before they land on me, her brows rising with surprise.

"Well, someone's eager."

I force a smile, not wanting to admit my exhaustion. Mama eyes me before taking a seat on the bed, patting the space next to her.

We sit silently for a moment, her hand creeping into mine. I grip it tightly, emotion a tight lump in the back of my throat.

"I'm scared, Mama," I admit, my voice shaking.

No matter that I've spent years in training at the Omega Hub, that I could recite the principles of being a good omega in my sleep, that I can cook, run a household and dance acceptably.

I'm eighteen years old, and I'm leaving my family to live in a house full of alphas who don't know me.

"What if they don't like me?" I ask, vulnerability stripping my tone raw.

*What if they look at me and they don't like what they see?*

My mother squeezes my hand. "If they don't like you,

sweetheart, then they're not the alphas you need. My brave, beautiful, brilliant daughter. Of course they'll love you. How could they not?"

A tear trickles down my chin. My mother doesn't always have the right words, but today, they're just the ones I needed to hear.

"The Trials are a time for you to get to know each other. The tests are inconsequential to that – just a box-ticking exercise for the Omega Hub to feel important. It will all happen naturally. But if anything doesn't feel right, you come straight back home to us. My door is always open to you, mated or not."

"Thank you, Mama." My voice shakes a little, but I take a deep breath, pushing the nerves back as I stand.

"What's the plan?" I ask.

Several hours later, I'm regretting my easy acquiescence as the hairdresser pours milk over my hair.

"Is this really necessary?" I wonder aloud, biting back a wince as the beautician rips another strip from my legs. "We spent all day yesterday making me presentable."

The other beta working on my face snaps her fingers for me to be still.

"We need to make sure your eyebrows are even!"

Jessalyn lies next to me with cucumber patches over her eyes. "You are the only person I know who would complain about a day of pampering, Si."

Some sort of oil is being rubbed into my feet, and I try to lie back and enjoy the day as I've been told. My mind keeps wandering back to the club – and to Jax, his petrichor scent and those searing violet eyes.

I shiver and feel a brush on my eyes.

"Gah!" The beautician throws up her hands. "I'll need to start again. Please stay still, Ms Michaels!"

"Sorry." Biting my lip, I ignore Jess's muffled laughter next to me.

Once I've been primped and prepped to within an inch of my life, I'm finally given a moment to myself. Walking up towards my room where I'll be dressed, I trail my hand over the photographs lining the staircase. Images of me, Elise, my mother and father – the jigsaw pieces that make up my life are all here, set out for easy viewing.

I pause, looking at an image of my parents on their Bonding Day. Their joy is incandescent, the camera merely an observer as they stare into each other's eyes.

My heart constricts as I think of Jax Cohen, and the pack that I'll be presented to today.

I'm too afraid to admit out loud that I *want* this. Like it's going to be snatched away from me if I dare give voice to the hope coiling inside my chest.

I want what my parents had – what they still have. I want it desperately.

And if my meeting with Jax was anything to go by, I might possibly have a chance of getting it.

Finally, there's a lick of excitement in my stomach. We're Soul Bonded. Today will be a celebration, a meeting, a joyous reunion.

My feet fly up the stairs, pausing as I enter the bedroom to my sheepish-looking Mama and a grinning Jessalyn.

"What's going on?" I look between them as my mother flushes lightly, wringing her hands.

"I realized, at the boutique, that you didn't seem particularly enthusiastic about any of the dresses. And today – today is special, Sienna. It's the start of your journey, and you deserve to have something that makes you feel like a princess."

She takes a step to the side, unzipping the long gray bag hanging over my wardrobe to reveal a dress.

Not a dress. This is a gown.

Even Jess stays silent as I raise my fingers to the very edges of the fine white gossamer lace.

"Mama," I whisper, blinking back tears. "It's beautiful."

Mama sniffs wetly. "Shall we try it on? I have your other gown here just in case we need it."

Jess balances me as I step into the dress, the lace barely a whisper against my skin. Mama does up the small pearl buttons at the back, both of them keeping me away from the mirror despite my protests.

"Just wait," orders Jessalyn softly. "You're perfect, Si."

The bodice fits tightly against me, the lace flaring out into a mermaid style with a small band of lace around the top of each arm.

"I feel very exposed," I murmur nervously.

"That's sort of the point," Jess reminds me. "For the scent marking."

Nodding, I focus on tracing the delicate whirls in the lace as my mother and Jess finish up. Then finally, they draw me around to look in the mirror.

My mother bursts into tears as I take my first look. "Oh, Sienna!"

Jess meets my eyes in the glass. "This is it, Si," she whispers. "This is your day."

13
# GRAYSON

Taking a last look in the mirror, I close my eyes and blow out a deep breath. A shrill tone sounds from the floor underneath me and I grimace at my reflection. No matter where Alicia may be, her voice can still be heard from at least a mile away. At least I can hear her coming and head the other way.

*For fuck's sake. How have we gotten into this mess?*

I got us into this mess.

I can't even blame Logan – it was me who persuaded him into a moment of madness outside the protective walls of our home. I just wanted to feel *normal* for a single moment, to be an alpha who could be with his chosen partner in public, even if we thought the car park was empty.

And now my whole pack is paying the price.

And not just us – Sienna Michaels too. Regret dulls my chest as I take a final moment to straighten the collar of my black shirt. Our long-awaited mate has no idea that she's walking into a living hell. Our only hope is that she withdraws immediately after the Bonding Trials – and she'd be fucking crazy not to, with what Alicia has planned. Once Sienna is free and far away from us, we can look for a way out of this whole fucking mess.

A brief knock sounds at the door, and I pull it open to Jax. His

EVELYN FLOOD

eyes barely glance at me before he looks away, his anger still pulsing in waves that fill the corridor around us.

"You ready?" His words are jerky, his normally vibrant violet eyes shadowed with the knowledge of exactly how today will go down. Like a fucking shitshow.

"Yeah." Hesitating, I reach out, setting my hand on his arm. "Jax, we didn't want to hide it from you. Logan wanted to tell you. I just didn't want to put you or Tris in a difficult position."

He shakes his head, pulling back from me. "We're supposed to be a pack, Gray. Even though I get it, I'm still fucking furious at you for not telling me. But we can't talk about it now. Let's get this over with."

Nodding, I follow him down to the kitchen. Tristan and Logan are there, matching in black tuxedos with black shirts. Normally alphas wear as little as possible on top to give the omega the best chance at scent matching – but this isn't a normal Bonding ceremony.

Tristan, his face dark but resolved, glances between us.

"Let's go."

"What about Alicia?" I ask, and Tristan scowls.

"She can meet us in the car."

"No need!" she trills. "I'm ready."

Turning, I bite back my snippy response. Alicia is clearly determined to stand out like a sore fucking thumb – her white gown billows around her, yards upon yards of tulle and sequins and I don't even know the fuck what.

Nobody wears white to a Bonding Ceremony. Only the omega.

"You look fucking ridiculous," Jax snarls, and Alicia pouts, her scarlet lips glistening.

"Don't be like that, Jaxy," she coos, patting him on the chest as he recoils in disgust. "That is not the look of a man in love."

"That's because I fucking hate you," he shoots back, and she scowls.

"We have an agreement," she snaps, stamping her stiletto-heeled foot. "Do we not, Tristan?"

"In public." But Tristan turns, wordlessly pulling open the front door as his shoulders bunch. Alicia drapes herself in a long green cape and marches after him, struggling to pull herself into the car thanks to the fucking meringue she's got on. We all stand there and watch until she screeches for help, Tristan reluctantly shoving her in before he gets behind the wheel.

Sliding in, I manage to claim an inch of space that isn't crammed with sequins. All of us sit in silence for the ride to the city, Alicia checking her makeup in the mirror.

"Now, do we all remember the plan?" she preens, clicking her compact closed. "Everybody understands what they have to do?"

"Unfortunately," Logan mutters.

Wordlessly I nod, keeping my attention outside the window. I'm not doing this shit for Alicia Erikkson. I'm doing it for Sienna, even if she never knows it.

Even though she'll hate us for it.

As we reach the courtyard area that's used to hold the opening of the Trials, Tristan parks up, throwing his keys to a beta valet who gapes at Alicia's monstrosity. She struggles out of the car, rearranging the cape to cover the majority of the dress.

"You need to leave now," Tristan orders. "We'll find you."

"Make sure you do." She flounces off towards the public entrance, where guests are starting to gather and leaving a bleak silence in her wake.

Tristan clears his throat. "We do this right, and we can make sure Sienna is free and clear of us before she even has to set foot in the house."

Jax swipes his hand over his face. "It's not fucking right, Tristan."

Tristan stares at him. "Nothing about this is right, Jax. The last thing I want to do is get up there and humiliate an omega who doesn't fucking deserve it. But better that than what's waiting for her if she stays around Alicia."

Agreed. I don't know what the fuck this omega did to make Alicia hate her so much, but the sheer poison of her hatred worries me, no matter what agreement Tristan made with Erikkson to try and protect her.

"Tristan?" a voice calls and we look over to see David beckoning us. The flash of pain across Tristan's face disappears in a flash, hidden behind the smooth mask of his political smile.

"Dad." He tenses as David wraps him in a hug.

David pulls back, his expression a little confused as he looks over our suits. "Black? Interesting choice for your Bonding Ceremony."

I try to smile. "We wanted to look our best."

"Of course." He gestures us through the small door into a preparation room.

"How are you all doing?" he asks. "Excited? I remember my Bonding Ceremony like it was yesterday."

"Can't wait," Jax drawls, a slight edge to his voice that makes Tristan give him a warning look.

"We're all a little nervous," he hedges to David.

"It wouldn't be a Bonding Ceremony if you weren't." David smiles before he takes a step back.

"As you know, Ollena Hayward is in charge of briefing your omega before the Trials begin. As Council Leader and the most senior Alpha representative on the Council, you have me to take you through your own pre-Trials briefing. Take a seat, and we'll get started."

We all sink into the comfortable chairs dotted around the room. Jax works a finger under his collar to loosen it slightly, his hands twitching. I wonder if he wants a drink as badly as I do right now.

I glance at Logan where he's determinedly staring at David. His eyes flick to me once before moving back, his face expressionless.

David's brows crease as he looks between us.

"On behalf of the Omega Hub, I'd like to formally welcome you to your Bonding Ceremony. This is step one of the Bonding Trials, where your matched omega will progress through a series of tests to assess her suitability before a final mating Ceremony takes place.

"The first trial, scent matching, will take place today. When you are announced by the Head of the Omega Hub, you move directly to your mate. Tristan, as Pack Leader, you'll be going first, then it's oldest to youngest.

"The purpose of scent matching is to ensure that both the omega and the proposed pack are attracted to each other on a biological level. To assess this, the omega must inhale your scent, and you hers. Not just that, but you must ensure that your scent is embedded into her skin, where it will remain for the duration of the trials. Should the Mating Ceremony not go ahead, the scent will fade.

"The first Trial and Bonding Ceremony can be extremely daunting for omegas, and as their future pack, it's your responsibility to make sure they feel at ease. Is that clear?"

"Crystal," Jax drawls, and grunts as Tristan kicks him.

David crosses his arms. "That's it. What's wrong?"

Tristan clears his throat. "Nothing, dad."

David looks between us, his eyes assessing, but we're a closed book. He sighs.

"I'm proud of you all, you know."

I swallow back the shame at his words. David has been more of a dad to me than my own damned father.

He talks us through some of the finer points of the Trials, pointing out particular things we need to pay attention to.

"Remember that failing any Trial brings the whole process to an end," he warns us. "There are no do-overs, but you'll be able to try again with a different omega."

"They can choose to withdraw, though, right?" I ask, and David raises an eyebrow.

"You are able to end the Trials at any time. Your omega does not have the same option. She can withdraw only once, with the permission of Ollena Hayward and only if Ollena feels that her safety and wellbeing is being put at risk. Outside of this, she is legally required to see the Trials through. If she does remove herself, she will be banned from participating in the Bonding Trials in the future – thus removing the option of a pack, and therefore children. It's not a decision that any omega makes lightly. I can't see that happening here, can you?"

We all exchange loaded glances. If she withdraws, then she's essentially excluding herself from the possibility of ever having a family of her own.

But if she doesn't… then we have to Deny her, if we can't find a way out of this mess.

It won't get that far. But fuck, the impossible situation we're in is weighing heavily on my shoulders.

## 14
## SIENNA

My dress swishes around my bare heels as I carefully make my way down the stairs. Jessalyn sniffles as she looks up at me, her eyes red-rimmed.

"You look beautiful, Si," she whispers as I pass her, and I reach out, grabbing her hand for a quick squeeze before I turn to my family.

My mother smiles softly at me. "You're perfect, sweetheart."

Turning to my dad, I bite back my tears as he steps forward, his own eyes damp.

"Oh, Sienna," he whispers. "Look at you. You're all grown up now."

He opens his arms, and I throw myself into them as they carefully close around me. My dad rocks me gently.

"No matter what, sweet girl," he whispers. "You always have a home here, with people who love you."

I bite back the reassurance, the knowledge that I'm walking to meet my Soul Bonded.

They'll find out soon enough.

Stepping back, I dab my eyes with the handkerchief my mother holds out with shaking hands. Steeling my spine, I turn towards the door, pausing only to ruffle Elise's hair as she scowls at me, her displeasure at being manhandled into a dress clear.

"Look after my room, you," I murmur to her, tugging on an errant curl that's escaped from her bun. "It's all yours now."

Her lip wobbles as she crashes into my waist, my mother gently admonishing her as I rock her gently from side to side.

Jessalyn clears her throat behind me. "It's time to go, Michaels family. Before I actually dissolve into a puddle of tears."

Snorting out a laugh, I take my father's outstretched arm, blowing out a breath as we turn to the door. Today, all eyes will be on me, and it starts the moment I leave my family home as a resident for the last time.

Dad squeezes my hand gently where it balances against his wrist. "Deep breath, sweetheart. The day will fly by."

Giving him a grateful smile, I nod towards the doors. "Let's go."

Cohen pack… here I come.

The ride to the Omega Hub is a blur. My father's comforting taps on my wrist act as an anchor, the conversation between my mother and Jess a blur as we fly through the streets of Navarre, people stopping to watch the omega on her way to the Bonding Trials. Ribbons trail behind us, white sashes draped strategically across every angle. Some people cheer, and I even manage a half-hearted smile, although it looks more like a grimace. I think a baby starts to cry.

*Need to practice that one before any Council events.*

Seven hundred years later (approximately) we pull up outside, mama and Jess fussing with my skirt as I step out, my bare feet warming from the sun on the clean bleached sandstone.

Ollena Hayward stands at the top of the stone steps, her green eyes watching as I smooth down the lace. "Welcome to the Bonding Trials, Sienna Michaels. Please, say your goodbyes and follow me."

This is it. Swallowing hard, I turn to Mama and Jess. They both stare back at me, eyes wide.

"Okay," Jess mutters. She gives me a careful hug, mindful of my gown. "You look like a freaking goddess, Sienna Michaels. Own that shit. They won't know what's hit 'em."

My mother lifts up her hand, carefully cupping my cheek. "I love you, sweetheart. We'll see you soon."

Her voice breaks, and my father draws her away, his arms wrapping around her as he whispers soothing words into her ear. They'll be at the ceremony, but I won't actually see my family or Jess now until the conclusion of the Trials.

The only exception is my father, who gets to escort me to the courtyard for my first trial. He holds out his arm, his eyes twinkling. "Shall we?"

I blow out a breath. "We shall," I say, carefully placing my hand in the crook of his arm. We follow slowly after Ollena, the lace of my gown trailing behind me up the steps. I pause, turning to give one final wave to Mama and Jess before I turn to face the day ahead.

Ollena leads us into a small but ornate room, gesturing for us to take a seat in the dark leather armchairs. I sit, but my father stands at my shoulder, his hand squeezing my shoulder in reassurance as Ollena settles herself opposite us.

"How are you feeling?" she asks, clasping her hands on her crossed knees. She's resplendent in vibrant green robes that match her eyes, her official Councilor garb to reflect her role in today's events.

"Fine." I bite my lip. "Excited?"

"It's normal to be a little nervous," she reassures me. "Today is a highly public event, but afterwards you'll have the chance to unwind and get to know your alphas properly, in the privacy of the home you'll share together should the Trial progress well."

When I nod, she drops her eyes to the slim folder in her lap. "There are four alphas in your pack. Tristan, Jax, Grayson and Logan Cohen. Although we discourage the meeting of mates ahead of the Trials, this pack is relatively high-profile, so you may well have met before."

When she raises a questioning eyebrow, I shake my head, guilt eating away at my tiny lie. It's not a *complete* lie. I've only met one. "I…ah… haven't met them before."

"Good," she says crisply. "Things tend to go more smoothly when that's the case. As you should know from your training, the first Trial is scent matching. The purpose of this is to make sure you and your potential mates are compatible. Scents are incredibly important in a relationship, and the first Trial is often the one most commonly failed."

"And if I fail, that's it? I can't try again?" It all suddenly feels very daunting.

Ollena nods. "That's correct."

"And if Sienna decides she doesn't want this pack?" my dad asks suddenly. "Where does she get a choice?"

Ollena cocks her head. "The Trials are… admittedly weighted towards the alpha's preferences. Once they begin, the Trials must be seen through by law. There is only one chance to withdraw. As the Head of the Omega Hub, I remain ultimately responsible for your wellbeing during these Trials. Should I see anything that concerns me, I am able to offer one single opportunity to withdraw. If that is refused, there is nothing more I can do until the Trials are concluded. If you withdraw outside of these permitted limits, then the same applies, and you will not be permitted to take part again. Packs, however, are able to withdraw at any point without penalty."

Meaning the Cohen pack is likely my first and only shot at having a family of my own.

With Jax as my Soul Bonded, I don't think my next question will be an issue, but I ask it anyway. "And if I am… Denied?"

A shadow crosses Ollena's face, her thin lips tightening. "It's an archaic practice, but I am yet to be successful in removing it from the laws around the Bonding Trials. A pack has the power to decide if an omega is completely unsuitable for mating. Not just them, but any alpha pack. They can choose to Deny their omega, and the omega in question will be banished from Navarre, over the wall."

My dad stiffens. "But that doesn't happen, right?"

Ollena nods. "We have never had a Denied omega. Nevertheless, the law is there, and so I choose to highlight it as part of the Trials process, so that omegas can enter the Trials fully informed."

She leans forward. "Do you have any further questions, Sienna?"

I have hundreds of questions, but I don't think the woman across from me will have the time or patience to deal with my insecurities, so I shake my head.

"Excellent. In that case, I have some paperwork for you to sign."

It's all very clinical, as she produces the forms. I scan the papers briefly, my dad gently confiscating them so he can have a read through too before he hands them back to me with a nod.

Ollena holds up her hand. "By signing this document, you agree to enter the Bonding Trials. From this moment on, you will be bound to the law regarding the Bonding Trials, and you will be unable to withdraw, aside from and unless the particular circumstances I have mentioned arise. Do you agree, Sienna Michaels?"

My mouth feels dry as she hands me an ornate fountain pen. "I do."

And then I sign my name.

Ollena smiles. "Good. It's very formal, I know. I'll give you a few minutes to compose yourself. When you're ready, please exit through the curtain. Your father may escort you to your position, but he then must return to his seat."

She waits for me to nod, before she disappears through the billowing curtain. Noise filters through, the chatting and laughter of Navarre society settling in to view the first of my Trials. I've never attended one, but many consider them opportunities for networking.

When I stand up, my dad walks around to face me. He lifts my hand, kissing it just like he did when I was a kid, playing princesses and demanding he be my knight in shining armor.

"I have never been so proud to be your father," he says softly. "And remember what I said. You always have a home with us, sweetheart. No matter what."

My eyes burn, but I swallow back the tears. "Thanks, dad."

Bracing myself, I turn and walk towards the curtain, my dad next to me.

Today is the first day of the rest of my life.

And my Soul Bonded are on the other side. Probably.

## 15
# TRISTAN

Our pack stands shoulder to shoulder, all four of us gathered at the end of the aisle leading up to the circular area where we'll complete the first Trial. White curtains flutter in the light breeze where our mate will soon make her appearance.

She has no idea what's in store for her.

The light blue carpeted aisle, littered with white flower petals, stretches out in front of us, surrounded on both sides by rows and rows of chairs, all filled with simpering, laughing people, all here to watch the latest Trials kick off. One group is more subdued as they make their way to a few chairs set aside in the front row.

Jax nudges me. "Think those are the in-laws?" he mutters.

I don't respond, but my eyes flick to the blonde-haired, still beautiful omega, and the younger girl she escorts protectively, an arm around her shoulders. They're followed by another omega with wild bronzed ringlets, who'd probably be the same age as our mate.

All of their eyes turn to us, taking us in with serious looks.

Definitely family.

I turn my eyes from them. They won't be our family. No matter how much I wish otherwise. Although, with our Soul Bonded out there somewhere according to Jax, this whole thing might just turn out to be a blessing in disguise. For us and Sienna Michaels.

There's a swell of murmuring and shocked looks, and I close my eyes as a familiar simper fills the air.

"Fucking hell," Gray mutters, and I crack them open to watch Alicia forcing herself down into the front row seat left open for her by Erikkson. His eyes are on me, filled with gleaming, oily satisfaction as his daughter whips off her cloak, unveiling the full fucking white blancmange monstrosity she's chosen to wear. Gasps ring out across the room, people craning their heads to get a good look.

The omega that walked in with the Michaels family leans forward, her mouth moving as she gestures. The blonde-haired omega says something back to her, not even looking in Alicia's direction, and the omega grits her teeth, throwing her bronze hair back in a huff as she follows Sienna's mothers lead and faces the circle.

This whole thing is a fucking farce. I'm just sorry they're caught in the middle of it.

There's movement ahead of us, and my muscles tighten as Ollena Hayward emerges from behind the curtain. She walks up to a podium, her arms opening wide as she addresses the crowd.

"Good afternoon, Navarre," she announces. "And welcome to the Bonding Trials. Today, we welcome the members of the Cohen pack, and one Sienna Michaels, to participate in their first Trial. The scent matching trial is performed in front of family and friends, to cement the bond that will hold true throughout their journey together."

Alicia simpers, a high-pitched, wheezing sound that makes a few heads turn. Ignoring her, I keep my eyes on the circle.

"I call upon Sienna Michaels," Ollena calls. "To join the circle and take her first steps towards becoming a Bonded omega."

The curtain moves, a pale hand separating the panels.

My whole body locks up as Sienna Michaels emerges from

behind the curtain, her hands white where they hold her father's arm.

Beside me, Jax inhales sharply. "*Tristan.*"

His voice is agonized. And I get it immediately, the same, potent fury washing through me as I take Sienna Michaels in. Her beautiful, elegant white lace dress hugs perfectly shaped curves as she kisses her father on the cheek, and he steps down to sit next to her mother.

She turns to face us, wide, petrified blue eyes in a pale face. And glorious, cascading pink curls.

My fists clench. Sienna Michaels isn't just our mate, selected for us by the powers that be that run the Bonding Trials.

She's our Soul Bonded. It hits me like a thunderbolt, the knowing, the urge to stride up there, scoop her up and carry her away nearly overwhelming.

"Fuck," Logan groans. "What do we do?"

Gray takes a half-step forward, but my hand shoots out, grabbing his wrist. I have to make a decision, and I have to make it now.

I just pray to God she'll forgive me.

"We carry on," I force out. "As planned."

"What?" Jax hisses. "You can't be serious. This changes everything!"

I shake my head, the movement miniscule. "No, it doesn't. We still have to protect her. Continue with the plan."

And even if she hates us for it now, maybe one day we can explain. As soon as we get this mess sorted out, we can throw ourselves at her feet for forgiveness.

But right now, we need her out of the firing line.

"Tristan Cohen," Ollena Hayward calls. "Step forward."

I brace myself. Beside me, Jax growls, but he doesn't say anything as I step away from my pack.

Towards my Soul Bonded.

16

# SIENNA

My father walks away from me, leaving me free to stare down the aisle at the four alphas in front of me.

There they are.

Oh, God.

Sunlight casts shadows across the path in front of me as Tristan Cohen takes a step forward, his fists clenched. My brow creases before I smooth it out, conscious of the watching eyes waiting to judge us.

He doesn't exactly look thrilled to be here. Maybe he's just as petrified as I am.

My body leans forward involuntarily as he stalks up the aisle, his face blank. Taking a deep breath, I choke as his scent hits me, sharp warmth like the bite of whiskey on a winter night wrapping around me. He smells like *home*. God, I want to rub myself up against him. My mother would be horrified if I did that in the middle of my Bonding Ceremony though.

Jubilation fills me as his eyes finally lift to mine, his nostrils flaring as he sucks in a breath of his own, his step stuttering slightly.

My lips lift in a tremulous smile, anticipation flipping my

stomach upside down as he reaches the circle. This is it. This is the moment he realizes that I'm his Soul Bonded.

Any second now.

Tristan pauses before he takes a step closer, his muscular body brushing against mine. I have to tip my head back to look into his face, his body brushing against mine. Tipping my head back, I stare into his eyes, wondering at the blaze of color. One the vibrant green of the forest lining the wall surrounding Navarre, the other the jeweled blue of the ocean.

Tristan studies me just as intently, his full lips tightened into a flat line.

"Hello." It's a whisper between us, dropping like a stone in the awkward silence that I'm met with on meeting my god damned Soul Bonded.

It's not supposed to be this awkward, right? I mean, I can feel him inside me. It's a yearning, a draw in my chest pulling me towards him, like I've suddenly discovered the North Star.

Maybe I've done something wrong? Frowning as my eyes slide down to his chest, I think back. I don't think I've missed anything. Tristan's face tightens and pulls into a scowl.

"Let's get this over with."

It takes me a second to process.

My mouth drops open as I stare at him wordlessly, hurt hitting me straight in the chest.

I mean, I'm not anything special, but…

"Don't you feel it?" I ask him. My lips feel numb. He cocks a perfect brow at me.

"Feel what?" he asks abruptly, glancing behind him. The crowd starts to murmur.

"We need to hurry this up. The others are waiting."

I lean around him, catching a glimpse of the others waiting. Jax's face is like thunder.

None of them look happy.

Oh god. They're… disappointed. Furious, even.

And we're stuck together, because there's absolutely no doubt in my mind that these alphas are my Soul Bonded.

My eyes burn, but I force myself to nod when Tristan turns his unsettling eyes back to me. "Of course. Do what you need to do."

His hands lift, hesitating, before he rests them on my shoulders. They tremble beneath his light grip, and he squeezes lightly before he glances away again.

His hands are gentle, completely at odds with his brusque manner as he tugs me towards him until we're pressed together, our breaths mingling. His scent grows impossibly warmer, deeper, and I soften against him until his hands slide behind my back, holding me up.

Slightly woozy, I blink up at him as he leans down. A hint of beard surprises me, making me shiver as he sinks his face into my bare neck. His hands clench against me, hot against the lace material as he inhales against my skin, the rasp of his stubble dragging down against my neck as his other hand moves to my neck, pulling gently until I'm completely bent for him, his leg between mine.

I don't know what his damn problem is, but it sure isn't lack of attraction. Because I can feel it in the harsh pants of our breathing mingling together, the desperation of his hands as they yank me towards him. I'm burning for him, fire twisting up my insides and licking into a molten furnace in my abdomen.

The whine that slips out is embarrassingly loud, and I blink as a few chuckles break through the air, belatedly remembering that we have an audience. Tristan's hands release in an instant, and I yelp as I tumble backwards, only his arm shooting out and grabbing my hand stopping me from falling.

His fingers grip mine, his eyes burning into me as he helps me stand upright. His fingers trace the inside of my wrist before he steps back, the expressionless mask falling back into place.

I stare at him in confusion as he turns on his heel, striding back down the aisle to where the rest of the Cohen pack waits. Tristan ignores them, and whispers start as he makes his way down past the assembled guests, every single one watching him avidly, apart from Jessalyn, who gives me a WTF look from her seat and fans her face dramatically. Even my mother is watching him, her mouth slightly open.

Every single person is watching my Soul Bonded as he stops in front of Alicia Erikkson. She smirks at him as he holds out a hand, his body tense.

Gasps echo across the room as my heart stops in my chest, the lance of pain so vicious that I stumble.

Because he's kissing her as though his life depends on it.

## 17
## JAX

The pain is blinding. I stumble but I'm already halfway to her and I'm not fucking stopping for anything.

My Bonded is rigid, her arms dangling loosely from her sides as she stares behind me, her face white.

I take the steps two at a time, and she blinks as I reach her, my hand reaching up to her face.

"Sienna." My growl is furious, and she shrinks back. Shit.

Dropping my hand, I watch her as I desperately try to think of a way out of this fucked up situation that doesn't hit my pack or my Bonded. And I've got nothing.

If we can get this shithouse of a ceremony over and done with, we can get back to the house, away from prying eyes and come up with a plan.

Ollena Hayward moves into sight, her normally serene face flushed with fury.

"Mr. Cohen," she says, her voice low and furious. "This is not how a Bonding Ceremony works."

Throat dry, I stare at Sienna in desperation. Her pain is still pulsing as she stares blankly out across the crowd.

Have to finish it.

Turning to Ollena, I nod in deference. "There's nothing in the Trial rules that says this isn't allowed, Councilor."

Self-loathing sits like ash on my tongue as Sienna flinches. The Councilor's mouth opens and closes several times as she glances between us. Finally, she settles on Sienna.

"Ms Michaels. Mr. Cohen is, in fact, correct. However, I strongly recommend that you withdraw from the Trials now. I would never normally offer this option so soon, but it's clear there are... extenuating circumstances. We can find you another pack."

Staunch refusal wars with hope in my chest. If Sienna withdraws, she'll be safe and away from that fucking psychopath.

But she'll be away from me.

Sienna moves her eyes slowly from Tristan and Alicia, settling on my face. I don't look her in the eye, waiting for the words to come, dreading the moment they do.

"No."

My head shoots up as Ollena gasps. "Ms Michaels—,"

"It's my choice." Her words are direct, even as her voice trembles. "And I choose to keep going."

*Fuck, fuck, fuck.*

"Don't be stupid," I snarl at her. "Withdraw!"

This is her only fucking chance. Her one and only option is to pull out and be able to take part in future, and she's turning it down.

But then, we're her Soul Bonded. *Fuck.*

Sienna takes a breath, visibly pulling herself together as she nods to the omega Councilor. "I'm ready to continue."

Ollena glances between us both, her mouth pursed, before she shakes her head and moves past us.

"Settle, please," she calls out. "The Trial continues."

I swear I hear a yelped *"What the actual fuck"* before the crowd quietens. Turning back to Sienna, I scan her face. She watches me just as carefully, the hope in her expression well and truly gone. She just looks... empty.

We did that to her.

"Sienna," I breathe, stepping forward. "Why didn't you withdraw?"

I drag her scent into my lungs, greedily inhaling every possible part of her I can.

"This isn't right," she whispers, and my head shoots up. "What?"

"This." She gestures between us. "You *know* what we are."

I hesitate, before I look away. If I say it, if I admit it out loud... I won't be able to do this. And that makes me the worst type of fucking coward, but I can't stop the thrill that whispers in my veins that she's still here, that she didn't choose to withdraw.

"You don't know what you're getting into," I warn. I take another step, drinking in the way her cheeks flush as she looks up at me, the emptiness replaced by a familiar need that mirrors my own. "You should withdraw," I whisper, leaning in and trailing my lips across her neck, tasting the flutter of her pulse, the spike of raspberries that makes me want to lick. To bite down. Fucking mouthwatering.

Sienna's head tips back, a cascade of glorious pink spilling down her back, sprinkled with flowers like some goddamn fairytale creature.

"I know," she murmurs. Her breathing stutters as my hand slides behind her neck, the possessive hold drawing the hint of a growl from my chest. I want this omega desperately. I'd walk through fire for her, do anything to make her smile, to see her spread out across my bed, to drink in the sound of her cries as I take her.

And I'd do anything to keep her safe.

I press one last kiss into her neck, stealing one last precious moment before I shatter us into a million pieces. "I'm sorry," I whisper.

And then I walk away, retracing Tristan's footsteps as Gray passes me, his jaw set.

Alicia grins at me maniacally, the flurry of whispers turning into hushed exclamations of shock as I grab her face between mine, squeezing just a little too hard as I smash my mouth against hers in a mockery of a kiss. I push her back after a scant second, taking my spot next to Tristan and ignoring the stabbing in my chest.

Ignoring my Soul Bonded. Her emotions are leaking out across us all like a damned homing beacon. If I look at her, I'll go to her. I won't be able to stop myself.

Squeezing my eyes shut, I wait.

## 18
# SIENNA

I don't know what I expected. But the devastation only grows inside me as the next alpha walks towards me, his copper hair glinting like rusted blood in the sunlight.

I expected more from Jax. And he just shattered my fragile hope like confetti. Took the last, tiny piece of my heart and crushed it beneath the shining black dress shoes he's worn to this farce of a Bonding Ceremony.

I should have withdrawn. Soul Bonded or not.

I don't smile as Grayson Cohen moves into position opposite me. And he doesn't either. Rather, he nods at me, almost respectfully.

"Shall we get this over with?" he offers, his voice low.

The lump in my throat grows. *Get it over with.* Like I'm an imposition. Some unwanted chore on the list.

Like the most important day of our lives isn't burning to the ground in front of us, helped along by a scarlet-haired beta bitch who's grinning at me from her front row seat to my humiliation.

"Let's."

The word drops like a stone into the heavy atmosphere as I tip my head to the side, and Grayson steps into the now familiar position, the heat of his body warming mine. I didn't realize how cold I felt, and I shake as he curls his hand around my neck.

Breathing in, I close my eyes at the warmth he's giving off, his campfire and toasted marshmallow scent surprisingly soft for such a harsh looking alpha.

*Three for three so far.*

The awareness that he's my Soul Bonded too, that moment of wonder, is swamped beneath the pain beating a vicious rhythm in my chest. It feels unbearable.

But I'll be damned if I don't see this through.

Instead of layering his scent, Grayson pulls me until our foreheads rest gently together. Squeezing my eyes shut, I wait for him to move.

"I'm so sorry," he whispers. His voice shakes a little. "Truly, Sienna."

The sob breaks out. Just one, but Grayson pulls back sharply.

"Come on," I whisper, my eyes still shut. "*Get it over with.*"

"Sienna."

My eyes fly open, meeting his electric blue gaze. He's so sad.

"No," I seethe. "You don't get to do that. You don't get to come here, to do this, and then do that."

I tilt my neck, pushing it towards him. He doesn't move.

"Do it!"

I feel his flinch, his hand on my neck slipping away as he takes a deep breath before he leans in, his cheek smooth as he traces the same path as his pack members before him. A low groan rumbles in his chest, his hand becoming a tight band as he yanks me tightly against him, his breathing harsh against my skin.

"Jesus. Your scent—,"

It's enough. Steeling myself, I reach up my arms and push him away. He staggers, rubbing a hand roughly down his face as he glances away.

"Shit – Sienna—,"

"Go." I didn't know I could be this cold. Could feel this cold. "Consider it *over with.*"

He swallows. "I deserve that."

And then he leaves me, too. I don't watch, the muttering of the crowd and the steady sobs of my mother enough to tell me exactly what is happening right now.

My eyes stay firmly fixed on the ground until a silhouette moves into view. "Sienna?"

Bracing myself, I glance up and into a pair of soulful chestnut eyes. Honey blonde hair falls in loose curls to Logan Cohen's shoulders, a hint of dark stubble not doing enough to hide the hint of a dimple. But he's not smiling now.

Logan shifts on his feet, and I stare him out. However uncomfortable he feels, it's nothing compared to how I feel right now.

Finally, he swallows, and takes a step forward. And it's the pain on his face, the realization of how desperately he doesn't want to be here, that tips me over the edge.

I take a step away from him, and he stops, his outstretched hand dropping to the side.

"Sienna." His voice is gruffer than I expected. Tristan's was smooth, like the whiskey scent embedded into his skin. And mine now, I guess. Jax's voice holds the promise of music in every word, like he's about to launch into the songs he's so well-known for. And Grayson, he was steady. Measured.

But I don't know why I'm focusing so hard on their voices. Or why I'm still standing here, when they so clearly don't want me. I can't force myself on them, Soul Bonded or not.

Logan takes another step, and I wave him off. "I need a minute."

Turning away from the sight of him, so close and yet so fucking far away, I stare blindly at the white gauze hanging between the pillars behind us until they blur, the tears starting to fall.

I tried so hard to hold out, to stand here and not let any of them see how badly this hurts. But I can't keep it in anymore.

I already feel like I *need* them. The need is a pulsing, pacing creature inside me. And it's not going anywhere, not now that I've found them. This craving will only get worse, this desire to be close to my Bonded. My parents don't leave each other's side. *It hurts more the longer you're separated,* my mother told me once. *But it doesn't matter, because there's nowhere else I'd rather be.*

My hand claws at my throat. I can't breathe. I'm drowning on dry land; there's not enough air and I can't fucking breathe. White spots dance in front of me as a pair of hands land on my shoulder, spinning me around and folding me into them.

"Shhh, Sienna." Logan is rocking me slowly, my face buried against his chest, his shirt growing damp as he whispers my name over and over. I breathe him in, sucking down lemon sherbet like an addict searching out my next fix, my hands clawing into his shirt.

"I—I can't-,"

I can't stop.

"You're alright." Logan continues to rock me. "This is fucked up, but you can't stop, Sienna. Not now you've refused to withdraw."

If I do, I'll fail the Trial and forfeit my chance at any future rematch. I gave up my one and only chance when I told Ollena I'd carry on. I won't have another.

"One more," Logan whispers. His rocking slows, then stops, but we don't move. "Just one more, sweetheart. Then we can leave. I'm so sorry."

I suck down a few more breaths until the shuddering stops, pushing him back with a nod. His hands slip to my face as he wipes my wet cheeks. "Are you ready?"

In answer, I open myself for him, my neck tilting once more for him to layer his scent into my skin.

"Good girl," he breathes as he leans in. The twisting, clenching in my abdomen spikes, and a low whine slips out. Logan freezes, his skin warm against mine. "Sienna?"

"Do it. Now, please," I force out through the mortification.

*Sure, Sienna. Cry all over the Soul Bonded who is very publically rejecting you and then whine when he rubs his face in your neck.*

I wait for Logan to grip my neck, but he slides his hand up and into my hair, underneath the layers of flowers to cradle the back of my head as his arm slips around my waist. He holds me like I'm something precious.

They all did. And that hurts most of all.

When he's done, fresh lemon sherbet sinking into my skin, he takes a step away, looking behind him before he glances back at me.

I wet my lips. "Are you waiting for permission?"

Turning, he makes his way down the aisle, and I catch a glimpse of Jessalyn glaring at him, my mother's hand clamped around her arm.

It's nearly over. Just one more humiliating moment to go.

I force myself to watch as Logan brushes a kiss over Alicia's glistening mouth. She continues to grin, even as they all walk away from her, back towards me as Ollena Hayward reappears, a white ribbon twisting uncertainly between her fingers.

Our normally unflappable omega Council representative is well and truly flapped. Her mouth opens, then closes again as the Cohen pack forms a circle, Tristan standing to my right.

Warmth brushes my arm as I stare straight ahead, my eyes on Ollena. She meets my eyes with a question as her head tilts to the side soundlessly, and I nod, straightening my back.

"Reach out your hands."

The words are almost sorrowful as the five of us lift our hands in unison, holding them out towards the center of the circle. Tristan's knuckles are white next to mine, his fists clenched as Ollena works between us, looping the ribbon around our wrists.

Stepping back, she blows out a breath before turning to the crowd.

"Tristan Cohen. Has your omega passed the Scent Marking ceremony?"

I brace myself, waiting for the tense alpha next to me to

finalize my humiliation. At least it'll stop here. They'll stop it, and I can go home, lick my wounds and try to figure out how the hell I move away from this, now that I've found them.

The ribbon pulls lightly against my wrist as he hesitates, before his voice rings out.

"She has. We accept Sienna Michaels as a potential Bonded."

Gasps of shock ring out around the room as I spin to Tristan, the ribbon pulling tightly at my wrist.

"Are you *serious*?" I snap.

He only looks at me, those mixed eyes impossibly dark before he looks away. "It's done."

19

# SIENNA

It's done?

It's fucking done?

"It's not done." My gaze swings to Jax and quickly moves to Grayson. "What the hell is this?"

Why the hell would they want to continue with this shitshow of a Bonding Trial when they have someone else? My eyes dart to Alicia Erikkson. She smiles widely, her hands smoothing down her elaborate gown before she lifts her fingers and wiggles them at me.

My eyes skip over my family. I can't face them right now.

"Why?" I ask quietly, facing forward. "This makes no sense, Tristan."

Unless their only goal is to cause me as much pain as possible.

His jaw works, but he doesn't give me anything more than an empty "I'm sorry."

The ribbon loosens, the ceremony complete, and his arm drops, sending a swirl of heated whiskey warmth my way. My stomach twists, wanting something that apparently isn't on the table. Or is. I'm not quite sure right now.

"Me too." I murmur. The rest of the pack glances towards me uncertainly as Ollena gestures us forward, brow furrowed.

Flinching, I try and pull my hand back when Tristan grabs it, and he turns to me.

"It's nearly over," he says through gritted teeth.

"It would have been over already if you'd done the decent thing, asshole," I snap back. His head whips towards me in surprise, a hint of color flaring on his cheeks. I bite back the meek apology on my lips, because he sure as hell doesn't deserve any forgiveness from me.

He takes a few steps forward, his huge hand still swallowing mine until I'm forced to follow, the others falling into line behind us.

Where there would normally be cheers and confetti, there is only silence. My mother actually whimpers as we walk past, hushed whispers of consolation coming from my father.

We make our way further down until we're level with Alicia.

"What a wonderful ceremony," she trills loudly. "Just lovely."

Tristan's hand tightens around mine and he carries on walking, until we reach the double doors, the promise of privacy and maybe some fucking answers tantalisingly close.

I'm trying really hard not to soak in the feel of his hand gripping mine, the protective promise and strength behind it. The doors ahead waver as my eyes fill up and I blink rapidly as they swing open, Tristan pulling me through until we all stand silently in the hallway.

I yank my hand away and move to the side, my arms wrapping around me as I shiver. The warmth of the day is leached away by the cool stone around us, and I hug myself to the wall as others storm through the doors after us, closing out the gossiping whispers.

A wide-shouldered alpha, dark-haired with lines of gray, approaches Tristan in a storm. His hand reaches out to grab Tristan's throat and I flinch back against the wall.

"Explain. Now." The words are sharpened steel. Tristan meets the gaze of who I'm guessing may be his father unflinchingly, despite the paleness of his face. "I can't. It's done."

"You damn well can." Straightening, I press my back against the cool stone as my father follows Tristan's dad through the doors. My throat grows thick as he raises a shaking finger to Tristan's face, the Cohen alphas moving to flank their pack leader.

"You," my father forces out, "don't deserve to be an alpha. And you sure as hell don't deserve my daughter."

"I agree." Tristan flinches as his own father chimes in.

Knees shaking, I slowly slide down the wall, grateful for the white muslin that gives me some semblance of privacy to pull myself together.

"Tristan," his dad starts, just a little softer. "This isn't you. What happened?"

I watch, hands clasped around my knees as Tristan stiffens. "Nothing. I simply realized that our outdated traditions also include the Bonding Trials. We shouldn't have to go through such a complicated process to find a partner, and nor should the omega."

Frowning, I stare down at my hands. *That... doesn't make sense.*

His father steps back, disbelief etched on his face. "So this is some sort of rebellion? Do you understand what today will cost you, Tristan? Your pack? Your omega?"

He nods. The others cross their arms and don't move, a clear sign that they're standing with Tristan.

My father spins around. "Where's Sienna?"

I squeeze my eyes shut, desperately hoping for a resolution to this mess that doesn't seem likely to come.

A hand touches my knee and I jump, blinking my eyes open. Jax stares down at me, his violet gaze empty. "Here," he says bluntly. The emptiness in his face *hurts*.

Is this what it feels like to be Soul Bonded? My whole body aches, twisting and burning. Just the promise of Jax, standing so close to me, feels like a cool glass of water on a scorching day. Sweet relief, just within my reach.

Or, you know, *not*.

He steps back, not helping me up as I scramble to my feet, awkward in the dress I was so excited to wear this morning.

Dad pushes him aside roughly, his hands landing on the sides of my face. "Sweetheart."

I force a smile, the edges of my lips tripping up slightly even as my chin wobbles. "I'm alright."

He studies me intently, then nods. "You're coming home with us. Your mama and Jess are outside."

"I'm afraid that's not possible." Ollena Hayward interjects, and I shove down the relief. I don't want to be here, with them.

I *don't*.

Tell that to my traitorous body, though.

"I'm afraid that Sienna turned down the opportunity to withdraw from the Trials," Ollena continues. "I offered it, and she declined. She passed the Trial. She is now required to participate."

"That's ridiculous," my father argues. "If she refuses?"

"Then she will be refused the opportunity to participate again."

I flinch. Blocked from ever having a pack of my own. My future, the children I might have all wiped away in a moment.

My fists clench. I can't make that decision. The Cohens have to withdraw, have to let me go.

They *have* to.

Dad swings back to me, his eyes searching mine. "Sienna?" he asks. His voice wavers.

I force a smile. "You can't fix this, Dad," I whisper. "I have to go now."

Face crumpling, he nods, his hands falling away from me as he turns back towards the Cohens.

"If you touch a hair on her head," he says slowly. "If you hurt my daughter in any way, no law of Navarre will save you. Do you understand me?"

Tristan inclines his head, before holding his arm towards the door. "After you."

His eyes barely cross my face before he turns, the others ignoring me as they follow his lead.

Swallowing, I pick up my skirts and take one more look at my dad. He offers me a shaking smile.

"Tell Mama and Jess I'll see them soon," I murmur. "Tell them I'm okay, Dad."

And then I walk out, my Soul Bonded following me in silence.

## 20

# TRISTAN

Sienna holds her head high as she sweeps past us, not sparing us a glance.

I don't blame her.

I can feel the shame coiling around my pack, bunching our shoulders, tightening our chests. It's a heavy weight.

But it will keep everyone safe.

That's what I tell myself as I leave, even as my chest burns to grab Sienna, to tell her everything. The pull is visceral, the yearning of my Soul Bonded almost impossible to ignore. The way my pack keeps reaching for their chests tells me they feel the same. I'm impressed that Sienna is as composed as she is.

Her composure lasts as long as it takes to spot Alicia and Councilor Erikkson waiting by the black car that transported us here. She stops short before turning to us, face expressionless but a hint of hurt in her eyes.

"I'll wait here," she says quietly.

Shaking my head, I take her arm. "She's coming with us."

Sienna inhales sharply, her feet dragging just for a second before she picks her steps up. "I see."

The stab of pain inside my chest doesn't belong to me. Logan swears softly behind me as we reach the pair responsible for today. I don't have the patience to be nice.

"Get in." I yank the door open forcefully, my hand dropping to the small of Sienna's back as I nudge her in before gesturing abruptly to Alicia.

She huffs, but Jax darts in front of her before she can climb in, pulling himself into the back of the car with a dark glance in my direction.

Alicia stamps her foot. "You're ruining my buzz, Tristan." Her whining, so high-pitched, pushes the building pressure in my head to a full-blown ache.

I sigh. "Sit in the front with me," I offer belatedly, and she whisks around to the passenger side with a smile. Erikkson comes up next to me, his hands folded behind his back.

"An interesting day," he remarks. Rounding on him with a snarl, I keep my voice low.

"Satisfied?"

"Not quite. But I will be, as long as you stick to our agreement."

Waving him off, I get into the driver's seat, slamming the door behind me and ignoring Alicia's yapping to just squeeze my eyes shut and take a goddamned breath. Letting it out, I glance in the rear-view mirror, meeting a pair of blue eyes.

Sienna glances away from me, looking out of the window. The silence emanating from the back is as painful as Alicia's yapping next to me.

Fingers flexing on the steering wheel, I put the car into drive.

## 21
# SIENNA

My fingers twist in my lap. Tension thickens the air around us until I can taste it on my tongue, an accompaniment to the ache in my chest. It pulses in tune with my heartbeat.

Next to me, Jax shifts, his leg pressing against mine in the cramped space. The heat from his skin soaks into my side, a tiny respite from the itch to reach out to *them*, to bury my face into them.

*Mine.*

My focus is thwarted by the feel of eyes on me. I flick my glance up to the mirror, but Tristan has already turned away.

I felt it though. Just like I felt every glance he's stolen over the last twenty minutes.

The car slows, entering through ornate black iron-wrought gates. Despite myself, I lean forward slightly, the omega in me unable to resist a glance at my home. At least, it's my home for the next four weeks. What happens after that is a question mark, polluting the air between me and the four alphas around me.

I purposefully don't think of Alicia. The urge to scream, to shriek and rage and stake my claim on the men around me is a noose around my neck, slowly tightening. Clearly, Soul Bonded are very possessive.

So I bite my lip savagely until the faint tang of iron fills my mouth. As the doors open, I exit the confined space, taking a deep breath to clear my head of their scent.

Then I take another as I look over the mansion in front of me.

Pale stone rises from the ground into the sky, tapering off into columns. Bright, wide windows line the walls, surrounding detailed carved dark wooden entry doors.

I take another breath. I couldn't have designed this house any better.

*Calm down, Si. It's not yours.*

As I turn away, yet another gut punch hitting me, I come face to face with Grayson. Both of us pause.

The warmth I saw earlier is gone now, his face shuttered. "Let's go inside."

His sharp tone has me scurrying after him into the house, following the others. Belatedly, I look around for my cases before I remember that we left without them.

"They'll be delivered tomorrow." Logan brushes past me, his hair glinting in the late afternoon light. Glancing back at me, he tips his head towards the house, unsmiling. "Come on."

*Okay then.*

I expected marble, towering ceilings, huge paintings of weird things that make no sense, but I'm met with well-worn wooden floors, cream walls, and very little in the way of furnishings.

It doesn't feel like it's cold, though. It just feels…paused. Like it's waiting for something.

My fingers itch, and I squeeze them together as I follow Logan down the hall to the kitchen area.

My head swivels, taking in the bright, airy, full of *everything-an-omega-could-want* kitchen. A huge wooden table with seats to spare sits in the middle, well-loved by the number of marks scuffing it.

God. The sheer perfection of this place is almost enough to finish me off.

Who the hell did I piss off in a previous life to deserve this?

*Hey Sienna, we're going to give you four absolutely gorgeous Soul Bonded who smell like the best type of snack. Then we'll throw in your perfect home, tailor made and ready for you to put those omega skills to work that you've spent the last five years perfecting. Oops – forgot to say, none of it is real. Your Bonded will hate you and you won't be able to stay. Actually, you might be forced to leave everything you've ever known and never talk to any of your family and friends again too. Sorry about that.*

A throat clears and I tune back into the room, my cheeks flushing when I notice everyone staring at me. Alicia scowls, throwing herself down into a chair as the rest follow. When I hesitate, my eyes scanning the remaining seats, Grayson yanks out a seat for me with a slight huff.

"Sit," he says abruptly, and I sink into the seat.

I glance around uneasily. Tristan gets up and brings some glasses to the table, sloshing dark liquid into them and passing them around. Alicia wrinkles her nose, and Tristan rolls his eyes before he leans back in his chair.

Tentatively, I sniff at the amber liquid and take a sip. It burns, my eyes watering as I choke out a cough. I take a second to get over the taste before I finish the rest in one, placing my glass slowly back on the table and swiveling to meet Tristan's slightly widened eyes.

Pressing my lips together, I stare down at the empty glass.

Someone coughs. "Sienna?"

Sucking in a breath, I steel myself and look up. "Yes?"

Tristan's eyes bore into me, that forest green flecked with gold close up. They don't give away any secrets though.

"I'm sure you're wondering what's going on here," he offers, and I nod, slowly.

"You could say that. Today wasn't exactly... what I expected."

"And what did you expect?" Grayson interjects, scowling when I look at him. "A pack of alphas, just waiting to fall at your feet?"

My mouth falls open as Alicia snorts. "Are you kidding me?"

Grayson leans back in his seat, his arms crossed. "In case it wasn't blindingly obvious by today's events, we don't want you here."

The barb hits home, my flinch obvious. Tristan holds up his hands. "Let's just take a second—"

"I don't understand," I blurt out. "You entered the Trials. Nobody forced you into it. So why say you don't want it? Why say I *passed*?"

"Because you did. Technically," a low voice sounds. Logan leans forward, his golden hair falling around his fix as he fixes me with an expressionless stare. "But it won't last forever. It's not the Trials that's the issue here. We just don't want *you*."

The atmosphere ratchets up a notch as I sink back in my seat, Logan's words burrowing into my chest like arrows. *So much for my Soul Bonded.*

They obviously don't feel the same pull as I do, the pain in my chest at the distance between us a background hum to our discussion.

Maybe we're not really Soul Bonded. But Jax – he definitely didn't act like this when we met at the club. I look towards him with a hint of desperation. "Jax?"

He doesn't even look up, his focus entirely on the amber liquid circling around his glass. "Agreed."

My small whimper is drowned out by Alicia's cackle. "Oh, this is just too good."

Rising from her seat, she slides onto Tristan's lap. His arm lifts to wrap around her stomach as she smiles lazily at me.

"Give it up, little omega," she purrs. "You're not trapping them. This pack is mine."

Agony sears my throat, the burning making it hard to force out the words. "Why didn't you stop this at the Trial? This could have been *done*. Why make me come here?"

Why humiliate me like this?

Tristan pauses. "It was easier this way. You can withdraw quietly, less publically."

"And if I don't?"

Everyone stiffens at my words, except Alicia. She just grins, a wide, red smile that's more than a little freaky. Like the prospect excites her.

Tristan gapes at me.

"Why wouldn't you?" he demands. Throwing his arm out, he gestures to the rest of the table. "Nobody wants you here, Sienna. You're just going to force yourself on us for these damn Trials? What happens at the end?"

His voice rises. "Do you want to be Denied?"

I glare at him. "I want you to tell me the truth!"

Something isn't right here.

Grayson chuckles humorlessly. "You want the truth, omega?"

Jax shifts in his seat, but he doesn't say anything as Grayson begins to lay into me.

"Do you really think that much of yourself?" he drawls. "Think you're so precious, such a *good omega*, that we'd throw ourselves at you? Is that it?"

"Don't try to pretend you don't feel this," I snap back at him, at all of them. "Don't try to pretend that what happened today is anything close to normal."

"What is she talking about?" Alicia pipes up, yanking at Tristan's sleeve. "Tristan?"

He shakes his head, patting her hand. "Nothing, Alicia."

Turning to me, he holds his hands out. "I'm sorry if we made you feel that this was going to be something more than it is, Sienna. But you've got it wrong. We're going through the motions of the Trials because we have to, but Alicia is the one we choose. Not you."

My head shakes in disbelief. I know what I feel.

I just don't know why they're pretending they don't feel it too.

"I'm tired," I say quietly, looking away. I don't have any more in me today. "Is there a room I can rest in?"

I'm not stupid enough to think they prepared any sort of space for my arrival. If they're this set on not having an omega, I'll be lucky to get a bed. Although from the size of this place, maybe I'll get lucky.

Tristan stands, but Alicia tugs him back down.

"I'll show our guest to her quarters," she insists. "We need to have a little chat, girl to girl."

Jax frowns. "Alicia."

She waves him off as she points to the door. "Come along, omega."

Gritting my teeth, I stand to follow her. I can't spend another second around this pack, even if it's tearing up my insides to walk away from them.

Following Alicia, I close the door on the silent men sitting at the table and follow her towards a beautiful stone staircase, set square in the middle of the grand hallway. A sweeping flight of stairs splits into two at the top, one running up in each direction.

"Come on," Alicia trills. She holds her arm out, and I stare at her blankly until she links her arm through mine and tows me forward.

"I am so sorry about today," she sings as we ascend the stairs. I keep a careful grip on the banister, not entirely trusting that she won't shove me backwards at any moment.

There's definitely something not quite right about her.

She suddenly stops and tilts her head. Belatedly, I nod.

"It wasn't what I expected," I murmur. *Understatement of the fucking century.*

Appeased, she pats my hand and continues pulling me upward.

"Well, these things don't always go to plan," she confides, her voice dropping to a whisper.

"And why is that?" I ask. We reach the top, and Alicia pulls me down towards the end of the corridor. An older-looking door is tucked away in the corner, and she opens it with a flourish. I glance inside, trying not to shrink back at the thick strands of cobwebs hanging from the ceiling.

Incredulous, I glance at her, and the vapid smile slides from her lips as she takes a step forward.

"Listen to me," she hisses, her finger reaching up to jab into my chest, sharp red nails catching on my thin dress. I move to take a step back, but she grabs my arm.

"The Cohen pack is mine. Do you understand? They belong to me. I don't care what some ridiculous law says. You will stay away from them."

I yank myself back, my breathing harsh in the small space between us. "I could be home right now," I say in frustration. "I didn't have to be here, Alicia. So, you tell me. Why the fuck am I here?"

She snarls, that stunning face changing in an instant. "Because I said so."

I stumble back, shock filling me. "What?" I demand. My voice fills the hallway around us. "What do you mean?"

She throws her head back and laughs, and I eye her carefully. This girl is definitely not right.

"I mean," she says triumphantly, "that you're here because I want you to be. And you'd better remember that, omega, if you want to make it out of these Trials."

Taking a step, she waves her hand towards the stairs. "After you."

I really don't want to go up there. But I don't have much of a choice. I can't withdraw from the Trials now. I can't go home. Not unless I give up everything I ever wanted.

So, I take a step. And then another. Trying to avoid the inches of dust lining the rails, I lift up my dress as best I can and climb until we reach... what is definitely not a bedroom.

Old boxes and various pieces of furniture dot around the room, covered in sheets and more fucking dust. There's a tiny mattress in the corner with a blanket folded on top, and I turn to Alicia with a raised brow.

She looks back at me, impassive. "What did you expect? Some

bedroom decked out for a queen? You're not wanted here. You'd best get used to it."

Turning, she flounces back down the stairs. I dart to the door after her, sighing in relief when the doorknob turns under my hand. I really don't want to be locked in here.

I test the switch and a small amount of light flickers to life in the bare lightbulb overhead. It swings back and forth lightly, sending shadows bouncing across the floor.

Making my way to the mattress, I check it gingerly for any left-behind critters before sinking down, my dress pillowing around me in clouds of ash-streaked white. Sighing, I lie back, hands reaching up to cover my face.

The ache in my belly pulses again, a constant reminder that I am very much alpha-less.

And the men who I'm pretty sure are my soulmates are downstairs, staring starry-eyed at a scarlet-haired bitch who apparently has a screw or ten loose.

*The best day of my life?*
*I don't think so.*

## 22
# GRAYSON

Jax snarls at me as the door clicks shut behind Sienna.

"What the *fuck*, Gray?"

Leaning back, I shrug. "The best way to get her to pull out is to make sure she knows we don't want her, Jax. Kinda have to tell her for that to happen."

Even if it feels like someone yanking a knife from my side.

Logan rubs at his chest absently. "Anyone else feel a...,"

I frown. "A what?"

He shakes his head. "Like a tugging, I guess. Towards her."

A sudden burst of envy colors my words. "Panting after her already? Why am I not surprised?"

His head shoots up, anger in his voice. "Go fuck yourself, Gray."

"Enough." Tristan slams his hand down on the table. "We're in more than enough shit already without fighting amongst ourselves. We made our decision, and we have to see it through. Gray's right. We have to make it obvious she's not wanted here."

"But she is wanted," Jax growls. "I want her. Are you seriously telling me you don't?"

Tristan stares at him. "It doesn't matter, Jax," he says gently. "We have to do this. We have to do this for her."

Jax erupts from his seat as he starts to pace. "No."

He whirls, pointing a finger at Tristan. "We need to find a way out of this, quickly, so we can claim her, Tristan. We did what we had to do today because we had no time. We've bought ourselves four weeks to fix this fucked-up mess, to give the Erikksons what they deserve and to claim Sienna."

He faces us with his fists clenched, his breathing erratic. "She's our Soul Bonded," he growls. "How can you sit there and pretend that anything about this is okay?"

"It's not okay," Logan mutters. My hands clench around the table at the defeat in his tone. "I'm sorry we made this happen, Jax."

"This isn't our fault," I insist, my throat thick. "If the Council weren't so backward in their ideas, this wouldn't even be an issue."

Tristan sighs. "You're right. Although I'm still pissed you didn't trust us with this. And there's my father to consider too."

"So where do we start?" Jax demands. "I don't think I can take much more of this, Tris. What we did today was enough to permanently damage any bond between us. We need to start fixing it ASA-fucking-P."

"And she's not stupid." My words are low, but everyone turns to me. "She knows something isn't right. The dots just don't add up."

"So we tell her," Logan suggests, but Tristan shakes his head. "I don't want her involved. The less she knows, the less the Erikksons will involve her."

"That's bullshit," Logan shoots back. "Alicia hates her. It's personal."

Jax makes for the door. "I'm going to check on them."

The door swings open before he reaches it. Alicia sashays back into the room, her hands on her hips. "We need to talk."

"Where's Sienna?" Jax growls, and Alicia points upwards. "In her room, of course," she purrs. "Where else would she be?"

"And you put her in the spare bedroom?" Tristan asks.

Alicia humphs. "She's perfectly comfortable. But she's suspicious. You're not paying me nearly enough attention, Tristan."

Jax scoffs. "We paid you more than enough attention at the Trial."

Alicia's foot stomps down again, her heels digging into our wooden floors and making me grit my teeth. "It's. Not. Enough!"

Her voice rises, and Tristan snarls back at her. "We're not your whipping boys, Alicia. You wanted us, you have us. We're doing exactly what you wanted. What more do you fucking want?"

She leans forward, nails sinking into the table. "I want you to look at me the way you look at *her*."

Jax huffs in sarcastic laughter. "Hell will freeze over before that happens."

"Stop it," Tristan snaps. Taking a deep breath, he tries to smile at Alicia. "I apologize if our deal isn't living up to your expectations, Alicia. But we're doing everything we agreed to. We're publically choosing you as our partner. We're rejecting Sienna as our Bonded omega."

"Even though—"

"Even though," Tristan says with a dark look at Jax, "We're naturally drawn to her, as any alpha is drawn to an omega. This arrangement will take some time to adjust to."

Alicia tosses her hair back. "Not too long, I hope. The Trials are only for four weeks."

"And we'll be much more settled in by then, I'm sure. In the meantime, why don't you settle in for the evening? We'll bring a tray to your room."

I frown. "You look... dusty."

Alicia stands abruptly, nodding. "I think you're right, Tristan. I need to make sure I get my full allocation of sleep. I'll see you all bright and early in the morning, hmm?"

Leaning forward, she offers puckered lips to Tristan. He eyes them like they're poison before quickly brushing his mouth against hers. "Goodnight."

"Good fucking riddance," Jax murmurs as she leaves again, and Logan kicks him under the table.

"So…," Logan looks around, making eye contact with everyone that isn't me. "What's the plan?"

Tristan steeples his fingers, his brow drawn. "Are we all certain that we're her Soul Bonded?"

Jax smirks. "One hundred and fifty fucking percent. Tell me you didn't feel it sucker punch you in the dick as you walked towards her."

Logan hesitates, but he nods in agreement. "I felt it."

I look away, ignoring the feel of Tristan's eyes on me. "Gray?"

Shrugging, I stand and push myself away from the table. "I felt something. I wouldn't say it was strong enough to be Soul Bonded."

*Lie. Lie, lie, fucking lie.*

Everything about her, from that wild fucking pink hair to her delicious raspberry scent with a hint of warm vanilla – everything about Sienna Michaels screams *mine*.

But I'm not giving up on Logan without a fight. And if that means I have to push her out of my thoughts, then I'll do it without question. This whole charade actually makes it easier, no matter that my words from earlier still taste bitter on my tongue.

Tristan's shoulders roll back, a considering look on his face.

"We need to leave Sienna alone as much as possible. If she's around, then we have to keep up the pretense. The next Trial is nesting."

"She has a nest," Jax insists. "It's there, waiting to be used."

"Alicia nixed it." Tris sighs again. "She wants to use the garage."

"The garage?" Even I balk at the idea. It's chock full of all sorts of shit we've collected over the years. I'd be surprised if she wasn't buried under a mountain of useless tat the second she opens the door.

"She's probably going to fail," Logan whispers. "We're not

exactly making her comfortable enough to feel the nesting instinct."

And if she fails, we lose her altogether. This is a fucking knife edge, and we have to tread carefully.

"We can't win this," I point out. Jax glowers at me, and I shrug. "We can't, Jax. We can't treat Sienna the way that we want to because of Alicia. Us treating her badly means she won't develop the instincts she needs to bond with us. Therefore, she fails her trials and we lose her anyway. She has enough of us, she withdraws, and guess what? We lose her anyway. We. Can't. Win. This."

"But she's our Soul Bonded," Logan interjects. "That means she's probably going to feel those instincts, right? Soul Bonding isn't built up over time, it's instant."

Tristan mulls it over before he nods. "It's a risk we'll have to take."

Jax groans loudly. "I'm not made for shit like this. I just want to go and find her."

Tristan waves his hand at the door. "Be my guest. Put her – put all of us – at risk. Or you can help me by distracting Alicia tomorrow so I can visit Erikkson and see what I can dig up."

Jax's face is a picture. "Distract her? You mean by knocking her out, right? Tying her up and dangling her off the roof?"

Ignoring him, Tristan moves to the door. "I'm going to my office."

Jax stomps after him, grumbling, and I slide my eyes to Logan, both of us meeting in the middle before we look away.

"Logan," I breathe. "Can we talk?"

Shaking his head, he gets up too. "It's done, Gray. I meant what I said."

My hands shake as I close them into fists. "You don't mean that. We're good together, Lo. Really good. Don't throw that away."

His scoff is dismissive. "So good you couldn't even admit it to our pack. And look how that turned out."

Regret sours my stomach. "I'm sorry. If I could go back—,"

"It's done now." Logan moves past as I fight the urge to grab him, to pull him towards me and beg him to make a different choice. "And for what it's worth, I'm sorry, too."

And then he's gone.

## 23
# SIENNA

Smoothing down my hair, I sigh at the absolute mess looking back at me in the cracked mirror.

Tangled, slightly greasy hair? Check.

A very crumpled, dirty Bonding gown? Check.

I look like I've stumbled straight out of a zombie story. My face is pale, dark circles under my eyes testifying to the hours I spent tossing and turning on that shitty little mattress last night, thanks to the fucking ache caused by the absence of my Bonds.

The ache stabs again under my hand. Better get used to that.

Time to face the music.

Exiting my shitty little excuse for a room, I retrace my steps from yesterday back to the kitchen. A rumble of voices filters out as I brace myself.

The voices cut into silence as I walk into the room. Jax and Logan are seated around the table, Tristan stirring a cup of sweet-smelling coffee that makes my mouth water.

Thankfully, Alicia is nowhere to be seen. Neither is Grayson, which is welcome because his nasty words from yesterday were the soundtrack to my shitty night's sleep, but also very fucking unwelcome because my stomach apparently doesn't care that he's an unfeeling asshole and would *liketoseehimverymuchrightnowifyouplease*. Wincing, I gesture towards the coffee.

"Could I have some of that, please?" I ask. Tristan steps away, motioning with his hand. "Help yourself."

His face is wiped of expression again as he takes a seat. Everyone unsubtly tries not to watch me as I approach the steam breathing alien machine that apparently makes their coffee. After a few minutes prodding buttons, I'm about to cry from a severe caffeine deficiency when a steaming cup is shoved under my chin.

"Here."

Logan frowns as he hands me his cup.

"Ah... thank you." I retreat, resisting the urge to bare my teeth at the metal monstrosity. Apparently I have more than one nemesis in this house.

Lingering, I awkwardly cradle Logan's coffee as everyone ignores me once again.

"Um... Logan?" I ask quietly. "Did you say my clothes might arrive today?"

He doesn't look up. "Do I look like your personal assistant?"

*Wow.*

I take a deep breath and pray for patience. "You sure as hell look like the alpha who told me my clothes would arrive today. I was hoping for a little more information, but don't worry about it. I'll just trail dust all over your house until I have something else to wear."

Jax whistles under his breath as Tristan glances over his newspaper with a frown. "Why are you so dirty?"

My cheeks flush. About to launch into a heated explanation of the absolute shittiness of my room, I'm thwarted as a voice drawls behind me, making my chest thump.

"I thought hygiene was something omegas were pretty keen on. Guess not."

Grayson isn't pulling his punches again today, I see. Humiliation brands my cheeks a rosy red as Jax takes pity on me and opens the chair next to him. "Sit down and have some breakfast."

I smooth down my dress self-consciously as I move around the table, angling myself so I don't touch Grayson as I pass. Settling down, I glance at the paltry offer and my fingers twitch again.

Clearing my throat, I draw Jax's attention. His violet eyes slide to mine with a question.

"I could cook?" My words are almost soundless. I don't want to insult him, but I have no idea how they maintain themselves if this is what they eat on the regular.

Besides – this is what I'm here to do. To take care of them. And they're supposed to take care of me, too.

"You cook?" Logan asks, a touch of hope in his tone. He scans the table mournfully. "We're not the best at it."

His words draw a smile. Because this? This, I can do. And it's better than hanging around on the outskirts, pathetically pining for a crumb of attention.

"Do you mind?" I ask, already eyeing the layout of the kitchen. Logan actually laughs.

"Go ahead."

"Don't poison us," Grayson grunts, and then grunts again.

"Ignore Gray," Jax murmurs. "He hasn't had his fix yet."

Gray strides across to the metal monster, pressing some buttons and then frowning. "Is the coffee machine broken?"

I try not to choke as he turns to me, looking accusingly at the cup in my hands.

"I, um. I tried to make coffee and it didn't work," I offer. "Maybe it was already broken?"

Gray curses. "Fucking perfect."

Skirting past him, I lose myself in getting to grips with their kitchen. The refrigerator is a monster just like their coffee machine, and whilst it's not exactly what I would call full (not unless you count dozens of cans of beer) it's still got enough for me to make something.

Logan appears beside me as I push the door shut, my arms full. "Need help?"

I shake my head. "I've got it," I offer. "Why don't you sit down?"

"Telling us what to do in our own kitchen," Gray's words deflate the tiny bit of confidence I have, and my hands shake as I put everything down on the counter.

"Sorry," I whisper. Logan inhales, a hint of his sweet lemon scent reaching my nose and making my knees shake.

"Don't be. Gray's an asshole."

The atmosphere changes, Gray's anger a sudden weight in my chest. I rub the pain away, fighting the urge to flinch.

"Jesus, Gray, tone it down," Tristan orders. The door slamming is the only response, and Logan sighs, moving away from me again.

Ignoring the weirdness of this situation, I break eggs and chop peppers and onion, whisking and seasoning until I'm carefully cutting the steaming tortilla into sections and setting it out on the table.

Logan and Jax immediately grab for the food, but Tristan casts his eye over the table and stands. "I'll eat at work," he says dismissively as he turns away. He grabs a set of keys from the side and disappears, the door slamming a moment later.

Eyes smarting, I quietly gather the dishes and pile them in the sink, starting the water running. A hand appears over mine, making me jump as it gently turns off the faucet.

"You need to eat too," a voice grumbles. Jax.

Vision blurry, I blink as a tear drips down my face.

Why is all of this so fucking hard?

Hands land on my shoulders, and Jax spins me slowly, bending until he can see into my lowered face. "Ah, Sienna. Don't cry."

"I'm not," I insist, my voice thick as I dash my hand over my face. "I just got some onion in there."

Jax's hand pats my shoulder as he maneuvers me towards the table. "Onion eye is the worst."

He sits me down and slides a full plate in front of me. "You didn't eat anything yesterday," he murmurs softly. "You need to eat, shortcake."

*Shortcake?*

The ache in my stomach intensifies as I stare at the food. I know that I'm hungry, but it's muted against the pain I can feel radiating through my body.

"Don't you feel it?" I whisper, looking up at him.

*Don't you feel any of this damned pain?*

Immediately, his face shutters and he takes a step away. "Eat."

Way to go, Sienna.

Biting my lip, I reach my hands out for a slice as the door opens behind me. "Morning!"

Alicia's shrillness makes my teeth ache, but Jax smiles at her easily enough. "Mornin', sweetheart."

And just like that, any appetite I had is swallowed by a spike of pain directly into my stomach. Coughing, I reach out for my coffee.

Alicia slides into a seat next to me. "Oh, is that eggs?"

She tugs the plate from in front of me with a sharp smile. "You don't mind, Sienna, right? I do hate to see good food go to waste."

Jax growls just a little, and Alicia's smile falters as she looks between us.

"Am I interrupting something?" she asks silkily.

Jax's jaw ticks, but he shakes his head, not saying anything as Alicia picks at the food.

I wrap my hands around the cup, trying to soak up the last of the warmth. Logan clears his throat. "What are your plans today, Sienna?"

I stare at him, a little lost. "My plans?"

I don't have any plans. I would have plans, lots of lovely fun plans, if this whole situation wasn't ten shades of fucked up.

*God, Jessalyn would lose her shit if she could see this.*

I shrug. "I don't know, to be honest."

Alicia laughs lightly. "Don't be silly! The Nesting Trial is a week away. Surely you want to prepare."

My mouth opens, and then closes again. Prepare for what? More rejection?

I'm not going to pass another Trial. We all know it.

Confused, I look between them all. "I'm not sure what you mean."

"Don't tell me you haven't shown Sienna her nesting space?" Alicia trills. "It's quite the spot, you know."

Dread grows in my stomach. This isn't gonna be good.

"I'll show her." Logan stands, pushing his chair back. "Come on, Sienna."

"She hasn't eaten anything," Jax snaps.

Alicia frowns. "She said she was full."

*Um. No, I did not.*

Quickly deciding that the need to get away from Alicia is more important than the gnawing hunger dancing around the Bonding ache, I stand to join Logan. "It's fine. I'll eat later."

Jax opens his mouth, but I'm already heading after Logan. He opens another door leading off the kitchen, and I follow him down an airy wooden hallway. It's bare, and something occurs to me.

"Don't you paint?" I ask his back hesitantly.

Why is this house so empty if Logan's a well-known painter?

He stops, shooting a dark look at me over his shoulder. "I don't really like being surrounded by my work."

Chewing over his answer, I follow him silently until we reach yet another door. This place is a damned maze. You could get lost in here.

"Here you go." He pushes the door open and stands back.

My history with doors and spaces in this place isn't great, but the state of the room beyond makes my reaction to my so-called bedroom pale in comparison.

Gaping, I look at him. "This is a nesting space?"

Logan's face flushes as his eyes flick to the room. "I know it's not ideal."

"Not ideal?"

Logan winces. My tone may be a little shrill. But who can blame me?

My supposed nesting space is top to toe with junk. Bulging boxes stack almost to the ceiling, surrounded by a thousand different things. I can see paint pots, canvases, music stands, even filing drawers from where I'm standing.

I fight back the urge to dissolve into tears. This isn't even a blink on my radar in comparison to everything else.

"Do you have to make everything so hard?" I ask weakly. "Am I that bad?"

Logan twitches. "You're not that bad."

I look at him incredulously, and he shrugs helplessly. "We're not supposed to help with the nesting."

My lips press together as I nod soundlessly. The unsaid words hang between us – *yes, I'm very aware of that, but we both know that all packs prepare a nesting space that their omega can tweak and play with until she's completely satisfied.*

There's helping, and then there's making things completely impossible.

I can't even see the floor or walls properly, but something tells me there's no blankets or softness waiting for me in there. That's even if I can clear it.

And I only have one week until Ollena appears to inspect it and tell me if I've passed.

Another realization hits me, and I pinch my nose. "My things, Logan. Are they arriving today?"

I need a pair of jeans. Desperately. I'm not going to get far while still stuck in my filthy Bonding gown.

Logan nods a little too quickly when I spin to him. "I'll make sure it does. Sienna...,"

I grit my teeth. "I know. You can't help me."

He shakes his head. "That wasn't... anyway. There's an empty room next door."

He points to the door as I blink. "And just so I'm clear, the empty room can't be a nesting space? It has to be this one?"

Of course. *Why give me an empty space when they can make me lug everything from one room to another?*

My shoulders slump. Should've eaten breakfast.

I step inside the room, and Logan clears his throat. "This wasn't what we wanted, you know."

"I know," I say, throwing up my hands. "You've all made that very clear to me. I'm just pushing into a pack that doesn't want me. Knocking on a door that isn't open. I get it, Logan. You don't have to try and hurt me anymore than you already have."

"That's not what I meant."

His low, husky voice hits me hard. Staring sightlessly into the room, I blink.

"Then what did you mean?"

Heat warms my back as he moves behind me. His warm breath ghosts across my neck, making me shudder.

"We wanted an omega," he whispers. His hand trails up my arm, goose pimples springing up on my skin as he traces a line with his fingers.

The ache dims just a little, and I list to the side as my neck tilts.

"What changed?" I whisper back.

I feel the loss of heat a half second before he speaks, his voice cold.

"Alicia."

Reality hits me in the face like a wet fish. *Nearly fell for that one, Sienna.*

"I see," I push out, my voice trembling. "I need to make a start here."

But when I turn around, Logan is gone.

## 24
# LOGAN

First, it's the canvases. Then it's the paint. The brushes. The white spirit.

I can't grab them fast enough, can't pull them together quickly enough, my fingers itching to get started. I'm holding my breath, unable to release until I finally have the brush in my hand.

And then I can finally breathe.

The knocking at the door rouses me, and I blink, taking a step back. My hands, my shirt, are covered in black. I run a hand through my hair, feeling the stiffness that tells me I'm covered just as much as the canvas in front of me.

But I'm grinning.

Turning, I stride to the door and pull it open. Gray's eyes widen as he takes me in.

"You're painting," he breathes.

I turn away, my head already pulled back to the picture in my mind, my fingers begging to add it to the canvas before it's forgotten, nothing more than a vague remembering.

Gray's footsteps follow as I pick up the palette, slowing until all I can hear is his breathing.

"Logan," he half whispers, half-groans.

Shaking my head, I carry on. "I don't need your judgment, Gray. Not today."

"I'm not judging." He sounds hurt. "Lo, this is… it's incredible."

"It's all her."

Sienna stares out at us, wide eyes sunken in undeniable pain. There's no color to this canvas, no vibrancy.

"Pink," I mutter, my fingers dancing over various tubes. "I need pink."

Not just pink – perfect, light, blush pink. A touch lighter than candyfloss.

Gray touches my arm, his face sad. "You've found your muse again."

Blowing out a breath, I nod. I already have more ideas in mind, but they're opaque, only the edges visible. I need more. More Sienna.

"I'm pleased for you." Gray's words are genuine, and I finally look at him properly, taking in the pale tint to his skin, the dark shadows under his eyes. My heart clenches, even as part of me wants to head straight to the sad omega carrying out her impossible task across the hall.

"I didn't want this." I repeat the same words I said to Sienna.

Gray takes a small step closer to me, his eyes darkening further. "So, what did you want?"

I hesitate. "I'm greedy, Gray. I want it all. I don't want to have to hide what we have from the world. I'm not ashamed of loving someone."

"Fuck," he says wretchedly. "I'm not ashamed of us, Lo. I never meant to make you feel that way. It's just… it's not just us we have to think about. We're a pack."

"And now there's Sienna…" My tongue curls around her name, the faint promise of raspberries.

"And now there's Sienna."

Gray's acknowledgement of my silent question settles something in my chest, and I turn to him.

"Love isn't limited to one person," I breathe. He looks away from me, and I touch his face, taking in the faint lines around his mouth, signs of laughter etched into his familiar features.

"I miss you," I say quietly. "So much, Gray. But I can't live like that again."

His face tightens. "Tell me what that means," he says, his tone urgent. "I'm not always good at reading between the lines, Logan. You need to tell me what you want."

"I want to step into the light," I breathe. "With you. And with Sienna, if she'll have me. Have *us*."

"Us." Gray looks uncertain.

"You want her," I accuse gently. "I saw your face when you walked away from her. It hit you even harder than the rest of us."

His forehead leans in until it rests against mine, our soft breathing mingling together in perfect familiarity. "I feel her," he confesses. "Fuck, Lo, I can barely breathe for feeling it."

I smile against his mouth. "You're going to look so good together. I can't wait to paint it."

He shudders, pressing into me so I can feel his cock harden "Fuck, Lo."

Gently, I push him back. "You need to take it easy. With her, I mean."

"I know," he groans. "I just… it's so hard to be around her and not touch her that it's easier to push her away."

"Don't push too far."

He swallows, stepping away. "I'll do better. For both of you. I swear."

I smile, feeling a little more hopeful. "I know."

## 25
## SIENNA

My arms shake as I try to lift another box down from the endless stack against the wall. Giving up for a moment, I sink down, sucking in gulps of breath as my head swims.

"Sienna?"

Spinning my head around, I scramble up, wiping my filthy hands on my dress as Grayson eyeballs me from the doorway. *Great.*

He's looking around the room, his brow furrowed. "This place is disgusting."

"Thanks for pointing it out. I had no idea," I deadpan.

Besides, it won't be by the time I'm finished with it. I'm determined to make them all eat their words. I will clean this shithole out, and I will build a decent nest by the time Ollena comes. Even if it kills me.

Which… it might. My head spins again, and I list to the side.

"Sienna?" Gray appears in front of me. Fuck, is that actual concern I can see on his face?

"Did you eat anything at breakfast?"

When I shake my head, he swears under his breath. "Stay here."

"I'm not going anywhere," I mumble as he ducks back to the

doorway and grabs something off the floor. When he turns, revealing the tray, my stomach growls its approval across the room.

And Grayson Cohen actually smiles.

It transforms his whole face. I thought he was handsome before – in the way that marble statues are handsome. Cold. But now... *holy shitballs*.

"I think you need this." He carries the tray over to a set of drawers and places it down, giving me a stern look. "Sit down."

And I sit. Abruptly. On my ass.

"Shit – are you okay?"

Because I'm laughing hysterically, except I'm not, because tears appear in a wild rush that says very clearly that *I am not fucking okay*.

"Fuck, Sienna."

And then Grayson is lifting me, and he's folding himself down on the floor with me curled around him, crying great big noisy snotty sobs directly into his very soft – possibly cashmere – sweater.

"Shhh, Sienna," he soothes, his hand rubbing down my back softly. "Fuck, please stop crying."

I'm trying my best, but these damn tears just keep flowing. I'm so tired, and hungry, and the pain is just slowly growing and growing in the background, and my whole body hurts. And they're just swimming along with Alicia without a care in the world.

"It hurts," I whimper. "It hurts, Gray."

"I'm sorry," he murmurs. "Fuck, sweetheart, I'm so sorry."

He doesn't understand. Hell, I don't understand. There isn't exactly a manual for Soul Bonded omegas, and the only source I have isn't here to ask. Not that I want my mother to know I'm Soul Bonded. Not like this.

So I continue to cry into Gray's chest until my sobs become quiet whimpers, my torrent of tears slowing to a trickle. Sniffing, I pull back in mortification and scuttle off him, trying not to trip myself up on this damned stupid dress that I now officially hate.

He watches me, his electric blue eyes examining me closely. I brush myself off before hugging my knees with my hands.

"Sorry about that."

"Don't be," he says softly. "You've held up remarkably well, considering."

When I look away, he reaches out for the tray, grabbing a bowl and holding it up to me.

"Jax made soup," he says with a wry smile. "It's the only edible thing he can cook. He was worried when you didn't eat breakfast."

My heart twinges at the idea of Jax making soup for me. When Gray lifts the spoon to my mouth, I open obediently. He feeds me in silence until the last of the soup is gone.

"Good girl."

The edge of a purr in his tone as he places the bowl back on the tray makes me stiffen, the atmosphere around us changing.

Gray reaches towards me, but I frown, taking a step backwards even though all I want to do is find out why he's reaching for me with that look in his eyes.

"I don't understand," I say helplessly, my palms out toward him. "You don't want me here, Gray."

He closes his eyes briefly. "I said that, didn't I?"

"You did." I eye him cautiously. "Did you mean it?"

Gray's hands drop to his sides. "I have to mean it."

Frustration scents the air around us. "I don't understand what that means!"

God fucking dammit. Why is every male in this house so *confusing*?

He takes another step, and then another, backing me up until I'm pressed against a not-completely-steady bunch of boxes. Gray's hands land on either side of my head, caging me in as I stare at him, wide-eyed. My breathing comes a little faster as he leans in, his mouth pressing against my ear.

"I wish I could explain," he murmurs. "But I can't, Sienna. I would if I could."

His mouth trails a line from my ear, barely touching the skin but heating every inch he traces. My eyes drift close as he presses in, taking a deep breath.

"You carry my scent."

His voice is deeper, the thrum of a growl reverberating up my spine. My moan is quiet, but he hears it, sliding a hand around my neck and tilting my face to the side, recreating the moment we shared in front of strangers.

Scent-marking.

"Raspberries," he growls. "I fucking love raspberries."

And then his mouth is on mine, and my arms are around his neck, and he's pushing into me, his hand sliding down to hook my leg around his waist. He's a perfect fit against me, our mouths dancing together as he presses against me.

"Sienna," he groans. His other hand slides from my neck until it's grasping at my bare leg, lifting the filthy lace and lifting me into him until his length is pressed directly into my panties.

And Gray Cohen is *built*.

"Gray," I gasp into his mouth as he does something with his hips that makes stars burst behind my eyes.

We should stop. This whole mess isn't gonna get sorted by both of us getting hot and heavy in this mess of a so-called nest.

But that ache. As Gray's warmth soaks into me, the ache that's been thrumming in my bones for the last twenty-four hours finally, blissfully recedes. Apparently a bit of heavy petting from one of my Soul Bonded feels like nirvana, ambrosia in my veins.

He surges against me again and again, both of us barely pausing for breath as he drinks down my gasps and whimpers.

"Give it to me," he groans. "*Sienna*."

His grip on my legs as he holds me tightly and the feel of his denim rubbing against my clit tips me over the edge. He swallows my cry with his mouth, his hand slowly lowering one leg and moving back to my neck to press our mouths together. The boxes behind us shift precariously, and I lose my balance, Gray toppling with me.

I laugh, feeling light for the first time since I arrived here. Pushing my hair back from my face, I lean up on my elbows, turning to face him.

But he doesn't look happy. He looks tortured.

"Gray?" I bite my lip. I guess we got a little carried away.

When he looks away, my happiness starts to ebb away. I swallow.

"Gray." There's a faint pleading note to my tone.

"I shouldn't have done that." My heart drops at his words, and he turns to me. "Shit, Sienna – I didn't mean it like that. You were…,"

"Don't," I whisper thickly. "It's not me, it's you, right?"

Gray hesitates. "It's not as clear cut as you think."

A sudden stab hits me in the stomach, making me bend over with a gasp. Gray grabs my arms. "Sienna!"

"I'm fine." I shift carefully to my feet, tugging my dress back into place. Shame is a leaden pit in my chest.

*Stupid, stupid, Sienna.*

Gray scrambles after me. "Sienna—"

"Could you leave, please? I have a lot of work to do."

He hesitates, but he doesn't argue. And as the door closes softly behind him, I'm left alone in a filthy room, in a filthy dress, after doing filthy things with an alpha who has just proved, yet again, that he doesn't want *me*.

And my heart cracks a little bit more.

26

JAX

Panting, I bring the speed down on the treadmill, slipping my headphones out of my ears and grimacing as those weird-ass fucking noises fill the gym.

When I desperately suggested the gym to Alicia, I wasn't expecting her to actually take me up on it. I was just relieved that I could distract her for a bit like I'd promised Tristan.

But the noises she makes – Jesus FC. She's like a rhino on steroids.

She grunts again as she stretches out her legs into a deep v, peeking over her shoulder to me before she bends over. The spandex stretches over her ass, and I shudder.

*That is one hell of a camel toe.*

Grabbing a towel, I wipe it over my face as I move towards the weights. Alicia bustles up next to me, selecting a dumbbell way too fucking heavy for her and letting out another one of those weird grunts as she lifts it.

I turn to her, pitching concern. "Is your stomach okay?"

She stares at me, dumbfounded. "Why?"

"Because those farts are something else."

I bite my cheek as her face flames in embarrassment. "I am not *farting*!" she says furiously. "Those are workout noises!"

"Hey, farting is completely natural. You might wanna get that checked out though. They sound painful."

Her annoyed shriek as she stalks off is the win I really fucking needed today.

A chime rings through the room, and I jog over to the security panel next to the door. There's a wild-haired chick glaring directly into the camera, mouthing something I can't hear.

When I pull the main door open, she switches her diatribe to me without blinking. "—swear to fucking god, I will pinch your balls off with a clamp if you've made her cry even one time, you little bitch."

I blink. "Excuse me?"

She huffs. "Where the fuck is my best friend?"

"Er— you're here for Sienna?"

This is awkward. We're not supposed to spend time with family and friends during the Trials. Special bonding time and all that shit.

But this isn't a completely normal Bonding, and plus, maybe this will give Sienna a much-needed pick me up.

"Sienna!" I holler loudly. "There's a crazy chick at the door asking for you!"

I smile genially as the wild cat hisses at me.

"If you bite me," I ask, "do I need to get a shot from the healers?"

Her retort stops short as Sienna flings herself past me. "Jessalyn!"

Her shoulders shake as she buries herself in wild chick's hair, and the harpy gives me a death glare as she draws her finger across her throat.

"Hey," she murmurs, using a much softer tone with Sienna. "Whose ass do I need to kick?"

Crossing one leg in front of the other, I nonchalantly hide my crown jewels just in case she attacks.

Sienna laughs as she pulls back, and Jessalyn the Wild Chick gives her a once over.

"Why the hell are you still wearing your Bonding gown?" she demands, outraged. "Where are your clothes?"

Sienna shrugs. "They're arriving today."

Jessalyn frowns, but she lets it go. "I know I'm not supposed to be here, but you left something behind."

She reaches forward and I back away rapidly. Giving me a toothy smile, Jessalyn grabs something leaning across the wall. My eyes widen, and I think I choke a little.

"Is that—"

"A guitar? Yes it is." The harpy is clearly smug as fuck as I stare at Sienna.

"You play?"

"Like a fucking queen," Jessalyn crows, but Sienna shushes her, shaking her head.

"I just dabble."

*Well, you can come right along and dabble with me, princess.*

"Thanks, Jess." Sienna strokes the battered leather case. *Dabble, my ass.* That case has seen some use. "I wish you could come in, but the rules…"

"Fuck the patriarchy, remember?" Jessalyn mutters, but she takes a step back anyway, her grin wobbling. "You're okay, though?"

"I'm okay. Pinky swear."

"Okay." Harpy wild girl blows out a breath. "Because I brought my knuckle duster."

"Jess!"

"I'm kidding!" She eyeballs me. "Maybe."

I back away, and Jessalyn wiggles her pinky at me. "Bye, Jax Cohen. See you soon."

*Fuck, that sounds like a threat.*

Hiding in the kitchen like the little bitch I apparently am, I skulk around until Sienna comes in, wiping at her eyes. The case is clutched tightly in her left hand.

"Oh, I—,"

Sliding off the counter, I saunter towards her. "You've been holding out on me, princess."

To her credit, she only frowns. "Hard to hold out on someone that doesn't speak to me."

I wince. "I deserve that."

"And more."

A *rat tat tat* grows louder in the distance, and I look between Sienna and the door, wanting more time with her. She watches me with a cute little line right between her eyes, this omega with the brave heart and the dirty dress.

Frowning, I make a note to check on her stuff. The harpy was right, it should have arrived by now.

"Jaxy! *There* you are."

I swear my balls shrivel up into raisins as Alicia stalks in, throwing her arms around my neck and pressing herself into me.

"I missed you," she purrs, her nails scratching a little too hard at my chest. "Did you miss me?"

"I saw you ten minutes ago," I mutter, straining over the top of her head to look for Sienna.

But she's gone.

A light sting draws my attention down to where Alicia is digging her pointy nails into my skin.

"Fuck, will you stop?" I bark, pushing her away.

Crossing her arms, her eyes shoot daggers in my direction. "You watch her like a puppy," she sneers. "It's pathetic."

"It's called biology, Alicia."

God, I'm so tired of this shit, and it's been less than twenty-four hours. Tristan better have found something during his little hustle to Councilor Erikkson's place.

Logan wanders in, covered in paint. "Lo?" I ask quickly. "When's Sienna's stuff getting here?"

He looks around, as though it's gonna magically appear in front of us. "It should've been here by now."

"Can you call and chase it up?"

Alicia coughs, inspecting her nails closely with a small smirk on her face. A *knowing* smirk.

"What have you done?" I ask through gritted teeth, and she bats her lashes.

"Me? Nothing! Although there were a few boxes of donations in the hallway this morning…"

She gasps in mock horror, bringing her hand over her mouth dramatically.

"Oh no! You don't think…. but they were so old and tattered, I assumed that they were to be disposed of."

My head starts to pound. "You threw her stuff away?"

She pouts. "Well, how was I supposed to know that pile of rags was hers?"

Taking a step closer to her, a snarl ripples out of me. "Where. Is. It?"

"Gone." Alicia's face twists as she snarls back at me. "Just like she will be soon enough. You're forgetting our agreement, Jax, and *I don't like it.*"

Logan intervenes, appearing between us, his hands held up placatingly. "We can buy her new stuff, Jax."

"It's not the same," I growl.

"No, but that's all we can do right now. Yeah?"

Stifling the urge to wrap my hands around Alicia's neck and squeeze, I step back with an abrupt nod. Spinning, I turn to walk away. Alicia grabs my arm and I shake her off with a snap of my teeth, making her jump back a step.

"Where are you going?" she demands shrilly.

"*Away from you.*"

## 27
# SIENNA

"Sienna."

Jax's smooth, low tone pulls me away from the box I'm elbow-deep in. This stuff is never ending. Every time I manage to drag something to the next room, I swear another three appear in its place.

"Mm?" I don't turn around. One encounter with my Soul Bonded is probably about as much as I can cope with today. I keep my eyes determinedly away from Jax's sculpted chest, snugly covered by his black cotton shirt, and zero in on the box of paint.

*Logan, we need to talk about your addiction to ochre yellow.*

Jax inhales. "About your things."

Now that gets my attention. "They're here?"

Thank fuck. I can finally get out of this goddamned dress.

"Uh." Jax rubs at his neck. "They *were* here."

Foreboding trickles down my spine. "Where are they?" I ask flatly, any euphoria I felt at the idea of clean clothes rapidly dwindling.

He swallows. "Alicia threw them out. I'm sorry."

*Alicia. Threw. My. Stuff. Out.*

Swinging back to the box I was clearing, I take a deep breath. Then another.

And hell, I take another one too.

My nails bite into my hands. That fucking bitch.

She takes my Soul Bonded. Humiliates me at my Bonding Ceremony. Threatens me. And now my stuff, too?

My photos.

Pain suffuses my chest. I packed a few of my favorite photos of me and Jess, my parents, Elise. All gone now.

"Sienna?" Jax asks quietly. "I'm really sorry."

Swinging around, I point a finger at him. "See, you say that like you actually mean it. Except you're not sorry. She's a *psychopath*, Jax. What are you doing with her?"

I hate that a whine drops into my voice. But *come on*. So they don't want me, fine (actually, not fine, but that's a whole other thing) but why the fuck would they want someone like *her*? They seem like decent men, assholery moments aside. Half the time it feels like they can barely stand her.

*This shit just doesn't make sense.*

Jax's face shutters. "It's—,"

"Ah – don't tell me. It's complicated. That's why I'm here, instead of home with my family, licking my wounds and gearing up for a second run with a pack that actually wants me."

A deep, throaty growl stops me short. Jax glares at me.

"You are not going to another pack," he snarls. I stare at him in disbelief.

"So what?" I say tiredly. "I'm just going to stay here? Live in the attic and be your little omega piece on the side while you parade Alicia around? Wait for the moments where you just can't help those pesky alpha hormones and come and rub yourself all over me, get us both off and then walk out? What's your endgame, Jax?"

I'm yelling by the time I reach the end of my impromptu little speech, and Jax looks understandably confused at my weirdly specific accusation.

"I don't know," he admits. Throwing my hands up, I stalk over and jab him in the chest.

"Well, you'd better figure it out fast, Jax. For all of us."

Dismissing him, I turn back to my boxes, hoping he'll leave so I can lick my wounds, and maybe scrounge up some spare clothes. A hand lands on my shoulder, softly squeezing.

"I'll get you something to wear," he says quietly. "I should've when you first arrived. Then we're going shopping."

"Don't do me any favors," I gripe.

But I really do want some clean clothes.

And some alone time with Jax… my heart leaps, a little pulse in my abdomen that tells me exactly how much my body likes that idea. *Traitorous, filthy little omega hormones.*

God, I wish I'd been born a beta. How easy would that be? No hormones, no heat to worry about, no fucking nesting instinct that claws at my skin and makes me drag hundreds of boxes from one room to the other.

No Bonding Trials.

And no Soul Bonded.

"Let's go." Jax interrupts my musings, splaying a large hand against my lower back and steering me out of the room. I squint as we head towards the stairs. "Where are we going?"

"My room." When I freeze, he takes a rapid step back, lifting his hands. "Not for that. To get you new clothes."

Relaxing slightly, I make my way up the winding staircase. "Somehow I can't see your clothes fitting me."

"You're so small, you can probably wear one of my sweatshirts as a dress."

I swat at him. "I am not small. I am perfectly formed."

"Damn right."

My mouth opens and closes again at his words, a flash of sadness that this isn't just a normal Bonding process. We're not getting to know each other, becoming more comfortable as we spend time in each other's company. That's not the end game here.

*Alicia. He has Alicia. Doesn't want you.*

Jax leads me to a doorway on the first floor, the other side from my little attic paradise. "You okay? Lost you for a moment there."

"Fine. What can I use?"

He frowns at my sharp tone but doesn't say anything. I stop abruptly at the doorway to his bedroom.

I expected a mess, but everything is perfectly placed around the room. A walnut-coloured queen-sized bed sits in the middle, surrounded by pale cream walls. I steer my eyes away quickly, sucking in a breath as I take a step forward and getting a lung full of musky rainfall for my trouble.

*Fuuuck, that's good. Jax could bottle that shit.*

But I'm distracted by the vast array of guitars lining his walls. There must be more than a dozen, every shade and type hanging perfectly. A cherry-coloured acoustic is propped up on a stand, and my fingers twitch.

I could really use a play.

Jax coughs. "Go ahead."

He waves a lazy hand towards the wall, but his eyes are focused firmly on me, a light in those violet eyes that dares me to step forwards.

God, do I want to rise to the challenge I can see there. To shock this alpha, this cocky, vibrant man into silence with what I can do.

Maybe he'd be excited. My stomach twists. It's what I'd hoped for from my Soul Bonded. To have someone to mess around with, to play with the words inside my head and bring them out through my hands.

I close my fingers into a loose fist. "The clothes?"

Jax frowns, his furrowed brow telling me he's disappointed, but he walks over to a closet and pulls out a black hooded sweatshirt.

"Try this. Weather's warm enough to get away with it as a dress."

I reach out and take the soft cotton, our fingers brushing together. For a moment, my eyes meet violet flecked with gold, and I pause.

But he turns away. "I'll wait outside, let you get dressed."

Nodding and gripping the sweatshirt, I swallow the lump in my throat as he walks out, not sparing me another glance.

I glance down. Finally, I can get out of this damn dress. If I'm quick, maybe I could even use Jax's shower.

…I am not quick.

Not even a little.

Ten minutes later, there's a knock on the door. "Uh, Sienna?"

"I need another minute," I gasp. My face feels blood red from the effort of trying to get this thing off me.

*Forget Alicia. Forget the demonic coffee machine. Fuck all of it. This dress is my real nemesis.*

Making one final attempt to reach the back, I strain with everything I've got but my arms just aren't that long.

"I need help," I grumble. There's silence on the other side of the door. Shit. I hope he hasn't left.

"Um, Jax?" I call out, my voice wobbling. "I think I need a hand with the back of my dress."

The door swings open, but Jax stays where he is, leaning against the doorframe with his eyebrow cocked, raven hair sticking up as though he's run his hands through it.

"You know that's the oldest trick in the book, right?"

My cheeks catch on fire. "No trick," I almost snarl. "Just get this thing off me."

He takes a step, and I spin, showing him the line of buttons edging down my spine. He whistles. "That's quite a dress, you know. How'd you take it off last night?"

"I didn't," I grumble. "So I'd appreciate it if you could help."

His hand gently presses against my back, and I feel the tug of the button being released from its loop. "So you slept in your dress? I can think of more comfortable sleeping choices."

I snort. "The dress is the least of my worries when it comes to comfort. I do want to be clean though."

His hand stops, halfway down my back. "Is your room not comfortable?"

I grit my teeth. "Oh, absolutely. Very pleasant."

*If you like a side of drafty, dusty attic and a mattress with broken springs, then it's a fucking dream come true.*

"Good." He actually has the nerve to sound genuine.

I blink. "Are… are you joking?" He can't be serious.

I can *feel* his frown. "No?"

Spinning, I gesture brusquely towards the door. "You know what? I've got it from here. Thanks."

He stares at me, hands still lifted. "What did I do?" he asks, in a slightly wounded tone.

Pinching my nose, I take a deep breath for patience. Fuck, I've mastered the deep breathing technique since being here. Any more time in this place and I'll become a damn Buddhist.

"I'm not in the mood for playing games," I say heavily. "I'm *trying*, Jax. Even after that farce of a ceremony, after being told again and again that I'm not wanted. I'm still here. I get that none of you want me, but you brought me here, and so I am trying. I want to make it through these Trials, go home, and try to sort my life out. Do you really have to make it so difficult?"

His eyes have darkened. "You can't go home," he snaps. "Have you forgotten that you're my—"

The words cut off as my own eyes widen. Anger makes my voice shake.

"I haven't forgotten. Not for a second. Pity I can't say the same for any of you."

My voice starts to break. Turning away, I shove the dress down to pool around my ankles, ignoring Jax standing right fucking there, his eyes burning into my back and raising the temperature by seven hundred degrees. Taking the sweatshirt, I yank it quickly over my head and push past Jax to the door. Fuck the shopping. I just want to find a quiet corner to curl up in.

Fuck this pack and all the bullshit.

"Sienna!" Jax growls as I collide with someone.

"Watch it," Alicia grunts. She takes a step back and looks me up and down.

"Is that… is that Jax's sweatshirt?" she breathes. Her face darkens. "Take it off."

"I wouldn't have to wear it if you hadn't thrown all of my things away, you psychopath," I snap.

She takes another step, and I don't move. "Take it off, now."

I grin in savage satisfaction.

"How about…nope. Don't think I will, actually."

Smoothing down the material, I shimmy in place, putting my hand on my hip. "Don't you think it suits me?"

"Aghth!" Alicia screeches unintelligibly, before she launches herself at me. Someone pushes in between us, a hint of smoke entering my nose.

"*Stop.*"

I freeze, Tristan's command enough to force me into place. But his bark doesn't have any effect on the beta in front of me. Alicia ducks around him, reaching her hand up and slapping me across the face.

I stumble, my shoulder slamming against the wall as more people join us in the hallway, gasping as my cheek starts to burn.

"They're mine," Alicia shrieks. "Not yours, you little omega *whore*. Know your place, and just fuck off."

Blinking, I glance around. Jax and Tristan both stand still, faces like stone and eyes wide.

But they don't say anything.

As I stare into Tristan's empty eyes, my throat starts to burn, the ache in my stomach sharpening to pulsating stabs of pain and radiating along my throbbing face.

*You know what? Gladly.*

My hands drop to the hem of this fucking sweatshirt, and Tristan's eyes widen. He takes a half step forward before the sweatshirt hits him in the face.

Jax twitches, his hands fisting as Alicia stands there triumphantly, her face wreathed in savage satisfaction.

The hallway is silent as I turn and walk away wearing nothing more than two-day old underwear and bruised pride.

And neither of my Soul Bonded says a word.

Reaching the door to the attic, I pull it open and traipse up, my whole body aching.

I reach the shitty little room, faint patches of light illuminating the mattress.

And I curl up, my breathing coming faster and faster as I bite down savagely on my lip until I taste the iron tang of blood.

But I don't cry.

No more tears. Not for them.

## 28
# TRISTAN

Soft footsteps pad away from us as my Soul Bonded walks away, her walk stilted and her head held high.

I switch my gaze to Alicia, anger a fist closing around my throat, closing off my breathing as a door closes softly.

I snarl, squaring up to her. "What the fuck was that?"

She glances down, fiddling with her nails. "She was wearing something that belonged to me."

"My clothes don't belong to you," Jax grits out. "And neither do I."

Alicia gasps as my hand shoots out, curling around her throat. Bending down, I growl in her face.

"You broke the agreement, Alicia. I told you not to hurt her."

"Please," she scoffs. "I barely touched her."

But her eyes are wide, glancing frantically between me and Jax. Our anger swells in the hallway, so potent that even Alicia, as a beta, can pick up on it.

"You hurt her," I rumble. My hand tightens around her neck, and she squeaks. Jax places a hand on my shoulder, but I shake it off.

"Tris," Jax murmurs in my ear. "You need to calm down."

My whole body shakes. I'm so fucking done with all of this. What's the fucking point?

Releasing Alicia, I take a step back as she braces herself against the wall, hands rubbing frantically at her throat.

"I'm done," I say in a low voice. "You hear me? This shit is over with, Alicia."

She straightens, keeping out of reach.

"Don't be ridiculous, Tristan. You can't just end this. My father will—,"

"I don't care," I growl. "You hear me? I'm done with this shit. Your father can do what he wants. I'll deal with it."

"Tristan," Jax's voice is low behind me. "I get it, but we need to think about this. It's not just about your dad."

My eyes squeeze shut. Fuck, but I hate that he's right. Breathing heavily, I turn away before swinging back to jab a finger towards Alicia. She shrinks back.

"Don't fucking touch her ever again," I growl. "Don't go near her, don't speak to her, don't touch a hair on her goddamned head. Do you understand?"

Without waiting for an answer, I take the steps two at a time, heading for my office and pouring a giant glass of scotch. Jax stalks in a few minutes later, his face pale.

"I knocked on her door," he says. "No answer."

"Are you surprised?" I say wearily. "She doesn't want to see us. And I don't blame her."

*Fuck.* Her face as she looked at us. Like we were the monsters.

*We are the fucking monsters.*

"She hasn't even got any clothes," Jax whispers. "Or any of that omega stuff they like. She's got nothing, and she's hurt, Tris."

I stare into my glass. "I'll sort it."

I'll sort everything. I just need time.

My fingers tap on the desk as I battle the urge to stride up there and check on her for myself. But Jax tried, and she didn't answer. After today, the last thing I want to do is force my company on her.

I can feel the lack of her like an itch under my skin. I'm fucking desperate to scratch it, but I need to set an example to my pack and keep my distance.

But... she needs clothes.

Standing up, I make for the door. Jax swivels in his seat.

"Where are you going?" he calls.

"Shopping."

Taking the stairs two at a time, I make a quick detour to my room before I arrive at her door. Rapping my knuckles against the wood, I wait, but she doesn't respond.

I clear my throat. "Sienna."

"Yes?"

Spinning, I take in the sight of her, all five foot nothing of fiery attitude. She leans against the bathroom door with her eyebrow raised and arms crossed, still barely dressed. My eyes flicker down before I move them up with some effort.

Tossing the sweatshirt at her, I rub my neck when she scoffs.

"No, thank you. I've already been down that road today, and it didn't end particularly well for me."

Her cheek still has a hint of red from Alicia's slap, and my fist curls.

"I'm sorry," I say in a low voice.

Now both of her eyebrows raise. "For?" she asks quietly.

"For not saying something. Or doing something. She shouldn't have done that to you."

Sienna huffs quietly, but I don't miss the way her chin quivers. My chest constricts.

"I thought we could go shopping," I offer. "Get you some of your own things to replace the ones you lost."

And just like that, the fire returns.

"The ones *I* lost?" Sienna advances on me, her finger jabbing my chest. "I think you mean the ones your psychopath girlfriend threw away. Right?"

"Er- yes. That is... correct. Yes."

Fucking hell. I'm supposed to be the next Council Leader and she's tying my tongue into knots.

Sienna stares up at me, our bodies so close she brushes against me as she breathes. I'm not breathing at all.

Then she spins, scooping up the discarded sweatshirt and tugging it over her head before turning back to me with a small smile.

"After you," she says primly, sweeping her hand towards the stairs.

Obediently, I turn and walk down, blinking as I wonder exactly what I've let myself in for.

I wait by the door, and Sienna pauses. "What are we waiting for?"

She sounds a little hesitant, and I wave towards her feet. "Shoes?"

"I don't have any."

Fucking hell.

"Sorry," I say again like a rock.

*Of course she doesn't, you idiot. All she brought was her dress.*

As we get into the car, I glance over to where Sienna sits quietly, her hands in her lap as she fidgets with the oversized sleeves. She jumps when I lean over her.

"What – what are you doing?"

"Buckling you in." I take a little longer than I need to, just savoring the feel of her close to me, wrapped up in my scent. The scents from the first Trial have faded slightly, I realize with a frown. Sienna freezes when I lean into her neck, taking a deep inhale.

"My scent is fading on your skin."

I don't mean to growl, but that's exactly how it comes out. Sienna lifts her face, her mouth a hairsbreadth from mine.

"And whose fault is that?" she whispers.

The soft graze of her lips against mine is enough to pull me back. Clearing my throat, I turn away from her and fix my eyes forward. "Mine, I know."

The lost moment grates on me throughout the silent drive. Sienna sits quietly, her previous fire all but gone as I steal glimpses of her at every opportunity. Her hair hangs down in a tangle, covering her face. My hands flex on the steering wheel.

The uncomfortable silence persists until we pull up at a well-known omega store. Sienna shrinks down further in her seat.

"Is this not right?" I ask with a frown, double checking the name. "I figured this would be the best place."

"It's fine," she says quietly. "Can we go in now?"

She's out of the car before I can respond, and I follow more slowly.

Walking through the doors is more of an experience than I expected. I'm assaulted by a plethora of sickly-sweet scents burning my nose, and I cough, waving it away.

"Jesus. What is that?"

Sienna shrugs, her face pale as she hugs her arms around herself. An assistant flounces forward, bright and bouncy with a practiced smile tugging up her mouth, anticipating a sale.

"Well, hello there! How can I… help you, today?"

Her smile freezes as she spots Sienna, her eyes flicking down to where Sienna is hiding one foot behind the other.

"Are you sure you're in the right place, dear?" she asks. Her pleasant demeanor slides away, replaced by a sneer. "There are some stores further down the road that might be more suited to you."

My eyes fly up. *Wow, what a bitch.*

But Sienna almost disappears in front of my eyes. Her shoulders hunch in, her hands gripping her elbows tightly as she stares at the floor. "Sorry," she whispers. "We just wanted…"

Something deeply protective stirs in my chest, and I step forward.

"Excuse me," I say quietly. "I must have it wrong. I was told that this was the best store for omegas in Navarre, but I must have been misinformed."

The assistant sputters as I reach out a hand, grasping Sienna gently and drawing her under my arm. I can feel her shaking lightly as my own anger rises.

"This is the best store in Navarre," she responds with her nose in the air. "And we don't allow—"

"The bonded mate of the future Council Leader?" I ask smoothly, my eyebrows raising. "You must have quite the criteria."

I see the moment she puts two and two together, her face leeching of color as she glances frantically between Sienna and me. "My apologies, Mr. Cohen, I didn't recognise—"

"I'm sure it was all just a terrible misunderstanding," I respond smoothly. I'm tempted to leave and go elsewhere, but this place is the best. And I want Sienna to have the best.

"I'm sure... Marcia, is it? I'm sure that you didn't mean any harm, and you'll take superb care of Sienna here. I want her to have absolutely everything."

Marcia's eyes round. I can almost see the moneybags dancing through them as I slide my black card from my wallet and gently close Sienna's fingers around it. She glances down and back to me, her blue eyes wide.

"Tristan," she whispers, and I shake my head.

"Whatever she wants," I say firmly. "No limit."

Marcia damn near wets herself with delight. "Of course, Sir. If you'll follow me, Ms Sienna, we'll get you all set up in no time. We've just had a beautiful selection of lingerie in that I'd be delighted to show you."

She gestures to Sienna, who follows her with her face flaming scarlet.

Not bothering to hide my grin, I take a seat on a tiny little couch and wait.

## 29
# SIENNA

Humiliation curdles my stomach as Marcia leads me happily to the back of the store, babbling away in high-pitched terror that we might take a huge order away from her.

She pauses to look me up and down, pursing her lips as she looks away.

"You'll definitely need the works," she mutters. "Lucky your alpha has that black card handy, huh?"

I stare at her. "I don't want the works."

She scoffs. "Don't be silly. A male like that needs someone well-groomed on his arm. You'll hardly do in your current state."

She pats my arm condescendingly. "But not to worry! We'll fix you right up."

Tempting as it is to blow Tristan's credit card limit on everything and then some, I refuse to bow to the pressure. "I need two pairs of pants, some underwear, one dress and a couple of tops. That's it."

Marcia scowls before her face smooths back into position. "That's not what the alpha said."

I give her a plastic smile back, gritting my teeth. "That's what *I'm* saying."

After some to-ing and fro-ing, I end up with two small bags

filled with a few essentials. At my insistence and much to Marcia's horror, I yank the tags off a few pieces and put them straight on, sighing with relief at the feel of actual clothes.

Tristan stands when I walk out, the bags clutched tightly in my hand. He cranes his head to look behind me.

"Where's the rest of it?"

Shaking my head, I brush past him. "I've got everything I need, thank you."

Tristan calls my name, but I exit the store and wait by the car, wrapping my hands around that constant throb in my stomach. He storms out after me.

"What was that?" he growls, caging me against the car. His hands come up on either side of me as he leans in. "I thought omegas wanted to be pampered?"

"I guess I'm defective," I snap. "I just wanted a change of clothes."

He throws his hands up, shaking his head. "I don't understand."

I take a deep breath. "You're *not* my alpha, Tristan. And I feel uncomfortable taking anything from you. I needed some stuff, but I don't need anything else!"

He actually snarls at me.

"What the hell is your problem?" I demand, anger shaking my voice. "I saved you some money today, Tristan. Back off."

"I don't know what to do with you," he grumbles. "Everything I do is wrong."

I try to push him away. "Are you serious? You think throwing money at me is going to make me – what, fall at your feet, after everything that's happened? Fuck right off, and then *fuck off some more*!"

I'm yelling, and he's snarling, and then the fucker kisses me.

And I kiss him back.

God *damn* it.

His lips smash into mine, his growl reverberating into my mouth as he grips my face in his hands. My mouth opens on a gasp and he surges inside, a hint of smoke and heat that's all Tristan.

We pull away, taking gasping breaths, but he doesn't let go of my face.

"Infuriating omega," he snarls, and then he kisses me *again*.

His hips press against mine, pinning me in place as I writhe against him, desperately seeking more as a whine vibrates in my throat. Tristan's hand slides to my throat, his hand gripping my neck in a hold that's weirdly comforting. I push myself into it, tipping my head to the side and baring my skin. His teeth sink into my neck gently, and I gasp. His other hand slides around my back, holding me to him as he tastes me.

"Fuck," he whispers. "Fuck, Sienna."

It's a confession and a curse. He pulls back, staring at me, his mismatched eyes wild and hair in disarray.

"What are you doing to me?" he asks. It's strangely vulnerable.

My breathing is erratic as I stare up at him.

"What is this, Tristan?" I ask, watching his face. "Is this… have your feelings changed? Because I'm getting a little whiplash here."

I brace myself, but it still stabs to watch his face close off, like a curtain falling at the end of a performance. The heated, passionate alpha I just had a glimpse of vanishes before my eyes.

"That's what I thought," I whisper.

My throat feels tight, an ache building as I blink rapidly.

"It's not going to happen, is it?" I mutter. "And yet every time, I fall for it."

Tristan flinches, his hand reaching out before it falls limply to his side. "Sienna."

It's a plea that I don't understand.

I wet my lips. "It should be easy, Tristan."

This should be the easiest thing in the world.

"You're my Soul Bonded," I force out. "All of you. We're

meant to be. And if what you've seen isn't enough by now, then it will never be enough. *I* will never be enough."

Every word feels like a stab through the gut as Tristan pales.

"It's not like that," he rasps. "It's not that simple."

I close my eyes. I'm so tired.

"But it should be," I whisper. "It should be that simple for us, Tristan."

He doesn't say anything. Fuck, there's nothing to say.

We ride back to the house in silence. The atmosphere grows colder and colder until I can almost taste ice on my tongue. The ache in my stomach burns a little more with every mile.

When we pull up, I get out without a word, collecting my bag and making my way into the house. Gray stands in the entrance, his eyes raking me as I pass without a word.

Heading to my weird nest, I place the bags carefully to one side before rolling up my sleeves and carrying on.

Collecting a pile of dirty tarps, I stagger towards the door to dump them in the other room. Pushing past one of the remaining piles of boxes, a sharp pain radiates through my leg and everything collapses to the floor, me included.

"Shit. Shit, shit, shit!"

I'm not sure what I'm most annoyed about – the nasty cut at the back of my calf or that my brand-new replacement jeans now have a massive rip in them.

Taking a deep breath, I grab one of the cloths and wrap it carefully around the cut. Turpentine is good for cuts, right? Because there's no way in hell I'm going down and asking for help from the Cohens. Not a chance.

Bracing myself, I stand up and take a careful step.

*Okay, that hurts.*

I bite my lip, taking another step. *Manageable. Definitely manageable.*

It has to be.

I have four days until Ollena comes. Four days to make this shitty little room into an acceptable nest.

I have no blankets. No lights. Not even a candle.
One thing at a time.
Clear the room. Clean the room. Fill the room.
*Four days. Let's go, Sienna.*
And no matter what, I will not think about them.
I will not cry over them. Or about *her*.
I will not break.

## 30
# LOGAN

I make my way towards Sienna's makeshift nesting space. We've barely seen her over the last three days. Our Soul Bonded is a ghost, a glimpse of pink hair before a door closes, a faint scent of raspberries in the kitchen, a dish or two drying on the side.

My chest aches. This whole situation needs to resolve itself. I don't even know if she'll be able to forgive us for the way we've been.

*We'll never stop making it up to you.*

I stop awkwardly at the doorway before I lift a hand to knock.

"Sienna?" I call softly. "It's Logan. Can I come in?"

There's a shuffling inside before the door pulls open, and I feel like I can finally take a proper breath for the first time in days.

It quickly fades though, concern taking its place.

"Sienna." I step closer, my hands gripping her arms lightly. "What's wrong?"

Because she's clearly not fucking well. Her previously vibrant hair hangs limply past her shoulders, her face bloodless as she looks up at me emotionlessly. "Logan."

Fuck. What's wrong with her?

Steering her into the room, I glance around for a spot for her to sit down, but the previously packed room is completely empty. When she stumbles, I look down with a frown, panic warring with protectiveness in my chest.

"Why are you limping?" I don't mean to bark at her, but I can't help it. She doesn't flinch though.

She doesn't do anything. Just stands there, her hands drooping at her sides.

"I hurt my leg," she whispers. "It's not a big deal."

The fuck?

"I'm taking a look at it," I tell her. "Come on."

She stiffens when I go to lift her, so I nudge her out of the room and across the hall into her room. She feels so frail under my hands, the fire that was present just a few days ago snuffed out. She sits obediently on the bed, her head hanging down, shoulders slumped.

She finally looks up at me, her blue eyes almost gray. "You don't need to do this."

My heart clenches in my chest, and I grit my teeth. "Yes, I do. Stay here."

I head to grab a first aid kit, slowing as I re-enter the bedroom and see what I missed the first time round. It's so tidy in here.

She hasn't settled in, hasn't made any changes to the room. I know how important that is to an omega. That she hasn't isn't a good sign.

*And whose fault is that, asshole?*

I need to talk to the guys. Something needs to change. *Now.*

"Hey," I murmur, tucking a strand of hair behind her ear. "Let's take a look at that leg."

She leans forward, her movements jerky, and rolls up the soft material of her yoga pants. My breathing hitches as my hand lifts to the rag covering her leg. It looks like one of the rags I use to mop up bits of paint. I had hundreds of them stashed in that room.

"Why didn't you tell us?" I scold her gently, but she flinches anyway and I bite back the admonishment. But something is seriously wrong here. As I unwrap it, she tenses, a low whine shaking her throat.

"Shhh," I soothe her, my hands shaking slightly. "It's okay. I've got you now."

A growl rises up my throat as I get a good look at her leg. The jagged gash is deeper than I expected, right across the back of her calf, inflamed and red with the early signs of infection. My fingers tighten over her knee. "How did this happen?"

"Something was sticking out," she murmurs. "I fell when I was carrying a box. Couldn't see."

And whatever it was, was probably rusty as fuck too.

"When?" I rasp. She shrugs a little. "A few days ago."

She moves, and I press her back into the bed. "You're not going anywhere until this cut is properly cleaned."

Sienna just blinks at me, slowly. "Why do you care?"

*Because you're my Soul Bonded.*

*Because you've taken all the shit we've thrown at you and just carried on.*

We're fucking assholes. All of us. We don't deserve her.

"I care," I say hoarsely. "Now stay still."

I'm no healer, but I clean out the cut as best I can. Sienna barely moves, her teeth chewing at already ragged lips until I pry them loose softly with my thumb.

"That's enough of that,"

When the cut is clean, I apply a soft white bandage before I pull the covers back on the bed, frowning. "It's like you haven't slept in here at all."

She begins to struggle. "I can't. I need to go back to the nest."

"Like fuck," I bark, toning it down a notch when she flinches. "Sienna, you're hurt, baby. You need to rest that leg for a while. Just for a little bit."

For the first time, her face shows a glimmer of emotion. *Fear.*

"The Trial is tomorrow," she whispers, dread lacing her words as she shudders. "I'm going to – I'm going to fail."

I stare down at her, realization sinking in. The empty room. It's still dirty, and there's nothing in it. No blankets, no soft lighting, nothing at all that suggests the space to be an omega's nest.

Sienna is right. She's not going to pass.

And we've just left her to struggle.

"I'll fix it," I murmur. "I promise, Sienna. I just need you to rest."

She blinks at me, but her eyes are already starting to drift closed. "Why would you do that?"

I try to smile. "You've worked so hard to clear it all. Least I can do."

"But you hate me," she whispers as her eyes close. Her breathing slows, her body growing lax as she falls into sleep.

"I don't hate you."

*The only person I hate right now is myself.*

I tug the blankets over her, wrapping her up and being careful of her leg before I turn and hightail it out of the room and down to Tristan's office, throwing the door open.

"What's wrong?" Tristan is nursing another glass of drink as he sits behind his desk. I haven't seen him at home without one on his hand since this shit started.

"We fucked up." I pace back and forth.

"I know," he sighs. "I'm working on it, Lo."

"No." Spinning, I slam my hand down on his desk. "We fucked up massively. She's sick, Tristan!"

He bolts upright, his face losing color. "What are you talking about?"

"She cut her leg open a few days ago in that fucking room and I just caught her about to pass out. She just wrapped a filthy rag around it and carried on because she's so worried about failing the Trial. Tristan, *we have fucked this up*."

He jumps to his feet. "Where is she?"

"I put her to bed in her room. Which looks completely untouched, by the way. I'm really worried about her, Tristan."

His eyes flicker past me, bouncing between the door and the papers on his desk. "I…,"

"This isn't working," I say quietly. "Whatever semblance of a plan we had is done, Tristan. I'm not doing it anymore."

"You're not *doing it anymore*?" he shouts. "Who the fuck do you think I'm doing this for? You want pictures of you and Gray splashed across every paper in Navarre?"

Pushing back the instinct to step back, I square up to him. "I never gave a fuck about that. The whole damn world can know for all I care."

Tristan's nostrils flare. "That's not what I thought."

"Well, you thought wrong. It's Gray that cares about that."

"What do I care about?"

Both Tristan and I startle, turning to Gray where he leans against the doorway. He looks as tired as the rest of us, this farcical charade leaving light grooves in his forehead that weren't there before.

"Nothing," I say quickly. "We need your help, though."

He straightens, looking at me properly for the first time in days. "What's wrong?"

"It's Sienna." Briefly, I explain as Gray frowns.

"She's hurt?"

"She's sleeping now. But the Trial is tomorrow, and she'll fail if Ollena gets a look at that room. There's no way it'll pass for a nest."

Gray hesitates. "Lo… maybe that would be best."

Tristan growls behind me. "You want her gone?"

Gray shrugs helplessly. "I want her safe. And fuck if we're not doing an all-around shitty job of that. At this point it would be safer for her to be as far away from us as possible."

My throat tightens, anxiety crawls at me. "You know what that'll mean?"

Gray nods, silent.

It means Sienna will fail the Bonding Trials. She'll have to leave, and she won't be allowed to come back. Not only that, but she'll never be able to participate in the Bonding Trials again.

We'll never be able to be together. She'll never be able to meet anyone else.

"She won't be Denied," Tristan says hoarsely behind me. "It's not as bad as that. She wouldn't be banished over the wall."

"But we're Soul Bonded. That's not something we can turn off, Tristan!"

"I know," he says, leaning back in his seat. "Fuck, Logan, I know. I get it. But we're no closer to getting Erikkson and Alicia off our backs."

"I said I don't care," I point out. "Let them all know, Tristan. Gray and I can ride this out. Your dad can ride this out."

Gray freezes. "Tell everyone?" he asks. "About us?"

I nod. "It's time, Gray. We can't call ourselves alphas if we keep putting our own needs above our omega. You didn't see her tonight. It's gone way beyond far enough. It needs to end."

Gray opens his mouth, but a voice cuts through.

"Well, this is touching," Alicia drawls. "Having a little pow-wow, Cohens?"

She saunters into the room. Jax appears behind her, an apology in his eyes.

"Alicia," Tristan says smoothly. "I thought you were staying at home this evening."

"But this is my home," she murmurs. "Isn't it?"

"No."

She swivels to face me, her smile not dimming. "No?" she queries, examining her nails.

"You know who I saw today? The most darling little child. So like her sister, it's uncanny."

Unease slithers up my spine as the room goes silent.

"Yes," Alicia murmurs. "Such a lovely shade of blue eyes. Quite unmistakable, really. And to think, she nearly fell into the road."

She laughs. "Why, if I hadn't grabbed her arm, who knows what would have happened?"

Jax grabs her arm, shaking her. "Threatening children now, Alicia?"

"No threats," Alicia says silkily. "It's more of a promise, really. Quite simple. You keep your word, and Elise Michaels remains unharmed."

Jax and Gray snarl in unison, and I look at Tristan. He's watching Alicia carefully, his hands folded.

"I think you're scared, Alicia," he says quietly. Gray and Jax stop their snarling, and Alicia straightens. "Excuse me?"

"I think you know," Tristan says in a low voice, "That this ruse isn't going to hold forever. It's going to unravel. And you'll try anything, won't you? So desperate to get what you want that you'll threaten a child."

"It's no threat," Alicia blusters. "I mean every word."

"I'm sure," Tristan says drily. "You think holding the safety of Elise Michaels over our heads will make us dance to your tune? Your father is already extorting us with what I strongly suspect is false evidence—,"

"It's not false!" she shrieks. Her composure is rapidly unraveling, spots of bright red appearing on her cheeks. "My father has you tied up, Tristan!"

"Maybe," he murmurs, surprisingly calmly. "But some knots unravel, Alicia."

He stands up. "Get out of my office."

Alicia's mouth falls open. "But—,"

"Get out."

Tristan's bark is enough to take the air from my lungs. Alicia backs up rapidly, the color leaching from her face.

"Don't worry," Tristan says softly, the faintest hint of menace in his tone that makes Alicia swallow as she backs through the door. "The agreement remains in place. For now."

As soon as she reaches the other side of the entrance, Jax slams the door in her face with enthusiasm, grinning at the outraged squawk the echoes through the wood.

"We're going to pay for that, but I don't give a fuck." Rubbing his hands together, he looks around. "What is it?"

But I'm watching Tristan. Watching the familiar tilt of his lips, that self-assured smirk that's been missing since this whole shitstorm started.

Catching my eye, he casually lifts his hand.

Gray chokes. "Is that what I think it is?"

Tristan grins. "It's something that'll help us win."

The recording device clicks as he presses a button, the tinny sounds of Alicia's voice filling the room.

*"...Quite simple. You keep your word, and Elise Michaels remains unharmed."*

Another click, and the recording switches off. Tristan looks around at us.

"I'm going to Erikkson's office tomorrow," he says in a low voice. "I'll see what else I can find. Then we take it all to my dad, but Logan is right. I'm done with this shit."

Gray clears his throat. "Does that mean everything comes out?"

I turn to face him, my fists clenched. "I'm done with hiding," I remind him, my jaw tight.

*You promised me, Gray Cohen.*

Gray's throat bobs, but he gives me a nod.

"That's it, then," he says hoarsely. "It's all coming out."

Tristan nods.

"As long as we have the evidence against the Erikksons, I'm confident we can get through it."

I take a deep breath before letting it go slowly. My chest tingles.

*Hope.*

"Where are you going?" Gray asks, as I turn and head for the door.

"You mean, where are we going," I toss over my shoulder. "Come on."

We have a nest to build.

31

# SIENNA

Grit lines my eyes as I crack them open a smidge, then blink. Sunlight fills my room. Actual, proper sunlight, not murky shadowed light crossed with dust and cobwebs and God knows what else.

Turning my head, I moan at the pain. Everything hurts.

That damn ache in my stomach has snowballed to epic proportions, and my leg is burning too.

Gradually pulling myself upright by sheer force of will, I glance around the room I slept in. It's nice. Too bad they couldn't have given me this one instead of the shitty attic.

*Way to make a point, Cohen pack.*

Groaning, I manage to wobble upright as a knock sounds on the door.

"I'm coming," I croak. I make my wobbly way to the door and pull it open. Jax takes a step back as he scans me.

"Sienna," he growls. "You look like shit."

"Thanks," I mutter sarcastically as I try to move past him.

"Whoa," he says softly, grabbing my arm. I don't have the strength to shake him off. "Where are you going?"

"Today is the Trial," I swallow back the pain as I force out the words. "I'm not going to pass, Jax. I'm going to get my stuff together."

There's nothing more I can do. The room is an empty shell, and Ollena will be here any minute. I'm not much better, and Jax growls slightly as I sag against the wall.

"You should be in bed," he mutters.

*No shit, Sherlock.*

"Trust me," I mutter, "It's the first thing on my list when I get home."

His grip flexes on my arm as he holds me steady. "You might be stuck with us for a little while yet, shortcake."

Frowning, I look towards the stairs as the doorbell rings. With a sigh, I pull my arm from his, moving away from the warmth of his touch to make my way unsteadily down the stairs. Jax lingers behind me.

"I don't think so, but we'll soon find out."

There's no sign of bitch-face Alicia, thank God, but the rest of my Soul Bonded are lingering in the hall, wearing matching looks of concern.

Tristan steps forward, his eyes scanning me. "Sienna," he breathes.

I wave at him half-heartedly. "I know, I look like shit. Let's get this over with."

My legs are shaking despite my bravado. They might be ready for me to leave, but the idea of being separated from them is enough to send my stomach into a twisting frenzy.

When I pause, letting out a sharp breath of pain, a hand appears at my elbow. Gray looks gutted when I glance up at him, his azure eyes blazing into mine.

"It's going to be alright," he whispers, and I look away from him as Logan pulls open the front door.

Ollena stares at us from the top step, her lips pressed together as she scans me up and down.

"Sienna Michaels," she says with a nod. "Cohens."

Her nod towards the pack is decidedly frostier as Tristan

welcomes her in. She looks back at me, her face tightening as she takes me in.

"Are you well?" she asks abruptly. "You look quite different from last week."

God. Has it only been a week?

Forcing a smile, I spread my hands out. "Unfortunate timing. I seem to have caught a bit of a sickness bug. I'm feeling a little better now."

Gray's arm slips around my waist. "Terrible timing. Just as we were getting to know one another," he says.

"Indeed." Ollena's eyes scan the hallway, peering past Jax. "Just us?"

When Tristan nods, her shoulders relax slightly, and she turns to me.

"I'm sure you know why I'm here," she begins. Gray continues to hold me, his arm taking more of my weight as I begin to sag. He holds me upright without complaint, his fingers gently caressing a circle on the skin at my waist.

"I do." Swallowing, I nod towards the nest. "The nest is this way."

We stroll down the hall, each step feeling like lead in my legs, weighing me down. Sweat beads on my brow as Gray looks down at me in concern.

"Si," he whispers. "You need to sit down."

"Shhh!" I swat at his arm. "After."

We pause in front of the door, and I brace myself.

Ollena sniffs. "The second Bonding Trial is to support your development as a cohesive pack. As a bond between alphas and the omega develops, the urge to nest grows greater, and you must produce an acceptable nesting area to pass the Trial. Do you have an area prepared?"

My mouth feels bone dry. "I—,"

"She does," Tristan interrupts, and I blink at him. Ollena frowns at the interruption, looking at me. Behind her, Jax nods exaggeratedly, so I jerkily mimic his head motion and he gives me a small smile.

"I do," I whisper.

*Maybe.*

Tristan turns the door handle to push the door open, and I blink. Then again. Very rapidly.

Because the space in front of me is not the room that I've spent the last week desperately trying to clear.

Dozens of flickering candles placed carefully onto low wooden shelving cast a soft light over the piles of cushions and soft-looking blankets lining the floor. The warm light flickers against the clean white walls, cleared of the oil and paint that flicked across them yesterday.

But it's the back wall that truly takes my breath away.

Inky black paint covers the entire wall. And over that... stars.

Dozens of stars. Constellations scatter across the space, making what would have been an open space cozy and inviting.

"Oh."

I think I gasp. Logan turns, a slight smile on his lips.

"I added the constellations earlier as a surprise," he murmurs to Ollena. But his eyes are glued to mine, soft and apologetic. "That's why it may smell a little of paint. I wanted to contribute a little something."

Ollena softens slightly. "They're lovely."

Turning to me, she tilts her head. "I must admit, I was concerned about the outcome of this Trial, Ms Michaels, given the events last week. However, I'm pleased to say that you've passed."

The sudden wave of relief nearly buckles me, but Gray remains steady. He presses a soft kiss to my hair. "Congratulations, Sienna."

Ollena looks around. "I know that the Trials may seem archaic," she says quietly, and we all lean forward. "But they are designed to help omegas and alphas have the strongest possible start to their Bonding. It ensures a successful pairing and is a process that offers protection to both sides." She looks at me, and I wonder how much she really sees.

Tristan nods.

"It wasn't my intention to insult the Trials," he responds. "However it may have looked."

Ollena gives him a considering look. "I know excitement when I see it, Mr. Cohen. Whatever happened between your Trial invitation and today, I'm pleased that it seems to have resolved itself."

Tristan hesitates, before offering a brief nod.

Chewing my lip, I follow Ollena, Tristan, Jax and Logan back to the main door, leaning heavily on Gray. My limp is getting worse, the burning in my leg stabbing with every step. But the stomachache has lessened again.

"Until the next Trial, Ms. Michaels," Ollena murmurs, turning to me. "Given your progress with your nest, I would expect your heat to arrive on schedule around seven to ten days from now."

Flushing, I nod as the alphas around me suddenly find the floor incredibly interesting. Jax audibly swallows. Gray's fingers flex on my skin. Tristan's ears have turned a rather fetching shade of scarlet.

"I'll be in touch. Good luck."

Ollena smiles at me, a little mischief in her eyes, before she turns and sweeps out of the door. Jax pushes it closed behind her before he sags against it.

"Thank fuck," he mutters. "That woman absolutely terrifies me."

Tristan strides towards me.

"You need to rest," he says with concern, placing his hand on my forehead. "You don't have a temperature, but you're clearly not well, Sienna."

"She's struggling to stand up," Gray chimes in, and I give him a dirty look. He raises his eyebrow, unrepentant. "What? You're going to fall over soon."

"'M not," I mutter petulantly. Just to show him, I pull away, biting my lip as wooziness threatens to knock me on my ass.

Jax muscles through, scooping me up. "Nuh uh. No fainting to prove a point. God, you're just as stubborn as Gray."

"Hey!" We both protest.

Tristan tucks a strand of hair behind my ear. "Rest," he says firmly. "We'll talk when you're feeling better."

I close my eyes as Jax carries me up.

"Do you need the bathroom?" he asks as he carefully places me down, and my eyes fly open.

"I've got it from here," I assure him, and he eyes me doubtfully.

"I'd rather make sure you get to bed," he states, crossing his arms. "I can wait."

Ugh.

"Please," I mutter. "I'm not going to die getting from the bathroom to the bed. I'll be fine, Jax."

He actually pouts at me. "I wanted to play nurse."

His humor nearly pulls a smile out of me, but I manage to resist. Fuck, he even has dimples.

"Shoo," I push him gently towards the stairs. "No omega likes an audience when she's in the bathroom."

He rubs his neck sheepishly. "Good point. I'll come and check on you in a bit. Bring you some soup."

"Is soup really the only thing you can cook?" I ask suspiciously. They eat a lot of soup.

Jax grins. "Rumbled. I wouldn't mind some more of that tortilla when you're feeling better."

Now I smile. "Maybe. If you're a good boy," I tease.

It's light-hearted, but Jax's eyes darken. I take a step back against the door as he leans in, crowding me.

"And if you're a good girl," he purrs into my ear, "then I'll make sure you're well rewarded."

Ooft. *And he scores a straight shot to my ovaries.*

With a squeak, I scramble backwards, nearly cursing as my leg jolts. Jax sees me wince and backs off, a penitent expression on his face. "Sorry, shortcake. I like playing with you."

"Another time?" I ask, before I bite my lip.

*Stupid, Sienna. Don't ask for promises.*

But Jax nods, leaning in to press a kiss against my forehead.

"Another time."

Hope flutters in my chest as he disappears downstairs with a final glance back.

Wincing, I limp my way into the bathroom. The sconce above the vanity highlights my flushed face and bright eyes in the mirror as I wash my hands.

"Stop it," I flick my hands at my reflection, spraying water droplets over the glass. "Don't get your hopes up."

Because Alicia is still hanging around, even if I've been lucky enough to avoid her for the last few days.

As I slowly make my way up the stairs to the attic, burning pain lances up my leg with every step. Carefully setting myself down on the mattress, I unwrap the bandage Logan placed on it.

*Shit, that looks bad.*

I gingerly poke at the wound, biting my lip on a curse as... *something*, oozes out.

Quickly wrapping it back up, I lie back on the bed, blowing out a shaky breath. The cream ceiling wavers above me, disappearing and reappearing with every slow blink. One of the coiled springs digs into my back, but I'm too tired to move.

This is fine. I'll get some sleep, and by the time I wake up, my leg will feel better. And if not, I'll ask the pack to take a look, maybe call a healer in.

It'll be fine tomorrow.

## 32
# GRAYSON

Early morning light spills against the wall in front of me, casting a golden glow across the room. Tapping my pen against the desk, I make another note on the plans in front of me. They need to be submitted this week, but I can't get my head in the game. My head bounces between thoughts of Sienna and thoughts of Logan until the pen cracks in my hand, black ink spilling out across the papers.

"Shit!" Grabbing some spare paper, I blot at the stain before pushing the plans away in frustration. The door cracks open, Logan's face peering around it.

"Can I come in?"

"You never used to ask permission," I snap. Logan frowns.

"Feeling a little irritated, are we?"

"I'm fine," I grumble. "Just…"

*Missing you.*

"Can I help you with something?" I manage to keep my voice steady as my eyes remain on my work. Logan circles around the desk, sliding in front of me. His hands cup my cheeks.

"Gray."

"What."

Instead of responding, Logan leans in, his mouth capturing

mine. My eyes slide shut as he takes leisurely sips at my mouth, my lips chasing his as he pulls back.

"What was that for?"

He grins lopsidedly. "I missed you, too."

Those soulful eyes burn into mine. "I think we'll do it, you know," he says quietly.

When I raise my brows questioningly, he waves his hand.

"I can feel it. Alicia, Erikkson... it's just temporary, Gray. We'll help Sienna pass the Trials, get them off our backs. And then..."

My chest constricts. "And then everyone will know."

He cups my face. "It's not such a bad thing, Gray," he whispers. "Maybe I thought it would be, once, but now... I want to walk down the street with you. I want everyone to know you're ours."

"Ours?"

"Mine... and Sienna's." Logan's cheeks flush a little.

"I've been painting," he admits. "The two of you have given me plenty to work with."

I sink back in my seat. "You sound so certain. We've fucked this up, Lo. From the start. We haven't treated her the way we should've."

His shoulders sag. "I know. It's not the way any of us wanted it to happen. But it'll come together."

I hope he's right. Leaning in, I rest my head against him, breathing in the comforting familiarity of his scent.

"I missed you," I admit on a mutter. His laughter shakes against me.

"I know."

"I don't function without you."

He pokes me. "I know that, too."

When I glance up, his face looks a little worried.

"We should check on Sienna. I didn't like the look of that leg."

I frown. I thought it was just a bad scrape. "Was it that bad?"

He shrugs. "It wasn't infected, but it looked like it might've gone that way if she'd left it. I cleaned it, wrapped it."

I might love this alpha, but he's the absolute worst at any kind of care. I watched him cut his hand open on glass once and put jello on it to 'soothe the burn'.

"Let's go." I stand abruptly, heading towards the door. Logan follows as I head upstairs, knocking loudly on Sienna's door.

"Gray, it's like... really early," Logan whispers.

I wince. Shit, I forgot.

But there's only silence.

"Why isn't she answering?" I mutter.

"Um, because she's sleeping?"

I shake my head. There's something tugging me, like a discomfort in my chest.

Something is wrong.

"This doesn't feel right," I turn to Logan, rubbing my chest. "Can you feel it?"

He frowns. "I've been feeling out of sorts for days. Figured it was the Bond acting crazy with everything happening."

I blink at him. That hadn't even occurred to me.

But it explains a lot.

I hammer on the door with more force. "Sienna!" I call. "Can we come in?"

A door opens down the hall, and Tristan sticks his head out. Dark circles sit under his eyes as he stares at us. "What's going on?"

"Sienna's not answering the door."

Jax is next to open his door. Yawning, he scratches absently at his chest as he wanders past Tristan. "Because it's early as fuck," he points out. "What are you even doing up?"

"Couldn't sleep," I mutter. Because something feels *off*.

"Don't you feel strange?" I ask Jax and Tris. "Sort of... numb, right here?"

I rub a spot in the center of my chest, and Tristan's brow furrows. He ducks back into his room and back, tugging a shirt over his head as he strides to the door.

"Sienna," he orders. "Open the door."

DENIED

Logan's face loses a little color. "We're making a lot of noise."

Tristan's hand shoots to the handle, twisting it. We crane our necks to look past him at… an empty room.

I blink. The bed is neatly made, not a sign of Sienna.

"What the hell?" Jax asks, following us in. "She's the tidiest person ever."

"No," Tristan growls. "Omegas make their spaces their own. She's not sleeping here."

He sounds *pissed*.

"So where is she?" I ask, and we all blink at each other.

"Split up," Tristan says tersely. "Find her."

The worry tugging at me grows with every room we check that comes up empty. Logan runs downstairs to check the nest. "Nothing," he calls up. His voice is anxious now, all of us picking up on the vibe that something isn't right here.

"Where's Alicia?" I shoot at Tristan. His fist clenches. "In her room, I hope."

*Fucking right off back to her father, I hope.*

I push her door open without knocking. She's snoring, a face mask turning her face a garish shade of green. I pull it closed without waking her, having no desire to bring that bitch into this discussion.

Shaking my head at Tristan, I watch as he starts to pace. "We've checked every room. Where can she be?"

Jax calls out. "We haven't checked everywhere."

His hand is on the door that leads up to the attic, and Tristan scowls. "We haven't been up there in years."

Logan sticks his head in as Jax opens the door, pulling back with a cough. "Well, someone has. There're footprints going up."

I'm pushing past him as the words register, Tristan close behind me as we thunder up the rickety wooden stairs, pushing cobwebs and fuck knows what out of the way.

My heart constricts. *What are you doing up here, baby?*

33

JAX

Gray's shout spurs me on, my feet hitting the stairs harder with every step as I follow behind Logan.

What the fuck is she doing up here?

Pushing into the low space, I take in the scene in front of me. Tristan and Gray are on their knees, Tristan leant over Sienna where she lies still on a shitty old mattress.

Too still.

"Is she—" I can't grasp the words.

"She's breathing," Tristan says shortly. Pulling myself together, I drop down next to Gray and scan her. She looks so damned small lying there, her eyes closed, blue veins tracing the pale skin. Even her lips look too pale.

My eyes catch on her leg, and I reach out, carefully rolling up her pants until the bandage is exposed. Peeling it away, I flinch back as Gray growls, low and furious next to me.

The angry gash is so dark it's almost black, little tendrils of darkness running down and into her leg.

"Fuck, Sienna!"

Her head lolls in Tristan's grip as he lifts her, his face ashen.

"Call Health Elio," he says urgently. "Now, Jax."

Tearing my eyes away, I fly down the stairs to my phone,

dialing the number of the Health Councilor with shaking fingers. The tone bleeps in my ear and I curse, starting again.

Come on, Elio. Pick up the fucking phone.

Tristan sweeps past me with our Soul Bonded clasped tightly in his arms, Gray following a step behind. I move after them as Elio's housekeeper picks up the phone.

"Emergency," I growl. "Cohen house. We have an omega with blood poisoning."

Seconds later, Elio's voice comes on the line, shooting questions at me.

"No...I don't know." My lips feel numb as I watch them stripping away the stained cloth on her leg. "She cut her leg a few days ago—"

"Four days ago," Logan interrupts, his voice hoarse. He's followed me in but he's standing well back, his face pale as his eyes sweep over Sienna's too-still form. "She cut her leg four days ago."

"You should've told us it was this bad," Gray growls, and Logan flinches.

"Four days," I say to Elio. "Come now, please. She's not waking up."

Hanging up as he promises to get here, I take a seat on the bed, wrapping Sienna's hand in mine. She's freezing, her hand hanging limply.

"We did this," I murmur. "This is our fault."

Nobody says anything. Because I'm fucking right.

"What the fuck was she doing up there?" Tristan snaps. "Sleeping on a shitty old mattress in the cold? Not even a fucking blanket? She had a room down here!"

"She had a room that Alicia showed her," Gray rumbles. "Should never have let them even be in the same room."

"Fuck," Tristan hisses. "I'm going to kill her."

His hand shakes where it hovers over Sienna, pushing a limp strand of pink hair away from her face.

"I'll wait by the door for Elio," Logan mumbles. Gray doesn't look away from Sienna, all of us zoning in on the tiny rise and fall of her chest.

"She'll be alright," Gray says. "She'll be fine."

The words drip with desperation.

And all the while, our omega lies silently on the bed.

No fire. No sass. No *Sienna*.

Just… silent.

*Come on, shortcake.*

*Wake up, and I'll do anything. Burn it all down.*

Just *wake up*.

## 34
# TRISTAN

Alicia bolts upright in the bed as I throw the door open, smashing it against the wall.

Her cucumber slice slides down, landing in the luminous green goop gunking up her face.

"Tristan!" she wails, scrabbling to cover herself.

"I don't give a fuck about your face," I snarl. Grabbing her throat, I curl my fingers around it and watch her eyes widen.

"Can you tell me why," I ask silkily. "Despite us putting a room aside for Sienna during the Trials, she seems to have been sleeping in the fucking attic? On a dirty little mattress? Care to explain, Alicia?"

She splutters around my hand. "I have no idea. Maybe she likes dirt!"

My fingers flex, and genuine fear enters her eyes.

"Talk."

My voice is grim. I'm in no mood to fuck around, not with my Soul Bonded hooked up to a dozen drips to get her stable enough to transport to the hospital.

"It was just a bit of fun," she whimpers. "I didn't mean anything by it. She's a wet rag, didn't even argue."

I battle back the urge to tighten my grip again.

"She's worth a hundred of you," I snarl, leaning down. "If anything happens to her, I will not be responsible for my actions. Nod to tell me you understand that."

Her head moves jerkily, and I release her. She rubs at her throat as she glares at me.

"I don't even know why I want you sometimes," she mutters.

Turning away, I head back to Sienna.

"Because you can't have me. Not when I'm *hers*."

The healers are removing Sienna as I stride back down the hall, carefully transporting her on a trolley as Jax and Gray hover alongside.

"Careful," Gray orders, and one of the healers gives him a dirty look.

"If she'd been taken care of like she should have been, we wouldn't be moving her at all," he mutters.

"Rath," Elio's voice is hard.

"Apologies, Healer."

But his words hang in the air, all of us picking up on the undertone.

They're right. If we'd looked after Sienna as we should have, taken on the role of her protectors, as her alphas, as her fucking Soul Bonded, then she wouldn't be lying on a trolley being carried out of the home where she should have been treated like a princess, not an unwanted toy.

Elio approaches me, his face inscrutable. "A word, Mr. Cohen, if you please."

When the door closes to my office, he rounds on me.

"I should remove Sienna Michaels from your care," he says tight. "You're clearly incapable of having an omega in your pack. I expected better from you, Tristan. Your father—"

"I know," I say quietly. "He's ashamed of me."

I haven't heard from him since the Bonding Ceremony. My father, my parents, both of whom would have been sniffing around regardless of the guidelines, have been silent. I know exactly what disapproval looks like, and it weighs heavy on my shoulders.

Elio sighs, his bushy white brows dropping low on his face.

"What's going on, Tristan? This isn't like you."

I've always liked Elio. He's solid, unwavering in his commitment to care for people, even when they don't always welcome it. But he's trusting, too. And he trusts his Councilors. There's no way I could confide in him.

I shake my head. "We were unprepared for the intensity of the Trials. We gave her some space, not realizing she was unwell. It won't happen again."

"See that it doesn't," Elio warns. "I'll let Ollena Hayward know. You can probably expect a visit."

He moves to leave. "Are you coming to the hospital?"

For any other pack, it wouldn't even be a question.

"Of course." Grabbing my keys, I head outside, Elio following. The ambulance is still outside, two healers crouched over Sienna as they work.

I force my lips to move. "Will she be alright?"

Elio pauses. "I believe so. She came very close to severe blood poisoning, but with the right care, she'll recover fully."

It's pointed.

"We'll make sure she's cared for."

Jax and Gray linger by the doors, Gray glancing back towards the house.

"Where's Logan?" I ask.

Gray shakes his head. "Beating himself up over Sienna. I'll get him and we'll meet you at the hospital."

The healer leans out. "Anyone getting in?"

Jax hauls himself up without hesitation. "Me. I'm staying with her."

Nodding, I shut the doors and watch as they pull off, jumping in the car. As they pull out onto the highway, I speed past them, taking an earlier exit.

I have a stop to make first.

Before I can face Sienna and ask her to forgive me.

## 35
## SIENNA

My leg is itching.

Rolling over, I try to reach down to scratch at it, but a large hand grabs mine, tugging it back up.

"No scratching," a deep voice commands. "Healers orders."

Healers' orders?

Confused, I crack my eyes open. They feel crusty and generally disgusting, and I squint through the crack at the face hovering close to mine.

"Sienna?"

A cool cloth presses gently over my forehead. "You with us, sweetheart?"

"Leave her alone," another voice chastises in the background. The cloth on my head gets taken away.

"What, so she can nearly die on us again?" The deep voice snaps back as I try to get my bearings.

When I finally manage to push my eyes open, I'm met with a dark metal railing. Frowning, I try to tally up my surroundings.

I went to bed in the attic. And I've woken up... where?

When I start to panic, struggling to push myself up, heavy hands land on my arms, pushing me back down. "Take it easy, Sienna. You've been out for a while."

*Out?*

My eyes finally focus on a rumpled Grayson. He looks up to meet my gaze and yanks his hands away, his jaw locked.

"How are you feeling?" someone else interjects. My head feels full of rocks, the effort to roll it over on my pillow surprisingly difficult. Logan looks even worse than Grayson, deep purple circles under his eyes hinting at sleepless nights.

I wet my dry lips, and Logan grabs a glass from the side, adding a straw and lifting it to my lips. "Take a drink."

Obediently, I suck down a tiny sip of water. It feels like nirvana, and I take greedy sucks, draining the glass before I shake my head and he removes it.

"What happened?" My voice is a croak as I glance between them with effort.

Gray folds his arms. "You nearly *died*. That's what happened."

He looks furious.

Confused, I glance around the room. I'm laid up in a metal bed, the large window opposite it showing somewhere that's definitely not the Cohen house.

The itch in my leg starts to niggle, and I try and rub it with my other one without either of them noticing. Gray sighs, reaching out to separate them.

"You had blood poisoning," he says shortly. He doesn't look at me as he pushes a white cotton pillow into the gap between my legs, stopping me from touching it. "We found you in the attic."

I snort. "Where else was I supposed to be, exactly?"

"In your room," another voice interjects. I turn stiffly to where Jax is standing in the doorway, looking just as pissed off as Gray. His expression softens as he walks over and sits on the edge of my bed, his hand pushing my hair back. "Which is definitely not the attic."

My head is spinning. There's cotton wool in my brain, my mouth is still dry as hell, and three of the four alphas who have been messing me around for the last two weeks are all gathered around me, looking seriously worried.

"Did I bang my head?" I ask. When they all look at me weirdly, I raise a hand with some effort. "Because you're all acting really strangely."

"We nearly lost you." Logan moves to sit opposite Jax, and Gray retreats, leaning his back against the wall. When Logan picks up my hand, it lies limp in his grip. "I'm so sorry, Sienna."

Something grips my chest, squeezes it. "What for?"

My voice is barely a whisper, and Logan exchanges a loaded glance with Jax before he looks down at me, his brown eyes darker than I've ever seen them.

"For everything," he says in a low voice. "Everything from the Bonding ceremony onwards. But especially for not realizing your leg was as bad as it was. You nearly died because of me."

It's an effort, but I manage to roll my eyes, even as hope flickers dangerously to life. "Oh, please. It was just a cut."

"It was not just a cut." Gray's voice cuts through the room like a whip. "You damn well cut the back of your leg open, and then you covered it with turpentine. Did you want to kill yourself?"

Jax and Logan both stiffen, and Jax moves so he's between me and Gray. Infuriated, I push uselessly at his back until he shifts.

"Would you have cared?" I snap back at Gray. "You've all been so concerned for my wellbeing so far, after all."

He takes a step closer to me, his nostrils flaring. "So this was a cry for attention?"

The back of my throat burns as anger pulses hotly in my veins.

"Of all the stupid, arrogant—,"

"Enough!" Logan raises his voice enough that we both look over at him, Gray looking as unsettled as I feel. "Stop it," Logan says to Gray in a low voice. "Just… stop, Gray."

Do they think I did this on purpose?

"I did not do this on purpose." My voice shakes, and how I fucking hate that it's wobbling when Gray is looking at me with mistrust in his eyes. "I tripped when I was trying to empty that absolutely *ridiculous* fucking excuse of a nesting space that you so kindly gave me. And unlike most other omegas in my situation, I don't have a caring pack to soothe my fucking ouchies, Gray!"

He opens his mouth to interrupt, but I am on a roll.

"So I wrapped it up, and I carried on because I was not about to fail the nesting trial when I am already failing at everything that being an omega should be. I don't even know why I bothered."

My voice breaks, and I close my eyes. "Just leave me alone."

I'm tired, and a little bit broken, and everything hurts, from the stupid stabbing pains in my stomach that have swept back in like the villain turning up in a horror movie sequel to my stupid poisoned leg.

I wait, but there's no movement, nothing to suggest that the three alphas in the room are even close to doing what I asked.

Big surprise. I mean, Tristan's not even here.

Groaning, I turn onto my side, tugging the pillow from my legs and hugging it.

"Just go away," I say tiredly. "Please."

A hand settles carefully over my shoulder, Jax's misty scent surrounding me as he leans in.

"We've got some making up to do, sweetheart," he says quietly. "But we will make it up to you."

"And when we leave here?" I ask tiredly. "Will Alicia be waiting for us?"

He hesitates, and I close my eyes. I'm so tired of opening myself up to keep getting smashed in the chest, over and over again.

How many hits can a heart take before it shatters completely?

"If you care at all," I say, my eyes still closed, "then you'll give me some peace."

My bedding shifts as Jax stands up, and there's a shuffling as they all make for the door. When it closes softly behind them, I try to curl up and get comfortable, but the shooting pain in my leg tells me that's definitely not the best idea I've ever had.

I tussle with the blankets, trying to shift into a comfortable position. The room is too bright, too open. I feel too exposed to rest here.

For the first time, I actually long for my nest at the Cohen house.

A knock at the door is closely followed by a cheery voice. "I hear our newest patient is awake."

Healer Elio sweeps in, his eyes moving over me in a way that's purely professional. He purses his lips, making a note on the chart he carries in his hand. We've never met before, although he treated my mother when she became ill several years ago. She's always spoken about him in glowing terms.

"Now, then," he sets the chart down, approaching and feeling my forehead. "No fever any longer, which is an excellent sign. How are you feeling, Ms Michaels?"

I decide on blunt honesty. "Like I've been hit by a truck."

He gives me a half-smile, his eyes narrowing. "You seem to have had an interesting few weeks. I've just gotten off the phone with Ollena Hayward."

I blanch. Why is he talking to the head of the Omega Hub?

When he sees my panic, he holds up a hand placatingly. "Nothing to concern yourself with." His tone is reassuring, firm, and I settle back against the pillow. "She was just concerned for your health, given... recent events."

*Like my Soul Bonded throwing me over at our Bonding Ceremony for a redheaded psychotic beta bitch with ridiculously good bone structure.*

He studies me closely, and when I don't respond, he opens up my chart. "All of your bloodwork is coming back clear, but you were very, very ill, Ms Michaels. Ollena is concerned – as I am – that your pack is not treating you appropriately."

My throat turns to dust as I read between the lines. "You're taking me away from them?"

He frowns. "I wish I could. But unfortunately, we're still bound by the law. And it's very clear that there are only a few, specific situations in which that can happen."

The tension lining my muscles releases, and Elio picks up on my relief, raising an eyebrow.

"You want to stay?" he asks. He's unusually direct in his approach. I kind of like it.

Turning his question over in my mind, I fidget with the bedding. "It's not as simple as that."

Nobody knows that we're Soul Bonded, and as much as I like the healer watching me with concern on his lined face, I want to keep it that way.

His eyes narrow, lips pursing in consideration. "You're Helena's daughter, aren't you?"

When I nod, his face turns considering. "I've always been very intrigued by your parents," he says quietly. His eyes don't move as I stiffen up. "Soul Bonding. It's such a rarity, but I've often wondered if it might be genetic."

Fuck, this alpha is perceptive. I force my face to stay as neutral as possible and stay completely quiet. I don't want to lie to him.

Elio tilts his head to the side. "There are very few records on Soul Bondings. But one thing that we do know, is that Soul Bonded cannot be separated. It causes physical pain, particularly for the omega. In extreme cases, it can cause the organs to shut down completely."

Well, shit. I try not to sweat as he peers at me.

"Well," he says at last, offering me a small smile. "I'm glad that's not something we need to worry about, given the current… situation."

He frowns again as he looks around the empty room. "I'm surprised they haven't stayed."

"They… they're not outside?"

When he shakes his head, my throat tightens up. I asked them to give me a little space, but they went home.

So much for making it up to me.

When the burning in my eyes threatens to spill out over my cheeks, I offer Health Elio a wobbly smile. "I'm feeling very tired, Healer."

"Of course. I'll let you get some rest." Flipping the chart closed, he leaves me in peace to wrestle with the stupid feelings tearing at my chest.

God, I wish Jessalyn was here. My mama. Dad. Elise.

People who actually care about me.

My stomach surges again, and I rest my hand over it. I'm trying not to panic at Health Elio's words, but if they're true... then there's a lot more at stake than being Denied.

Like my actual life.

36

# TRISTAN

"Is Councilor Erikkson here?"

The beta housemaid glances behind her uncertainly. "He's not, I'm afraid."

Smiling easily, I jump up the steps, brushing past her. "No problem. I'm happy to wait."

She's clearly flustered, glancing between me and the door. "Oh, well, I'm not sure that the Councilor would—"

"Nonsense," I interrupt. "The Councilor is a good friend. He won't mind me waiting."

My mouth nearly chokes on the words. Some fucking friend.

The housemaid clearly doesn't know what to do. I hide my smirk and nod to the padded bench in the entryway. "I'll wait right here. Promise not to move."

When I smile at her again, she finally capitulates. "I'm sure he won't be long."

Nodding, I set myself down. "As I said, I'm happy to wait."

When she lingers, glancing desperately down the hallway, I lean forward.

"I don't mind," I whisper conspiratorially, "if you need to get on with work, I mean."

She swallows. "It's just – the Councilor is very precise."

Winking, I wave her off. "Go on. I know how he can be."

Don't I just.

The maid wanders off, glancing behind her every so often. I lean my head back against the wall, stretching my legs out in front of me.

It was worth waiting two hours outside until the butler left. I doubt I would have had quite the same welcome. The itch to go to Sienna, to make sure she's safe, is clawing at me.

But if I want her to be safe, then I'm exactly where I need to be. My pack will contact me if there's anything.

When the sound of vacuuming echoes faintly, I stand up and move to the office door next to me.

If it's locked, this is over before it's begun.

But it opens easily under my hand, and I slip in, pushing it shut behind me and flicking the lock.

Heading to the large desk, I start searching, carefully pulling out drawers and working my way through pointless pieces of paper, invoices, email print outs – none of it what I'm looking for.

*Come on, you bastard. Give me something. Anything.*

But there's nothing here. Irritated, I push the last drawer shut, but my hand catches on something. I tap the wood lightly, the hollow sound bringing a smile to my face.

*There you are.*

Flicking up the false bottom, I grab the papers, scanning them over quickly.

The fuck?

I drop into Erikkson's chair, reading through the correspondence in my hand with growing horror.

I hoped to find something to get us out of this fucking deal, but this... I didn't expect.

> *Erikkson,*
> *Thanks for the update. Would appreciate a timescale on when you expect the omega to arrive. We have several buyers interested. If you*

*can expand the number of Denied omegas as discussed it would be worth your while.*
   *Samuels*

Nausea flips my stomach as I read the words again, my eyes flicking to Erikkson's scrawl underneath. Several pack names are listed, ones I recognise from my training. None of them have gone through the Trials yet.

Except one. Ours.

*Cohen* is circled several times, red pen indenting the page.

This is what he wants. *This* is Erikkson's endgame.

Alicia wanting me, my pack, that just fell straight into his hands. Because what he really wants is to sell our Soul Bonded to some asshole on the other side of the Wall for a fuckload of money.

And if we Denied Sienna, then she'd be sent over the wall. Completely cut off from her family, friends, her *life*.

There for the taking. And we'd never even know.

My hands clench on the paper. I don't want Erikkson to find me snooping around, especially now.

Carefully placing the papers exactly as I found them, I replace the false lid and slide them back into place. My hands shake, and I scrunch them into fists, pushing down the anger.

I need to be sensible. Logical.

And I'm taking that bastard down, before he gets anywhere near my fucking Soul Bonded.

I slide out of the door, listening out for the return of the maid as I take my seat. When she rounds the corner, face red with exertion, I'm exactly where she left me, casually scrolling through my phone.

"Councilor Erikkson is on his way home, Sir. He's asked that I show you to the sitting room."

I bet he has.

Giving her a smile, I gesture as I unfold myself from the bench. "After you."

I've barely been sitting for a few minutes, a coffee tray set out on the low, dark wooden table in front of me, when there's a commotion. Erikkson bustles into the room with a patently false grin on his face.

"Tristan! What a surprise."

Aware of the maid lingering in the doorway, I incline my head. "Councilor. I was hoping we might speak."

The civility feels like fucking ashes in my mouth, but Erikkson waves towards the door. "Of course!"

When the door to his study closes behind us, he drops his jovial façade, replacing it with a sneer that looks much more natural on his slimy face. "What do you want?"

I lean back in my chair, forcing my gaze away from where I know the evidence that could save us all is sitting.

"Alicia," I drawl, "is becoming a problem. Sienna Michaels nearly died today."

I make a concerted effort to unclench my fingers as I lean forward. "We had a deal, Erikkson. She is actively causing harm to an omega in my care. Whatever my feelings, we agreed that she would stay well away."

Erikkson actually sits up, paying attention. "What do you mean?"

Of course he's worried. Worried about losing his investment. Disgust curdles my stomach as I lay it out for him, but this is one thing that can work to my advantage. Erikkson wants Sienna whole and unharmed just as much as we do. For now, at least.

"I want her out of my house."

My tone is resolute. I might need to play a longer game in respect of Erikkson and his plans, but this is the one thing I can do for Sienna. For all of us.

With Alicia out of the house, we can all breathe a little easier.

Erikkson raises an eyebrow, but I can see him considering it. "That wasn't our agreement."

"I don't want a dead omega on my hands, Erikkson." There's a burning sensation in my chest at just the thought of anything else happening to her.

"If you want Alicia to stand at my side when I ascend to Council leader, then we need to tread very carefully," I continue. "Eyes are watching us. Many people are unhappy about how the Bonding Trials are unfolding. People are starting to question if I'm the right person to take on the role at all."

And if I don't, then Erikkson misses out on the second part of his plans to grab power any way he can.

He humphs, but nods begrudgingly. "Agreed. The rest of the agreement remains in place. You will still Deny the omega at the conclusion of the Trials."

"As agreed," I say darkly. I can't wait to take this bastard down.

But for now, I'll take the small victory for what it is. Getting Alicia away from Sienna, away from all of us.

Standing, I move to the door. "I'll send her along with her things shortly."

I'm looking forward to dragging her out of our house. But it can wait.

It's time to face the consequences with our Soul Bonded.

## 37
# SIENNA

The next time I wake up, it's to a large hand cupping my cheek.

I roll into the caress like a cat, butting my head against it for more before realization hits hard.

My head jerks back so quickly I'm pretty sure I just gave myself whiplash, and I stare up at Tristan, wide-eyed and confused. He's perched on the side of my bed, a sad smile on his face as he watches me.

"How are you feeling?" he asks. His tone is softer than I think I've ever heard it. More subdued.

"Better," I say cautiously. Giving myself a mental check-in, I realize it's true. The burning in my leg has subsided to a dull ache, and my stomach seems to have settled, at least for the time being.

Pushing away that little sack of crap to work through later, I focus on Tristan. "What are you doing here, Tristan?"

He's unusually hesitant, his hand tugging at the collar of one of the shirts he always wears. This one is black, perfectly tailored to his body. I refuse to be distracted, though.

Even if he does look deliciously rumpled.

"I owe you an apology," he says quietly. "One so big that I'm not even sure how to phrase it."

The lump in my throat reappears. This again.

It feels physically painful to tear my gaze away from him, to roll over and give him my back.

"No more apologies, Tristan. I've got a collection, and they don't mean anything."

He inhales. "I deserve that. And you deserve a lot more than what we've given you."

I squeeze my eyes together. "Yes, I do."

I might not be a hotshot future Council leader, or a superstar in the making. I didn't design a whole building when I was fourteen, and I sure as hell can't draw for shit, despite years of trying during my training.

"I am worth more than this," I say just as quietly, both of us keeping our voices low. "I might not seem like much to you, Tristan. But I am worth more."

My voice breaks at the end of my words. A low growl ripples through the room, making me jump.

Tristan's voice is furious. "I hate hearing that you think that. It's so opposite from the damn truth—,"

I spin around, my refusal to look at him forgotten in my anger. "What the hell am I supposed to think?" I demand hotly. My voice rises, filling the room. "You have pushed me away and rejected me at every single stage of these Trials, Tristan. You're all giving me whiplash with your mood swings, and your changing minds. Just tell me what the hell you want from me!"

"Everything," he says. He almost sounds defeated. "We want everything from you."

I shake my head. "No, you don't. You made that really fucking clear when you turned away from me – at our Bonding Ceremony – and kissed another woman, Tristan."

My chest aches. "We are supposed to be fated. Soul Bonded. Chosen by someone higher than us to be together, to be perfect together. And you threw it back in my face."

"Sienna."

"No." I push away his hand when he reaches for mine. "No, Tristan."

My stomach pulses in a low thrum of pain as I put distance between us.

"I don't believe you," I say brokenly. "Every time I do, it breaks me a little bit more when you prove that it's all bullshit."

He closes his eyes. "I did this. I know I did," he admits. "It's the last thing I wanted, Sienna. I swear to you. I want it all with you. If I could take it back, I would, but I am asking you to forgive me."

"I don't really have a choice, do I?" My lips feel numb as I force the words out. "This isn't something I can just walk away from."

His face drops, those eyes of his darkening. "Do you want to walk away? From us?"

I drop my eyes to the bedding. "I should."

But I can't say the words out loud. Regardless, it doesn't matter. I don't have a choice but to see this through, not when Elio confirmed my suspicions that the pain I've been feeling isn't just because I'm out of sorts.

I need them. I physically need them to survive.

I don't mention it to Tristan. I don't think he knows, and the last thing I need is for that to be used against me.

Or for them to take me on because they have to.

I think I'd prefer the alternative than living my life shackled to a group of alphas who want someone else.

I refocus on Tristan, taking in the furrow in his brow, the press of his lips. "Where is Alicia?"

"Going," he says immediately. "She's leaving tonight, Sienna."

"Wow." I laugh, a bitter, broken sound. "So you'll just toss her aside because you've suddenly decided on me?"

Tristan looks a little bewildered. "I thought…,"

I know what he thought. And I hate that my chest leaps at the idea of her leaving, at them turning their backs on her.

But maybe she and I aren't so different. Both told one thing, then the next minute our worlds flip again.

I never thought I'd feel any sort of empathy with Alicia Erikkson.

Jess would flip her shit if she could hear me.

Tristan is still waiting for my response, and I don't have one to give him. "It's not… not that clear cut for me, Tristan. I'm not suddenly going to be your little omega because you've pulled exactly the same stunt on Alicia that you've pulled on me."

His face flushes. "This is not the same," he snarls. "Not even a little."

"Maybe from your perspective."

He opens his mouth before closing it again, letting out a tired sigh as he squeezes the bridge between his eyes.

"Come home," he says softly. "Please, Sienna. Let us do this right, this time."

God, the temptation to do just that. To try again. The sudden burst of want hits me hard, every part of me crying out for exactly that.

But I can't be stupid. I can't just roll over.

I watch him. "One more chance, Tristan." His head shoots up, his eyes meeting mine hopefully. "You'll come back?"

I press my lips together before I nod. "One more time," I warn. "I can't *do* this again, Tristan. Soul Bonded or not."

Not when every small piece of me is suspended, waiting for that final crack before I fly into a million pieces.

I want them. I need them. And I'll go back, try one more time.

But if this fails…

Well. I'll cross that bridge when I come to it. Just the thought sends a spike of pain into me, strong enough to make me flinch. Tristan picks up it immediately as he turns his frame to face me, his eyes scanning over me. "Are you in pain?"

I shrug. "Well, I am in the Healers Center, so… yes?"

"I'm sorry. I'm pushing you, and you should be resting." He gets off the bed. "I'll leave you to it."

"You're leaving too?" I could kick myself for the vulnerability spilling out as Tristan whirls, his face masked in surprise.

"I thought you'd prefer it," he says slowly, taking a step towards me. "But… I could stay. I'd like to stay. With you. Here. If you want?"

I bite my lip, unexpectedly charmed as he fumbles through his words. Wordlessly, I shift over on the bed, leaving a space for him as he approaches.

Turning onto my side, I hold my breath as Tristan climbs behind me. The size difference between us becomes more than apparent, the little space available pushing us together until I'm pressed against him, my back to his chest, both of us breathing quietly. He curves over me, his warm whiskey scent curling around me like a blanket.

Hesitantly, his arm wraps around me. "Is this okay?"

I drink in the feel of him, the peacefulness as we both lie there. The stabbing pain ebbs away, chased back by his closeness. "This is okay."

Everything else can wait until tomorrow.

For tonight, at least, this is enough.

## 38
## JAX

I stare down at the brightly lit screen of my phone, taking in the absolutely fucking precious gift Tristan has just handed to me.

I'm pissed that he gets to stay with Sienna tonight when we had to leave, but this kind of makes up for it.

It's with absolute, unbridled glee that I stalk into the bedroom, flipping the switch on and sending the bright light spilling out across the room.

"Rise and shine, sleeping beauty," I sing. "Or should I call you Maleficent?"

On second thoughts, that's a fucking disservice to Maleficent.

Alicia sticks her head up, looking like a fucking horror story with yet another garish load of goop gunked on her face. This one is bright pink.

"What the hell, Jax!" she screeches. "Do none of you understand how important it is to get eight hours of sleep?"

"Oh, I do." It's with sheer delight that I rip off the covers, sending Alicia scrambling as I grab her ankle and yank her off. She lands in an inelegant sprawl in the middle with a yelp, blinking up at me. A cucumber slice slides into her goop, giving her a demented zombie flamenco look that actually suits her personality.

"Time to go home, crazy flamenco girl." Whistling, I yank out her suitcases from under the bed, tossing shit in without looking at it. When I reach for the drawers, Alicia screams, diving after me and latching onto my arm. "That's my underwear, you illiterate toad!"

"Ew." Giving the drawer a wide berth, I keep throwing everything I can see that might belong to the she-witch onto the bed. Alicia stares at me, a bit of comprehension finally dawning in that empty little head of hers.

"You can't throw me out," she says haughtily. "We have an agreement."

"Yeah, with your dad." Zipping up a case, I take nothing but pleasure as I yank it out to the hall and toss it over the railing. Something smashes underneath.

Eh. Worth it.

Alicia wails, running out to look. "You've gone mad," she hisses, coming back in and snatching away the shoes in my hand as she hugs them to her chest. "Stark, raving mad, Jax Cohen!"

"Oh, no." I wag my finger at her, enjoying the moment far too much. "You are most definitely the psycho bitch in this nonexistent enemalationship, Alicia. And it's time to get the fuck out of our house."

She frowns. "What's an enema....lationship?"

I roll my eyes. "Obviously, it's a mix-up of enemies and relationship. Also, an enema is where they inject liquid up your ass so you spray everywhere."

I throw the second case, enjoying the look on her face as it breaks open. "You're an enema in human form and I am flushing you the *fuck* out."

Does that make sense? Maybe not. It makes sense in my head, anyway.

I hear a shout from downstairs, a curse. "Jax!" Gray's bellow is furious. "You broke my model!"

I wince. Shit. Might've got a little carried away.

Scanning the room, I check everything is gone before I turn to

Alicia. She squawks as I approach, flapping her hands at me in a way that makes absolutely not an iota of difference as I flip her over my shoulder.

She screams at me the entire way down the stairs, beating at my back like a mosquito with an attitude problem.

"If it makes you feel better," I say casually when she pauses for breath, "I voted to sling you over the wall. But your father wants you home, so I'm afraid it's goodbye for now, Alicia."

I dump her on the doorstep, grabbing the cases and chucking them out after her.

Her hair is wild, sticking up in gloopy pink clumps as she wails. "How do I get home?"

"You're an inventive little thing," I shoot back. "I'm sure you'll work it out."

"Jax!"

"Don't let the gates hit you in the ass on the way out!" I call cheerfully, before I slam the door shut hard enough to rattle the walls.

I stick my hand in my pockets and turn to Logan and Gray. They both stare at me, lost for words, and I grin.

"Just takin' out the trash."

God, that felt good. I bounce on my toes as I point to the stairs, both of them looking a bit shell shocked as they follow my finger.

"Time to clean up, pack," I announce. "Our Soul Bonded is coming home tomorrow, and I want the Alicia stink gone before she steps through the door."

39

# LOGAN

"Stop it." Gray slaps my hand away.

I frown at the elaborate display of pale pink flowers in front of me. "Do you think she'll like it?"

Gray rolls his eyes. "All omegas like flowers."

Jax glares over at him. "She's not just any omega. Or have you forgotten?"

I watch Gray closely, picking up on the flex in his jaw as he looks down at the ground. Something is going on with him, but we don't have time to debate it now. Sienna and Tristan are due back any minute, and we've scoured the house to within an inch of its life.

It's not enough.

I don't even know how we begin to come back from the way we've treated the omega who's supposed to be our fated mate.

Somehow, I don't think a bunch of flowers is gonna help.

There's a rustle at the door, and then she's there, Tristan fussing over her as she limps inside. I swallow as I take her in. I don't think I've really *looked* at Sienna properly, really taken her in since our Bonding Ceremony… and she doesn't look like she did then.

Gray is frowning when I glance across at him, his blue eyes

taking in the sharp edges of her shoulders beneath her thin tank top. The curves that drew my eye have all but disappeared, her eyes sunken and her lips chapped as she glances around at us uncertainly. Her hair hangs limply around her face, the vibrancy of the pink curls dulled.

My heart feels like there's a fucking fist clamped tightly around it, squeezing.

This is what we did to her. She's a shell of the girl that came to us two weeks ago.

What the *fuck* have we done?

Tristan's arm is a gentle hold around her frail shoulders, his eyes full of emotion when he looks at me, the same shame I feel reflected in his gaze as he looks back down to Sienna.

"Hi," she whispers, tucking some stray hair back behind her ears.

Jax clears his throat, stepping forward. "Hey, shortcake."

She flushes, her cheeks deepening to a beautiful shade of pink as Jax carefully wraps his arms around her. Her eyes close as he gently squeezes her, and the sheer longing on her face sends a giant crack right down the middle of my heart.

I get in line behind Jax, waiting my turn. Sienna glances up at me shyly, chewing on her lip as I lean in and wrap her up. She feels like fine china, nothing like the omega I scent marked at the first trial. I can't scent myself on her any longer, the tangy lemon replaced by her own delicious raspberry ripple entwined with Tristan's deep, tangy scent.

I can't resist rubbing my cheek against her hair, desperate to leave some small part of myself behind as we pull apart.

"Are you hungry?" I offer. "I'm gonna cook breakfast."

She tilts her head. "You are?"

I rub at the back of my head at the slight suspicion. She already knows none of us are great cooks, but I can manage some eggs. "You need to eat," I tell her, tempering my tone so I'm not demanding it.

She glances down at herself, her arms wrapping around her defensively. "I guess I could eat."

Tristan is already ahead of me, fussing around the refrigerator as he yanks out the different fruits we bought at the grocery store first thing this morning.

Jax sticks close to Sienna, sliding out a chair for her to take a seat. Gray appears a few moments later, his manner subdued as he takes a seat towards the end of the table.

The atmosphere is undeniably awkward as Tristan and I hustle, Tristan chopping enough fruit to feed most of Navarre. I crack eggs into the pan, whisking them up into scrambled eggs, adding a pinch of salt and some pepper before tipping them out into a bowl and grabbing some plates.

When we're all sat down, Tristan serves Sienna first. We all watch her nibble at a piece of apple, and she glances around. "Are you eating?"

I spoon eggs into my mouth without paying much attention, too focused on the way she's picking at her food. Tristan's face pulls into a scowl, but he tempers his expression as she pushes her plate away.

"I was hoping we could have a conversation," he says. "About us."

"Okay." Sienna's shoulders bunch up like she's bracing for a blow. Jax pulls his chair in a little closer, his arm laying out across the back of her chair in silent support.

"We haven't been good alphas. Good *Soul Bonded*."

Sienna relaxes a little as she peeks up at Tristan.

"We haven't been good alphas," he continues, "and we'd like to change that. We have some ideas, but I think we'd all like to hear from you. What would you like from us? What do you need, to make you feel comfortable?"

Our omega's eyes widen as she looks around. "From you?"

We all nod, even Gray from the end of the table. Jax edges even closer, his hand creeping out to play with a lock of her hair.

"We're starting over, shortcake," he says firmly. "And we've got a lot of making up to do."

"So," Tristan presses. "Tell us what you want."

Sienna looks flustered, her eyes darting around us. "I... I don't want anything, really."

Her hands cross over her stomach, a defensive move that Tristan takes in with a curved brow. "Maybe you could have a think about it, and let us know?"

Sienna nods hastily, relief crossing her features. "I'll do that."

But then Gray throws a bomb into the mix. He leans forward, his face serious.

"Sienna... your heat will be coming in soon."

Everybody freezes. Sienna turns a cute but deep, deep shade of purple.

"Gray," I say, my teeth gritted. "I don't think we need to talk about that now."

I've obviously never seen an omega in heat, but I hear it's... an experience. Days of intense need, excessive fucking until it's over without pause.

I swallow, my jeans suddenly feeling much tighter than they normally do. Even Tristan looks flustered, his usual stoic face replaced with two flares of color on his cheeks. We're all trying really hard not to look at Sienna but her sudden burst of sweet raspberry scent into the room gives away that her thoughts are probably more than similar to mine.

"This," Gray says hoarsely, "is why we need to talk about it."

He looks at Sienna, his face softening for the first time since she walked in. "We know what it feels like when the hormones are in control. I'd like to know how you want to handle it before the choice is taken out of our hands and rational discussion goes out the window."

Jax nods, slowly. "He's right, Si. You deserve to have a choice in how you handle your heat. And if you feel you're not ready for that to be with us, then we should look at other options."

Sienna pales. "I'd fail the Trial," she whispers, but Tristan is shaking his head.

"We'll work something out. Lie if we have to. You won't be failing this Trial, Sienna. We only have two left, and then we're free to make our own decisions about how we move forward. I'm sorry that you're in this position because of us."

Sienna looks so damn lost it makes me want to pull her onto my lap. My fists clench on the table. We're not there yet.

"I'll think about it." Her fingers trace patterns over the dark wood of our dining table, her discomfort clear.

We all glance around. Jax widens his eyes at me, so I take the lead and stand up. "I was thinking I could show you your room?"

"I know where my room is, Logan," Sienna says tiredly, but she stands up all the same. "I just need to follow the dust."

I can feel my jaw tightening at the reminder of fucking Alicia and her little games. "Not the attic. That was never supposed to be your room."

Her eyebrows draw together in a frown. "It wasn't?"

"Nuh-uh," Jax chimes in. "Your room is two doors down from mine, shortcake."

He winks at her, and her plush lips press together firmly as she looks down. The smirk slides off Jax's face and I shake my head at him as I walk past, not waiting for Sienna to answer. Her soft footsteps pad after mine as we walk up the stairs, the distance between us feeling like a mountain. And I have no idea how to climb it.

Her breathing deepens, and I turn around, noticing that her leg is landing a little heavier on the one side. Concern tightens my chest. "Is your leg okay?"

Sienna pauses, leaning heavily on the banister. "It's a little sore. Think we should put more turps on it?"

I swing around, but she's smiling, biting on her lip as she shuffles past me. "I'm fine, Logan."

She's waiting at the top of the stairs, and I point to the room that was always meant to be hers. She raises her eyebrow. "So I was supposed to be here all along? What happened?"

"Alicia." The word trips apologetically off my tongue, but I don't miss the way she flinches as she moves slowly towards her room. "Of course."

There's a bitterness to her words. Of course there is. As far as she's concerned, we paraded Alicia in front of her at our Bonding Ceremony. I'm amazed she's even giving us the time of day.

And there's a whole clusterfuck to untangle. Alicia might be gone, but our problems aren't over. Erikkson is still expecting us to Deny Sienna at the closure of the Trials, and I have no idea how we're going to call him off without Gray and I becoming public enemy number one for the whole of Navarre society.

And Gray and I are a special cluster-what-the-actual-fuck all on our own. I don't even know how the hell to explain that to Sienna. If we even should.

Maybe we should let things lie.

The thought sends pain lancing through my chest, a direct hit. I don't want to be without Gray. To live our lives standing alongside him, unable to touch him the way I want to. Need to, even.

I need him, just as much as I need the omega in front of me. And all I'm doing is making a damned mess with both of them.

Rubbing my neck, I turn away. "I'll let you rest," I say abruptly. Not waiting for an answer, I take the stairs two at a time.

I need to lose myself in some art for a while.

# 40
# SIENNA

I'm left staring at Logan's back as he throws himself down the stairs, getting away from me as fast as he possibly can. I shove down the little spike of sorrow, locking it into an already overflowing box of rejection.

This is the slow game. It's not all going to be fixed in a day.

As confirmed by my reaction to Gray's comments.

Taking a few steps into the room, I hug my elbows as I look around. Someone has already brought my few belongings down, stacking them in the middle of the giant bed like a little shrine to how stupidly pathetic they are.

Shoving them aside, I wriggle awkwardly until I'm lying on my back, staring up at the white muslin canopy of the four-poster bed.

Makes a change from the filthy beams in the attic.

I stretch my leg out experimentally, wiggling my toes and biting back a wince at the pain in my calf. Yup, definitely not magically healed. My arms flop out to my sides as I blow out a frustrated breath, my thoughts shifting to the four alphas somewhere beneath me.

I have no *idea* what I'm doing here.

I'm rudderless. I thought I knew my way forward. Thought I knew what being an omega was all about, thought I knew what the Bonding Trials would bring, but now?

It all feels *tainted*. And the thought of going through my heat, of being so vulnerable to them when we've barely even started to work through this shitshow is not making me feel any kind of warm and cozy. It actually makes me want to curl up in a ball and hide until all of this magically goes away.

I don't... I don't want them for my heat. Soul Bonded or not. Not right now. Maybe we'll find our way through – it's not like I have much of a choice, with my own body firmly on their side.

I don't have an option here, unless Tristan can make good on his promise to find an alternative.

I stay where I am for a while longer, until the silence is full of my own screaming insecurities. None of them have come to check on me, to see if I'm alright.

When I can't cope with it anymore, I push myself upright, bracing myself to hobble back down the stairs. I can't stay in this barren, bland room for a minute longer, staring at my sad little stash and waiting for one of my freaking supposed soulmates to stick their head around the door.

Pausing at the doorway, I debate having a hot shower. I feel disgusting, all the grime from the last few days sticking to me like oil on my skin. But the urge to find Tristan, to confess that I can't see myself going through heat with them and try and work out a way forward that doesn't involve just rolling over and taking a knot – that feels like the most important thing I can do right now.

They need to understand that this isn't going to work – unless *they* do.

I'm not sure where I'm going. The kitchen is empty, so I work my way down the hallway, gingerly knocking on doors and pressing my ear against them to try and pick up some noise. God, the doors in this place are thick. I work my way down the hall until I finally pick up something.

I'm so focused on what I'm going to say and how to explain to them that I'm not comfortable with them being part of my heat that I barge straight in.

And I really, really wish I hadn't.

## 41
# GRAY

Stalking into Logan's studio, I slam the door behind me hard enough to jerk Logan out of his focused stare. He turns to me, bemused. "Where's the fire?"

"This," I say abruptly, pointing between us, "is the fire, Logan."

That he even rolls his eyes at me stokes the fucking flames in my chest. We've fucked everything up for the sake of our relationship. And I can't even touch him. I hate the distance that's opened up between us.

Fuck that. *This* is something I can fix.

His palette drops as I tug on his arm, and then my lips are on his, his face gripped between my hands as I devour him, pouring all of my frustration and need over the bruised omega resting upstairs, this soul-damned fucking clawing need for the man in front of me who's been avoiding my eyes for way too long.

His mouth opens under mine, my fingers entangled in the messy waves of his blonde hair as we grapple. Logan shoves me away, his chest heaving. "The fuck, Gray!"

"I cannot do this," I force out. My throat feels sealed closed, desperation clawing with nowhere to go. "I cannot do this, all of this, without you. Tell me that we are not done, Lo."

His deep brown eyes narrow, and then he's on me, yanking my arm around and shoving my back into the canvas. Wet paint sticks to my back, and I don't give a fuck because he's there, filling my veins with fire as he yanks my neck to the side, his mouth kissing up my skin a touch in a way that's not even a little bit gentle.

I'm gasping when he pulls back, his lips puffy as he growls at me. "Get on your fucking knees, Grayson. Get on your fucking knees and suck my cock like a good boy."

*Yes.*

My knees hit the hard ground of the studio with a thud, relief and hazy lust softening my bones enough that I don't think I could stand now if you paid me. Logan is unzipping his jeans, pulling out his beautifully carved cock as he grips my chin.

"Open up, Grayson. Since you've missed it so much, I'm going to fuck your face, and you're going to take it."

My eyes close in euphoria as he pushes his way in, no finesse as he nudges the back of my throat. He's all around me, his hands in my hair, grabbing the back of my head as he yanks me into him enough that I have to grip the back of his thighs. Logan's pace is relentless as he pounds into me, giving me everything I need.

How could I ever give this up? Give him up?

He swells impossibly harder, his knot nudging my chin as he teases me with it.

"Should I knot your mouth, Gray? Hold you here, your mouth full of my cum. Fucking filthy."

I groan, the sound reverberating around his cock as he ups his pace furiously. This is who we are. Stolen moments where we can be us, just Gray and Logan, the way that we want to be.

And stolen moments are all we'll ever have.

Logan grunts, the barest hint of warning before his legs tense beneath my grip, hot pulses shooting down my throat. I chase every drop, greedy for every little hint of him that I can take. This moment will have to be enough for now. We're risking a lot as it is.

I don't take my eyes from his face. He watches me clean him, brown eyes lazy and half-lidded, a smirk on his face as he pulls away and leans down, drawing me into a long, slow kiss.

"Bad, *bad* alpha," he chides laughingly, and I push him back with a snicker of my own.

And that's when awareness filters in, when he's far away enough that I can finally take a breath.

*Raspberries.*

My head whips around, taking in the sight of Sienna holding onto the doorway. Her eyes are saucers in her too-pale face as she looks between us.

"I… sorry."

"Sienna, wait!" Logan is cursing as he tries to zip himself up, but there's no explaining away what our Soul Bonded just saw. She slips out of the room, but she can't get far on her leg.

"Fuck," I snap.

I reach out to help, but Logan slaps my hand away.

"I can do it," he says shortly. He turns away from me, tidying himself up and shoving his hair away from his face, smoothing down the mess I made with my hands. Erasing me.

"She had to find out at some point," I say quietly. I'm still on my knees, the taste of him still in my mouth as he strides towards the door. He looks back at me, and for the first time, I see disgust in his face.

"Not like this, she didn't."

## 42
# SIENNA

I move as fast as I can, needing to get away, needing to hide and process what the fuck I just saw. I guess I know why Gray was so quick to push me away, now. He already has someone.

Logan.

Tears blur my eyes as I stagger into my so-called nest.

My safe space.

What a joke.

Logan's mural taunts me, the stars scattered against the far wall mocking in their beauty.

He didn't do that for me. He did it just so they didn't get pulled up by Ollena Hayward.

How many more fucking times?

It only takes a few minutes for them to find me. I'm curled up against the far corner of the too-big room, a blanket pulled over my head to try to create the soothing, contained environment that a nest should be.

I can't stop crying.

"Sienna," Logan says urgently. He tugs the covers down, away from my face, but I pull them back up with bared teeth.

"Leave me alone, Logan. Or have you come to really dig the knife in?"

Twist it a little more. Really shred my heart into ribbons, like what it's been through already isn't enough.

Now Gray kneels next to me, his chiseled face serious. "Please."

That fucking, soul-damned pain is back with a vengeance, pulsing low, agonising waves in my stomach.

Everything just fucking hurts.

I turn away, into the wall, burying my face inside my blankets so I don't have to look at the two alphas next to me.

And the worst thing? I'm not crying because I'm mad.

I'm breaking apart because I'm *jealous*.

Pure, shiny green with sheer fucking envy at how easily they touched each other. At the fucking love in Gray's eyes as he stared up at Logan like he was the sun and the stars and every little piece in between.

At the way Logan held him, when I've had to beg and scrape for every little piece of attention they deign to offer up, the barest scraps not enough to stop the agony happening inside me.

I'll never be enough, and the realization is breaking me.

Gray's hand touches my shoulder and I flinch instinctively, a low, pained whine slipping out from between my lips.

"Sienna," Gray murmurs hoarsely. "Please. Let us explain."

I stay exactly where I am, wrapped up in the tiny comfort offered by the blanket. In fact, I think I'll stay here until I die.

It'll probably happen sooner rather than later, the way things are going.

There's movement, and I choke as the blankets are pulled away and I'm deposited between two strong sets of arms. Logan and Gray press against me on either side, all of us sitting with our backs against the wall as Logan moves my legs around like a ragdoll.

I wipe my face with my arm abruptly, staring at the opposite, empty wall. "Happy now?"

"Not even a little," Logan says quietly. "You deserve an explanation, Sienna."

"Is this where you tell me it's not me, it's you? Again? Because that definitely looked like a *you* thing." My voice rings too high-pitched to pull off the snarky tone I'm aiming for, too shaky and fucking vulnerable, so I shut up, waiting for an explanation.

Aaaaaand... still waiting.

"This is the part where you talk," I mumble.

Logan inhales, a soft sound echoing in the room. "I'm trying to work out where we should begin."

"At the start would be good."

It's Gray who takes one for the team. "We've been... together, I guess, for a while."

Is that a month? A year? "You're not giving me much to work with here, you know."

"I know." Gray rubs the back of his neck. "It's difficult to explain, because... we've never really defined it. Us, I mean."

Ooo-kay. The sudden tension in the room is making me feel very awkward.

"You want me to leave?" I ask abruptly. "So you can *define* it?"

"No!" Logan grabs my hand like he genuinely thinks I'm a flight risk. I look down at our entangled fingers, mine lying loose in his grip.

"Gray and I care about each other," he says quietly. "But that doesn't mean we don't care about you too, Sienna."

I can't stop the slightly hysterical laugh that bubbles out of me. "Sure you do."

"We do." Gray takes my other hand. "We wanted an omega, Sienna. We wanted the Trials. We wanted you."

My heart flops over, beating out a dangerously familiar pattern. "So... what happened?"

I'm trying to jam the puzzle pieces together in my head, but they don't fit.

Gray and Logan exchange a glance over my head, and my shoulders tighten. "You told me I deserved an explanation."

And if they're serious about wanting me, then they'll give it to me. I'm tired of stumbling around in the dark.

"Alicia… she had photos of us. Together."

And it *clicks*.

"So she blackmailed you?" I ask numbly. Gray nods next to me.

"We didn't know what to do, Sienna. It wasn't just about us. It was the effect those photos could have on our pack. On Tristan, and Jax. So we made the call to play along, and hope that we'd work out something to fix it along the way."

There's something churning in my chest, and I don't quite know what it is.

"What did she want?" I ask. I can't look at them, my eyes still focused on the blank wall opposite.

I feel them both hesitate, and I swallow. "The truth, please."

"She wanted us to Deny you," Logan says quietly. "I'm so sorry, Sienna."

My eyes slide closed.

All of this. All because of *her*.

I wet my lips. "I'd like to be alone now, please."

They take a moment before they release my hands. Logan turns to me as Gray clambers up.

"We mean it," he says softly. "We do want you, Sienna. And Gray and I… we have some things to work out. But if it's a deal breaker for you—,"

I see Gray's face before a mask descends, icy calm covering up the agony that flashed across his face before he hides it away.

I shake my head rapidly. "That's not a problem to me. You being together. But everything else, I just… I need some time to process."

Gray's jaw locks up as he stares at me. "I thought…,"

"You thought I'd hate you?" I say softly. "Then you really don't know me at all, Gray. You never gave me a chance to show you otherwise."

My point hits home, and he looks down.

"We'll give you some time," Logan says. Fingers nudge my chin, and I turn to him in surprise. "But we've got a lot of making up to do, and we've wasted enough time thanks to our decisions."

I clear my throat. "Speaking of decisions... I've decided. About my heat."

Both of them freeze, and I look down, picking at a loose thread on my jeans. "I'm not ready," I admit quietly. "Not when things are like this. I know we might not have a choice... but I'd like to look at options."

Logan swallows. "We'll work something out. I promise, Sienna. You won't have to do anything you're not comfortable with."

Because my time here so far has been so comfortable. Like a luxury resort. I can't stop the sarcastic snort from slipping out.

As they move towards the door, I call out. "Is that it?"

Gray turns back to me, eyebrows bunched. "It?"

I eye them suspiciously, my stomach churning. "Is that everything? No more secrets?"

They look at each other, and the dread solidifies. What else can there fucking be?

"Nothing," Logan says finally. He clears his throat, and Gray shakes his head slowly.

"That's everything." His voice is hoarse.

Nodding, I curl back up and tug my blanket over me in a silent dismissal.

When I'm alone with my own thoughts, I turn over their words inside my head, replaying every interaction from the first time I watched them all walk towards me at the Bonding Ceremony. The difference in Jax, the way he changed from meeting at the club to then.

Everything I thought was off, that didn't feel quite right, makes sense now.

But if anything, my anger is only growing. They threw me under the bus without even considering how their actions would make me feel. All on the assumption that I'd just simper and forgive them?

They can all fuck off.

## 43
# TRISTAN

Jax is last to slip through the door, an overconfident smile on his lips as he pushes it shut. "I think we're making progress here."

"That's what you think," says Gray heavily. "Have you even seen Sienna this afternoon?"

He's slumped in an armchair, nursing a glass of amber liquor and looking like someone trampled his grandma. Sitting up, I give him my full attention. "Tell me."

"We fucked up." He gestures between him and Logan. "Sienna saw us. Together."

Jax whistles, and I fight the urge to sink my head into my hands. "What the hell, Gray?"

"I'm sorry!" He raises his hands defensively. "We got carried away. She just walked in."

"And what?" I swing my gaze to Logan. "What happened?"

He visibly swallows, looking away. Twin spots of color flare high on his cheeks. "We told her Alicia blackmailed us with photos."

"You fucking *what*?" I bellow, loud enough that they both shrink back from me as I jump to my feet, my hands slamming down against my desk. "Have you completely fucking lost it?"

"We had no choice," Gray interjects. "We had to tell her something, Tristan. Maybe it's not the full truth, but it's part of it, at least."

"She deserves the whole truth." Jax folds his arms. "I don't see why we can't tell her."

I sink back into my seat. There's so much to unpack here, I don't know where to start. It's clear that the threads I've been desperately trying to wrangle are unraveling before my eyes, and at the center of it is my Soul Bonded.

Resting my elbows on the desk, I press hard on my temples, trying to work away the ache that's coming through. "Because there's more, Jax. Shit that you don't even know yet. Jesus."

They all start talking at the same time, not shutting up even when I hold up my hand. The growl that rattles my chest does the job, though. Despite our informality as a pack, not one of them has the dominance I do, not even Jax. And I'm going to need every piece of it to get us all through this.

"Enough." My hand swipes through the air, and they all settle down. "I haven't had a chance to tell you what I found yesterday. At Erikksons."

"Wait." Jax steps forward. "You went to Erikksons? Yesterday?"

"It's why I was late to the hospital." I pull out my phone and swipe through to find the photos I took of Erikkson's messages across the wall, tossing it to Jax.

He clenches his jaw as he reads through. "What the actual fuck." His growl makes Gray and Logan straighten and pay attention, both of them leaning in to read together before dual curses explode from them.

"I'm going to kill him," Gray says grimly. "Now."

Logan grabs his arm as he moves towards the door. "Don't be stupid—,"

"Don't be *stupid*?" he rumbles, swinging back around. "Did you see what I saw? He's going to sell our fucking Soul Bonded to traffickers, Logan. Fucking sex traffickers. And you just want to sit there?"

Logan growls back at him. "I'm just as angry as you are. But we can't just rush into something, Gray!"

"I disagree," Jax says, walking forward to stand shoulder to shoulder with Gray. "He needs to be taken down now. We've got the evidence. What the fuck are we waiting for?"

I stay in my seat, resisting the push to square up to them. "*Sit down.*"

Gray drops into a seat first. Jax wavers on his feet, his fists clenching before he turns and throws himself down. "Go on then, *pack leader*. Enlighten us."

My jaw tightens, but I ignore his jab. "We have Alicia's recording and the photos of Erikkson's messages. They have the information about my father, and about Gray and Logan. If we try to reveal it now, Erikkson could weasel his way out of it in private. He has allies on the Council. Him and Justice Milo are cut from the same cloth. Milo will try and get him off."

"So what then?" Logan asks quietly.

I look around, my heart heavy. "We have to do it in public. Make such a scene that they can't just make it go away."

It's Gray who gets it first, his face darkening. "No. Fucking hell, Tristan. We can't do that to her again!"

Jax and Logan catch on, their faces turning slack. "Are you for real?" Jax demands. "Have we not fucked everything up enough? The final ceremony is our do-over. Our promise that we're serious about putting her first, Tristan."

I wince. "I know. I know, Jax, but I've thought and thought about it. This is the only way we can force them to pay attention. And I don't trust Erikkson not to take Alicia and run. I want them both arrested for what they've done. This isn't just about Sienna. It's about every other omega who bonds with the packs on that list. They're *all* at risk."

They don't understand. It's clear from the disbelief in Logan's eyes, the way Jax looks away from me and Gray's fists are clenched on the arms of the chair.

"For the record," Jax shoots. "I think this is a shit idea. But if you're so fucking insistent that you know best, then we need to tell Sienna everything. Right the fuck now."

"Absolutely not."

He jumps to his feet. I can see the tension in his jaw as he works it, his violet eyes darker than I've ever seen them. "Don't do this, Tristan. It won't end well."

His voice is low, pleading. For a second, I doubt myself.

But this is my job. I have to make the tough decisions. Even if my pack doesn't agree with them.

"We tell her nothing," I say slowly. "We keep her out of it as much as possible. It will help, in case things don't go the way we want."

"She could end up Denied, Tristan," Logan pleads, but I shake my head.

"There's no chance of that. Whatever happens, we're not Denying her even if everything else falls apart. That's the only way she gets sent across the wall, and those words won't cross our lips."

"If we do this," Gray interrupts. His face is pale against the copper of his hair as he runs his hand through it, sticking it up in tufts. "Everything comes out. Your father, me and Logan... there's no way we can pull that off without Erikkson coming back at us."

"I know." I look down, pushing down the ache in my throat. "I'm trusting that my father is the man that I think he is, and he'll have an explanation."

It's what I wanted to do from the start.

"And us?" Logan whispers. Gray reaches out and threads their hands together, the first sign of affection I've seen from them in front of us. Jax follows the movement, realization sinking in as his gaze shifts to mine. He nods, slowly.

I speak directly to them. "It's a risk. But this way, we call them out. There is *no law* against the two of you being together. It's not illegal. People are assholes, but times have changed. Someone has to be the first to speak out. And I want you both to be free to live the future you want to live. Not hiding in the shadows. We'll stand with you. But we have to stand."

"So we speak out," Logan murmurs. He looks at Gray uncertainly. "Gray?"

An undercurrent passes between them that I don't recognise. Another kick to my chest.

How did I not see this?

Gray nods. "It's time."

We're all on the same page. But Jax still looks tortured. "I don't want to leave her out of this," he mutters. "We promised her a fresh start, Tristan."

"This is our fresh start. We just have to fight for it."

And maybe I'm relying a little too heavily on us being Soul Bonded. We can work through anything, including this.

I'm certain of it.

44
## SIENNA

I'm rummaging around in the refrigerator when a low voice sounds behind me. "Sienna?"

I jump, banging my head on a shelf and wincing. I didn't know seeing stars was an actual thing.

Hands grasp my hips and tug me backwards. Head spinning, I collapse into a very male, very naked chest.

Oh, wow. That is warm. And muscled.

Swallowing, I blink away the spots and turn slowly, taking a moment to appreciate the sleekly muscled beauty that is Tristan Cohen. His mismatched eyes stare down at me, both impossibly dark as I breathe in, trying not to be too obvious as I grasp for a lungful of scent.

Just a little bit. What I'm getting from them isn't nearly enough.

"You okay?" he asks, his eyes scanning me. "You're a bit clumsy, you know."

*And the moment is gone.*

Stepping back with a huff, I turn my back on the snack in front of me to do an inventory check on the ingredients I've collected. His heat brushes up against me again as he peers over my shoulder.

Seriously. Does he not even realize how hot he is?

There's only so much an omega can take, so I duck beneath his arm, taking my goods to the counter and pulling out a knife. He follows me, sinking into a seat at the kitchen counter with a yawn.

I've never seen him look so rumpled, not even after he stayed with me in the Healers Center. He somehow woke up looking just as perfect as when we went to sleep, but now his eyes are hooded, his hair adorably tousled as he scratches absently at his chest.

My eyes swing down, and I bite back a groan.

Holy mother of gray sweatpants. Those bad boys do nothing to hide the outline of his significant looking cock.

Someone up there has it in for me, I'm sure of it. He looks lickable, and I don't think he'd appreciate it if I crawled into his lap and followed that tempting line up his throat with my tongue.

Or down in the other direction. My eyes follow the light trail of dark brown hair, ending at the edge of his sweatpants.

I *want*.

God. I suddenly feel completely flustered, my skin heating up as I bite down savagely on my lip until I taste blood.

What the hell is wrong with me? I'm acting like a cat in—

*Oh. Oh, no. No, no, no. Not happening.*

"Sienna?" Tristan looks a little more awake now, frowning as he leans forward. "Are you okay?"

"Fine!" My yelp is a little too high-pitched to be completely convincing, so I try again, pitching it lower. "I mean, I'm fine. Totally fine."

He tilts his head. "Do you have a bad throat? You just dropped about four octaves."

Someone save me.

Thank fuck Jax waltzes through the door, saving me from explaining why I suddenly sound like I've smoked fifty cigars.

His eyes light up. "Shortcake," he murmurs, caging me in with his arms as I shrink back against the counter. "You look like my favorite type of snack this morning."

On second thoughts, Jax is absolutely the worst of my Soul

Bonded for pushing boundaries. I grab the mixing bowl from the counter, shoving it between us. "I'm making breakfast."

"So I can see." He prowls after me as I skirt around the counter, trying to put some distance between us. "You smell absolutely fucking divine, you know that?"

I squeak, my scent picking the absolute worst time to erupt out of me like an ice-cream scented waterfall. Jax's nostrils flare, and he takes another step towards me.

"Sienna." His own voice drops, his violet eyes dark as he stalks me across the kitchen.

"Pretty, pretty Sienna. You smell like sin, shortcake. Come here."

He crooks his finger at me.

Before I can physically melt into a puddle, Tristan grabs Jax's shoulder. "Knock it off," he orders, shoving him down into a seat. His eyes meet mine, dragging just a little too long over my thin camisole. My nipples peak, standing to attention like a damn homing beacon.

Oh, god. I'm *definitely* approaching my heat.

Tristan grabs Jax's arm and tows him across the kitchen, throwing open the double doors that lead to the gardens I haven't even seen yet. Jax makes to move back towards me, and Tristan actually grabs his ear like a little boy.

"Get a hold of yourself." Shoving Jax outside, he glances back at me. "We'll eat outside."

I nod, but he's already gone.

This is good, I tell myself as I pull together a full-blown breakfast spread. I like to cook when I'm anxious, and by the time Gray enters the kitchen, Logan following behind, I've got two batches of muffins cooling on the counter and cookies in the oven.

"Ooh." Logan sniffs the air. My back tenses. "Are those cookies?"

Thank fuck for that. My tension releases in a whoosh, but I'm not about to risk a meal in the constrained space. I might end up knotted over the counter.

My hands clench on the wood. On second thoughts…

"We're eating outside," I blurt. "Outside. In the air. Fresh air."

"Sounds great." Gray gives me a soft smile, one sweeter than I've seen previously. "This all looks amazing, Sienna."

He heads straight outside, but Logan moves straight for me. He leans down, tracing his lips across my cheek in a gentle kiss and cupping my cheek. "Morning."

I blink as he follows Gray, leaving me with a final stroke across my skin.

This feels… promising. Definitely promising.

And I am definitely not just going to roll over for them.

Absolutely not.

Definitely… knot?

My thoughts go downhill as I start carrying out the first batch of food. Tristan's eyes flicker over me, relief in them as he stands up to give me a hand.

"Thanks," I say shyly, when he picks up the plates. He frowns down at them.

"You don't need to thank me for doing what I should've been doing all along."

And on that little bombshell, he nudges me outside and into a seat. I watch as his hands hover over the dishes, his eyes moving to me and back as he makes me up a plate.

"Thanks. Again." My cheeks crease as I take it from him. I actually feel hungry today. The soul pain doesn't seem to be making much of an appearance.

I don't want to ruin the nice atmosphere as everyone tucks in. I really don't. It's the first time where we've all been together, and it actually feels right.

But I'm still not happy about the Alicia situation. And I'm still not convinced over my heat, which by recent events could erupt any damn second.

"Um." I push my hair out of my face. "Tristan?"

He gives me his full attention immediately, turning to look down at me. "Yes?"

"Ah…," everyone else pauses to look at me too. "Did Gray or Logan tell you about my heat?"

Gray winces, and Logan turns a dark red. "Shit," Gray says. "I'm so sorry, Sienna. With everything – I didn't have a chance last night."

Wow. Good to know my heat means that much to them.

Tristan frowns as he looks around. "What's the matter?"

God, I wish they'd told him. Then I wouldn't have to have this discussion.

I square my shoulders defensively. "It's my heat. I don't think I'm ready, Tristan."

He picks up on my meaning immediately. Jax shifts in his seat, his mouth opening, but Tristan shuts him down with a look before he turns back to me.

"I understand," he says softly. "We all do, Sienna. We need to earn your trust back."

Jax nods silently.

I chew the inside of my mouth. "I don't know if it's possible, though."

I've never heard of an omega putting off her heat or getting through it without being knotted. I do know it's painful at first, and the pain goes away once the alphas get involved.

My stomach clenches at the idea of more pain. I don't know why they paint omegas as the weakest of the three designations. Do people even realize how much shit we have to put up with?

Tristan hesitates before his hand covers mine. He squeezes softly before withdrawing. "We'll need to keep it quiet, but I'll see what I can find out."

A tinkling sound comes from the kitchen behind us, and Jax jumps up. "I've got it."

"The doorbell," Gray clarifies for me. Jax comes back with an envelope in his hands and a frown on his face.

"It's for you." He hands it to Tristan, and we watch as he slides it open. His face darkens as his eyes scan the text.

"What is it?" Jax pushes. "Tris?"

Tristan growls, a low, furious sound that makes me flinch. He stops immediately, turning to me. "I'm sorry."

"I'm fine," I whisper. "What's the matter?"

He hesitates, before his hand reaches up. He cups the back of my neck, his fingers massaging softly. "The Council wants to see us. It's about... what happened before. With Alicia, and the healing. Ollena Hayward has put forward a motion to have you removed from the Trials."

My muscles lock into place. Jax jumps up. "The fuck? What's that all about?"

"Safeguarding," Tristan mutters, looking back down to the letter. "She's worried about Sienna's health. She's asking for a legal exemption."

Ollena is worried... about me?

"What does this mean?" I look at Tristan, and he stares back at me helplessly. "Tristan?"

My breathing is starting to speed up, panic building in my muscles. They want to take me away from them. From my pack.

"They can't do that," I whisper. "They can't take me away. They can't force me."

Tristan swallows. "If this was another pack and I was looking in... I'd agree with them, Sienna."

He wants me to go?

My whine rings out, all of them turning to me as it sounds low and agonized in my chest.

"No, no." Tristan stands, and in a second he has me lifted out of my seat, wrapping his arms around me as he presses my head gently into his chest. "Sienna. Baby, you're not going anywhere."

I'm shaking, my body vibrating. "They can't take me away. It's not up to them."

They're my Soul Bonded.

But the Council doesn't know that. And if I tried to tell them... they might not believe me. How could we prove it? After everything that's happened? No-one in their right mind would believe us, not when my parents are the polar opposite of everything the Council has seen.

"Shhhh," Tristan rocks me gently. "We're not going to let that happen, sweetheart. You're staying right here with us."

"If my heat is an issue," I blurt, my heart racing, "we can do it. It doesn't matter."

Tristan's arms clench around me. "It does matter," he says forcefully. His fingers grip my chin, pushing it up so I have no choice but to look at him. "Your choices matter, Sienna."

Relief and terror war for space inside my chest. "What are we going to do?"

Tristan runs his hand down my back. "We're going to do as they say and attend the meeting they've requested. We'll sort this out. You don't need to attend, Sienna. Unless you want to?"

I'm shaking my head before he finishes. I don't want to go anywhere near the Council. Especially with my heat on the way. "When is the meeting?"

"In two days." Tristan looks worried. "They're not accounting for the third Trial. You could go into heat at any time."

"Go. It won't be that long. I'll be fine."

He blows out a breath. "We'll see what we can find. Worst case scenario, maybe we can get something that will help you sleep through most of it."

I… like that idea. His eyebrows raise, and I nod. "That sounds like the best option to me."

"Then that's what we'll look at first."

He sounds so certain; it helps calm the pounding inside my chest. I lay my head back, listening to the reassuring thump in his heartbeat.

I have to trust them. I have to, if we're going to move forward.

"Okay."

## 45
## JAX

I stop short as I'm passing Sienna's room, my ears pricking up.
*At fucking last.*

I ease the door open, not at all ashamed that I'm invading her privacy when I can hear exactly what she's doing. My little shortcake may think she's being quiet, but I can pick up the thrum of a high note from a thousand feet away.

I slowly tilt my head around the door, taking in the beautiful sight of my Soul Bonded. She's hunched over, her fingers tracing chords on a freaking gorgeous but battered white acoustic. Her fingers fly as she immerses herself, her eyes sliding closed.

She doesn't even realize I'm here. And it's the sexiest thing I've ever seen as she loses herself in a melody I've never heard before.

I stay exactly where I am, barely breathing as she loses herself in the music. Serenity like I've never seen is plastered across her face, a peace I've never seen when she's been around us.

My heart pounds.

She finally opens her eyes, glancing over. Her fingers slide off the strings with a screech. "Jax!"

"Again." I cross the room to sit at the end of her bed, desperate for more. "Give me more, shortcake."

She bites her lip. "I shouldn't."

"You absolutely fucking should." I reach out and tug her battered lip free, soothing the small hurt with my finger. She stares at me, all wide blue eyes and pink fucking candyfloss and Sienna.

"I want you to look like that every day," I murmur, pulling my hand away with regret.

A cute little frown appears on her forehead. "Like what?"

"Happy."

She looks away from me, closing off those baby blues. "Jax."

"We can be happy, Sienna." Fuck. I didn't come in here to pressure her. I've been all about taking it slowly, giving her as much space as I can, as per the orders of King Tris.

But I'm only an alpha. And this omega could bring me to my knees.

"I know." She swallows, her fingers tracing the curved pattern of her guitar.

"It's beautiful," I say, admiring it. I know my instruments, and that one's a classic.

"My dad gave it to me." A smile crosses her lips, her whole face brightening. "He found me playing with it one day, and then it just appeared at the bottom of my bed. He put a bow on it and everything."

"You're close to your family." It isn't a question. It's right there in the softness of her smile as she talks about her dad. My mind flashes back to the Bonding Ceremony, the rage on his face. He obviously adores her.

Who wouldn't?

She nods, her head wobbling. "I am. My mama – we're very different, but we're still close. My sister Elise too."

She looks down again. "I miss them, Jax. And Jessalyn."

"Ah, yes. The wildcat."

Amusement lightens her face. "She wouldn't actually attack you. Not unless she was really pissed."

I'm still giving that omega a wide-as-fuck berth.

"So...," I coax hopefully. I even throw in some eyelash batting for good measure. "Play for me?"

Her lip twitches. "You're a bad influence, Jax Cohen."

But she picks up the guitar, strumming it in a way that goes straight to my dick, hardening inside my jeans. Fuck, this girl was made for me.

And she plays. I sit there silently, soaking her in. What I wouldn't give to run to my room and get my own guitar, for us to play together. There'll be plenty of time for that once this mess is sorted out, though. I can be patient.

Maybe.

When she finishes, I clap, and she flushes in pleasure. "You liked it?"

"You're amazing," I say honestly. She's better than most of the people I've played with.

She smooths down the covers between us. "Jax? Do you think the Council will try and separate us?"

I don't want to lie to her. "I don't know, shortcake. But we won't let that happen. I'd go over the wall before I let them take you away."

She looks up at me, her next words vulnerable. "You would?"

God. She hurts my heart. Clearing my throat, I reach over and wrap my fingers around hers.

"I'm going to spend the rest of my life," I say seriously, "making sure that you never, ever have any reason to doubt us again, Sienna."

"You promise?" she whispers.

"I swear it. On everything I am."

## 46
# SIENNA

I'm exploring the absolutely insane amount of garden my Soul Bonded own the next day when Tristan finds me. I turn from the rosebush as he holds a white paper bag out to me.

"I…ah. I found something that might help during your heat."

Oh.

Taking it, I gingerly peer inside. "Is it pills?"

"An injection. But you can take it yourself as soon as you start to feel… unwell. It should make you sleep for the duration."

"Okay." My voice is subdued. "Thanks, Tristan."

He rocks back and forth on his heels, his eyes scanning me. "Unless you've changed your mind?"

My breathing speeds up as I shake my head.

I haven't changed my mind, no matter how kind they've been to me in the last few days. This pack still doesn't feel like mine in my head, even if my heart is crying out for them, the Soul Bond a constant thrum in the background. I'm always aware of them, aware when they're not here, when they're close.

"I still have time to decide, right?" I force a smile. Tristan's eyes widen, and he nods slowly. "Yes. Absolutely. We'll go with whatever you decide."

He falls into step next to me as I start the trek back to the house. The gardens are a maze, what feels like dozens of different paths splitting off, something different down every single one. I've found fountains, sculptures, even a bike shed that's clearly Jax's domain, smothered in his heavy scent.

"What time are you leaving?" I ask. The council meeting is happening this afternoon, all of them leaving to attend. I'm trying really hard not to let on how much I don't want them all to leave me. My rationality is slowly sliding away as my heat creeps closer, making me crave things like hugs and shirts and fuzzy socks.

I *really* wish I had fuzzy socks.

I'm kind of regretting not taking Tristan up on the offer of his black card when we went on the disastrous shopping trip. What use is the moral high ground when my toes are bereft of cozy comfort?

He hasn't touched me since then, aside from the comfort he gave when the Council letter arrived. Logan and Gray have progressed to small touches, brushes of their hands against mine, and Jax has absolutely no boundaries whatsoever. But Tristan is a closed book.

"Soon." Hands tucked in his pockets as we walk, he looks down at me. "Do you need anything from us before we go?"

I shake my head. Maybe he'd touch me if I told him I was struggling. But I shouldn't *have* to tell him. Should I?

I grew up watching my parents fall more in love with each other every day. Two halves of the same soul. So completely entwined with the other that it almost felt like they were psychic.

I don't feel like that. Not even a little bit.

So, I bite my tongue as they leave, as Tristan nods formally, Jax ducks in to kiss me on the forehead, Logan squeezing my hand and Gray brushing against my arm.

"It'll be okay," he assures me. "We'll be back soon."

I force a smile as he turns away from me and strides down the steps. I stay where I am, watching as they climb into Tristan's car and it pulls off, moving at a slow crawl through the open gates.

None of them turn their head, my waiting hand dropping to my side when it becomes obvious that none of them would see me wave.

That's fine. They have a lot on their minds.

The nerves I've kept bottled up tightly in front of them spill out, my legs starting to shake as I head up to my room. I'm still not completely comfortable in the nest, the enclosed space of my four-poster bed helping to get me through the pangs for somewhere safe.

Yanking the curtains closed, I curl up under the covers, trying to keep my breathing even. I only last a few minutes before I push them back off. I'm too *warm*. My hair sticks to the back of my neck, damp under my fingers when I reach around to pry the strands free.

Sliding back out of bed, I shuffle into the bathroom. The shower feels too hot, and I have to turn it down until it feels cool against my overheated skin, closing my eyes in bliss.

It's an effort to get out, even when my skin is covered in goosebumps, but the moment I do, it's like I've stepped into an oven.

Great. I almost want my heat to get here so I don't have to go through these weird-as-fuck symptoms every other hour.

Reluctantly, I crawl back into bed, forcing my eyes closed. I'll sleep this little episode off. By the time I wake up, the pack might even be back, everything sorted out.

47

# TRISTAN

My father won't even look at me.

We've been here for fucking *hours*, arguing back and forth over the technicalities of the fucking ridiculous Bonding laws in Navarre. Even Ollena Hayward looks flustered as she leans back in her chair.

I can feel the frustration leaking out of my pack, making my skin itch as I shift in my seat. It feels wrong to be away from Sienna when she's so close to her heat.

"Milo," she says forcefully. "This is ridiculous. The law may be the law, but it is severely outdated. This particular process has highlighted some significant weaknesses that we, as the Council, have a moral duty to consider!"

Justice Milo only sneers. Whilst Ollena has been pushing heavily for Sienna to be pulled from the Trials, Milo has been an unlikely ally.

Or maybe not so unlikely, given he's bosom buddies with Erikkson.

"As I have said, and will continue to say, Ollena, no matter how many times you try to change my mind. The law may be harsh, but it is the *law*. It is here to protect the majority, to provide much needed structure and order to Navarre. If we change every little part at the drop of a hat, then it will cease to have meaning."

"This is ridiculous," she retorts furiously. "We have to consider the wellbeing of the omegas involved in the Trials. Sienna Michaels has been severely neglected through the actions of the Cohen pack. Their match clearly needs to be disbanded!"

Jax growls under his breath where he's slumped in the seat next to me, his arms crossed. We're squeezed into the most uncomfortable fucking wooden chairs, facing the Council in invisible battle lines.

Ollena turns to my father. "David." There's a clear appeal in her voice. Whilst my dad has always been a neutral voice, his views have often landed with Ollena's perspective, he, Ollena and Elio are natural allies against the often regressive views of Erikkson and Milo.

My dad meets my eyes for a single moment. The disappointment filling them is enough to gut me.

Sighing, he turns to Elio. "You've been quiet, Elio. What are your thoughts? You treated Sienna Michaels following her blood poisoning."

Health Elio steeples his fingers together, his eyes considering as he looks us over.

"I'm afraid," he says heavily. "That I have to agree with Ollena. Unless you can give us a reason to think otherwise, Tristan?"

My jaw tightens. "I have said everything I need to say. Whilst we had a rocky start, and I fully acknowledge the role played by my pack in that, we are completely invested in a future with Sienna as our Bonded."

Elio nods slowly, but he looks disappointed.

There's a lot of that going around.

My father sighs. "Given that Ollena is seeking an exception, not a change in law, I believe a vote will suffice, rather than a unanimous decision. Milo?"

The Justice Councilor nods as he stares down his nose at me. "I disagree with the premise of making an exception. The laws are in place for a reason. Sienna Michaels stays where she is, and the Trials should be completed."

Erikkson finally stirs. "I quite agree, Milo. Maintaining the integrity of the law in Navarre is paramount."

Ollena scoffs, but she doesn't say anything.

Elio frowns. "Whilst I disagree profusely with the actions taken by the Cohen pack, I believe that Sienna Michaels should remain where she is."

Ollena swings her head around to him, disbelief written all over her face. "Elio?"

He tilts his head. "There is much to play out here, Ollena. The pack deserves a final chance."

Ollena purses her lips. "That could cost Sienna Michaels everything. I vote to remove her from the Cohen pack."

I can feel the relief from my pack that the voting is leaning in our favor, but it does nothing for the discomfort coursing through my chest. Frowning, I rub at my chest. Jax turns to me.

"You feel that?" he mutters. "I thought it was this shit, but now...,"

I nod as my father stands, pushing the feeling away. He finally looks at me, but the disappointment is still firmly front and center.

"I agree that the Cohen pack should be given another chance," he says slowly. "Although I am highly tempted to say otherwise."

"Of course you would," Ollena mutters. My dad turns to her.

"I understand your frustration, Ollena. And I swear that I will not be so lenient, should the matter arise again."

He turns back to us. "I trust that you will take this as the warning it is. Should any further incidents take place, we will remove the omega from your care. Is this understood?"

I have to unclench my jaw to force the words out. "Understood."

My dad bangs the gavel down on the wooden desk in front of him. "Council dismissed."

I watch, hands clenching on the arms of my rickety chair as he walks out. He doesn't look back.

The discomfort in my chest shifts, developing into a weird burning sensation, just bordering on pain. When I glance around, everybody seems to be feeling the same. Logan is rubbing at his chest, and he looks at me. "Any idea why I suddenly have the worst case of heartburn?"

Gray twigs first, his face paling. "Sienna? Could it be her heat?"

Jax springs to his feet, the chair toppling over behind him. "We need to go. Right the fuck now."

I glance at the rest of the Council. Erikkson is watching me with a gleam in his beady eye. He nods his head mockingly, before he drops his eyes down to the phone in his hand.

"Let's go," I say hoarsely.

It'll be fine. She has the serum; she knows how to use it.

But the burning sensation only grows.

## 48
# SIENNA

I wake up groggy as hell, my hand sliding down to cover the dragging sensation in my abdomen. The sheets around me are twisted, soaked in sweat from my tossing and turning. I don't know how long I've been asleep, but it can't have been that long. The sun is still blasting through my window when I yank the covers around my bed back, causing a spike of pain in my head as it hits my eyes.

I don't feel any better. I feel much, much worse. As I try to stand, the dragging sensation intensifies, my legs buckling beneath me. Grabbing the wooden beam of the bed, I use it to prop myself upright, my breathing deepening.

I think this might be it. The dragging deepens into a sharp, spiked pulse of need, the strength enough to send me to my knees.

Oh god. I didn't expect it to be this... intense.

The need grows in a swell, my core clenching as my slick makes an appearance, my normally sweet raspberry scent sharpening into something sharper, more acidic.

Fucking hell. I say a mental prayer for the bedroom carpet as I sway over to the door, my balance listing to the side. I only make it to the hallway before I lose my balance, the deluge hitting me harder with every movement. My vision goes hazy, black specks dotting across my eyeline as I struggle to get to the stairs.

I left Tristan's paper bag on the kitchen counter. I just need to get that far.

I don't care if I pass out down there. I just need this feeling to go away.

The stairs take an eternity. By the time my toes touch the marble floor at the bottom, my breathing is see-sawing out of me, incoherent sobs punctuating the air as I crawl towards the kitchen. My whole body is shaking, my arms barely holding me up. When my energy threatens to give out entirely, all of it focused on the painful squeezing need in my abdomen, I drop down into a presenting position. There's a small touch of relief as my head rests on my hands, but it only lasts for a moment before the wave hits me even harder.

I feel empty. Empty, clawing, savage need.

I need a knot.

I need *their* knots.

But they're not here, and a raw, agonized whine escapes my throat.

Want my pack. Need them here.

The light streaming through the patio doors assaults my senses as I blindly haul myself through the doors, moving a scant few inches with each pull of my arms. The distance to the counter feels like an eternity as I reach up with my hand, weakly grasping the edge.

Just a little more. A little more, and then I can sleep.

Even though sleeping feels like the last thing I want to do.

I can feel my rational thoughts starting to trickle away, replaced by the haze of heat hormones and fuckery that will end up with me on my back and my pack buried balls deep inside me.

My inner muscles squeeze aggressively around my empty core.

Shit. Must not think about that.

My fingers grasp the bag at the same time as a banging on the door rings through the house. I let out a whimper as I drag it down to the floor with me, turning to face the endless expanse that I've just crossed. It feels like miles.

But they're here. They felt it. They're coming for me.

The bag slips from my fingers as a new burst of energy propels me back out of the doors and down the hallway.

My mind is hazy, something niggling there, but it's suffocated under the blanket of want.

Once they're here, it will all be better.

It takes an eternity to pull myself up using the ornate bronze handle, for my shaking fingers to fumble with the latch.

*They'reherethey'reherethey'rehere.*

It pulses in my chest. Tristan will know what to do.

I slump against the doorframe as I finally manage to haul it open, my hazy eyes desperately seeking the familiar sight of my Soul Bonded.

Wrong.

Wrong scent, wrong person.

Not my Soul Bonded.

Flaming red hair swims in my shaky vision, bright red lips stretching into a slow, victorious smile.

"Well, isn't this interesting?"

Backing away, my legs give out as I collapse. A hand grips my arm, sharply pointed nails digging into the soft skin underneath. "Where are my Cohens, little omega bitch?"

I try fruitlessly to pull away from her grip, the small bite of pain nothing in comparison to the burning inside me. "Get... away."

My words slur into the air.

"Don't be silly," the voice coos. "There's nobody here to help you, omega. Seems like I came along at just the right time, hmm? And I know exactly what you need."

The fingers tighten further, and then I'm being dragged back down the hall, back into the bright light of the kitchen that makes a whine curl up the back of my throat. My feet slide across the cold stone of the floor before cool air hits my face.

I try to unclasp the fingers gripping me, but there's a slapping sound, my head reeling to the side. Nausea swims up my throat as I gag.

"Disgusting. Come along now. We don't have all day. Good job I planned for this, hmm?"

Little slices of pain erupt across my knees, my legs as she pulls me along the path, my skin embedding in the gravel.

"Of course, I had thought I'd be here for the grand finale. But it's funny how things turn out."

There's a clunking sound, the squeal of rusty doors opening.

The gravel under my skin gives way to cold concrete.

"In you go." The fingers withdraw suddenly, and I land heavily on my hip, crying out as I roll over. The jolt shakes the barest amount of clarity back into my mind. Shaking, I curl up into a ball, my eyes blinking up at Alicia as she stands over me.

I wet my lips. "They're…coming."

My voice is faltering, the slurring worse.

She smirks. "Maybe. But not without a little pain first. I wonder how long it'll take them to pick up your scent? Especially given the little *extra* I stashed away."

She disappears, returning a few seconds later with a heavy can in her hands. She jiggles it at me, and I struggle to make out the text.

"Good old de-scenter," she coos. "Quite efficient, I hear. I have the spray version too. Guess we'll find out."

The liquid soaks me, cold and oily. I try to reach out, but the savage urgency in my core flares with a burning pulse, and I curl up again, my hands grabbing at my abdomen as if I can stop the tidal wave of my heat.

Alicia's feet move away from me. "I'd say good luck, but… well. I hear some omegas die without an alpha in their first heat. Guess we'll see what you're made of, *Sienna Michaels*."

The door hinges squeal, rust flaking off to land in little red flakes around me as she pulls it shut.

I hear the clanking as she secures the chains.

After I've caught my breath, I manage to make it to the door, my fingers scrabbling, tugging uselessly at the handle.

"Jax," I rasp. "Tristan."

My throat burns with the fire of the heat taking over my body. But I try, calling for them until the fire douses my voice.

There's nothing. No sound. No footsteps.

And then I don't hear anything else. Not for a long time.

## 49
# LOGAN

The burning sensation only intensifies the closer we get to the house.

"This must be her heat," I rasp. "It makes sense."

Jax turns from his position in the front, Tristan not responding except to press on the accelerator even more. I'm pretty sure we're breaking every traffic law in Navarre, but I don't give a fuck.

*We're coming, baby.*

"We left her," Jax growls. "Left her alone to sit through that fucking circus."

"We had to," Gray points out. "If we hadn't, they would have just come to the house to take her."

Jax scoffs. "I'd like to see them fucking try."

"Enough," Tristan slashes his hand through the air. "We're getting close. If she's in heat, hopefully she managed to take the medication. If not, then we need to prepare for what we might find."

An image bursts into my mind. Sienna, in heat, eyes dark as she beckons me forward. Presenting for me. For my knot.

*Shiiiiit.*

My cock hardens instantly in my suit pants. Gray stiffens next to me, his eyes sliding down as he swallows.

Fuck, I can't wait to see them together.

But that's not the plan for this heat. I understand, as much as I fucking hate that she's chosen to drug herself rather than rely on us.

Because we're not trustworthy enough to see her through. The shame coils in my stomach, the warmth of a moment ago evaporating.

This is the consequence. And it's a fucking light one, considering. I'll do everything I can to make sure she's comfortable.

We spill out of the car as Tristan pulls up, Jax flinging himself out before the car's even stopped. Tristan curses as he fights to unbuckle himself. "Jax! Get back here!"

Jax is gone, the front doors left open as we pound up the steps behind him.

Gray and I tangle as we reach the door, Tristan shoving us through.

Jax has disappeared, and I can hear him calling out for Sienna. He appears at the top of the stairs, his hair wild. "She's not here."

Tristan looks around, like she's magically going to spring out from a corner with a party blower. "That's not possible. She has to be here."

I head down for the nest, shoving the door open. There's nothing. I check my studio, Gray's office and the bathroom on my way back up the hall, but there's nothing.

As I walk back up to my pack, I pick up on something I missed the first time around. My head lifts as I sniff at the air. It smells like iron. Almost... metallic?

Now that I've noticed it, it seems to grow until the scent is pushing up my nose unpleasantly. Grimacing, I turn to Gray. "Can you smell that?"

He sniffs, shaking his head. "You've got the best nose."

"It's weird. Smells like metal."

Tristan walks out from the kitchen, his face tight. He's

clutching the paper bag in his hand that he brought home this morning.

A sick feeling enters my gut. "Was it open?"

He shakes his head. "It was on the floor. Something's not right. I can feel it. We need to find her."

"I'm checking the gardens." Jax shoulders past Tristan. "She's not in the house."

I move to follow him. "I'll help."

"We'll do a second run around the house, in case we've missed anything." Tristan nods to Gray and they turn for the stairs as Jax throws the patio doors open. "You take that one," he points to one of the two main paths branching off. "I'll do this one."

"'Kay. God, I hope she's alright."

"She'll be fine. Shortcake's tougher than we think." But his brows crease in worry as he jogs away from me.

I follow the scent of my nose. That weird metallic taste is back, burning the back of my throat as it grows in intensity. Coupled with the discomfort in my chest, my instincts are screaming at me to find Sienna.

Shouting her name, I run down every single path I come across. This whole place is a damned maze, a leftover from some rich bastard who had this place before we bought it. If Sienna is out here, she could easily have gotten lost. We don't even know how far back it really goes.

We even have a few outbuildings scattered around. She could be in one of them. I stop off at Jax's bike shed, scanning it quickly before ducking back out. There's a shed at the back, but it's secured with chains around it that Jax bought last summer to stash some of his pricier bike parts.

I nearly stride past it, but something niggles at me, enough that I slow to a stop, my eyes scanning it.

She can't be in there, not with the chains fastened to the door. But something stops me from moving on, enough that I take a few steps towards it.

Enough to catch the faintest, sharpest hint of raspberries. But it smells wrong. Off.

I take rapid steps to the doors, rattling them. I have no idea where the key is, but that scent is growing stronger, the sickening in my stomach telling me that something is really fucking wrong here.

I pause, and that's when I hear it.

A whimper.

50

# SIENNA

I burn.
Every inch of me is on fire, the flames racing up down my veins and into the demand bowing my back in intensity.

My hips pump, seeking something to fill, to consume. But there's nothing, only endless clenching peaks of pain that empty my throat of screams.

I have no voice. No sound comes from my throat any longer, only a rasping, choking noise that isn't enough to get the help I need.

My hands move desperately over my body, a pathetic replacement for the feel of larger, harder alpha hands I'm longing for. My fingers are soaked with my attempts to help myself; each try only making things worse. The oily liquid Alicia threw over me covers me like oil, metal burning the insides of my nose as I twist in agony.

Nobody is coming. My body twists, bending and unfolding as I try to ease the pain. I'm lost to the torture being inflicted on my body, so much so that I don't hear the banging on the door at first. The shouting.

It's when the door gets kicked in, splinters of wood hitting me as I slide pain-hazed eyes towards the light. My hand reaches out, and someone catches it.

The sob catches in my throat as violet eyes fill my vision, black pupils blown wide as Jax leans in, desperately kissing the tears away from my face.

"Sienna," he breathes, his face tortured. "Sweetheart. It's alright. We're here now."

I open my mouth to ask, to beg him, but Jax turns to snarl something. The anger remains in his eyes when he turns back to me, his hand tightening around mine.

A choked, strangled whimper catches in my throat. My hand tugs at his, pulling it down, to where I need him to be. His brows lower, his face uncertain.

"Sienna, the medication... Tristan is coming."

I shake my head violently. I don't want the medication.

Gray's face appears over Jax's shoulder, his eyes flicking over my face. "Tristan's here," he murmurs, and I yank my hand away with a whine.

This isn't what I need. The fire is too strong. I need them, but they're not listening. Jax is pulled away, his protests filling the confined space. I'm gagging on the metallic scent in my mouth, the movement and noise too much and not enough as Tristan takes his place.

"Sienna." Tristan strokes my damp hair out of my face, his fingers sliding through the oil. He pulls his hand back, rubbing them together, before he turns away. My blurry eyes follow his every move, my body flinching when he yanks out the syringe.

"No," I slur. My words aren't coming out properly, a garbled, hoarse mash that makes Tristan pat my hand softly. Like I'm a *dog*.

"I know it hurts," he murmurs. "This will make it better."

I force my muscles to move, to push with my legs so I scrabble away from the syringe in his hand. This is all wrong. They should want to be with me during my heat.

I'm their Soul Bonded.

My back hits a wall, my head banging against the iron sheet as Tristan moves closer, his hands out like he's calming a rabid animal. I can see the hormones affecting him, his eyes darker than I've ever seen them, sweat beading along his hairline and the outline of his dick pressing against his trousers.

Launching forward, I throw my arms around his neck, catching him by surprise as we topple over. He rolls so his back takes the brunt of the fall, grunting as his chest connects with mine. The coarse fabric isn't the skin contact I want, but it's better, and I rub myself against him desperately, my throat trying to push out the words to tell him. I've made my choice.

His hips settle against mine, and a low keen slips from my lips as the thickness of his cock presses directly against my slit.

Tristan's breathing deepens, his mismatched eyes staring into mine before he squeezes them shut. His hands slide down my arms, taking my hands and pressing them above my head as he leans forward, pressing a kiss against my forehead.

"I promised you," he whispers. "You don't understand now. But you will."

The haze of want inside my brain takes a moment to catch up, and then a tendril of fear snakes in. Tristan looks up, and I strain against his grip. His voice is dark. "Hold her."

Voices shout, and I hear Jax cursing Tristan. An argument breaks out, and I thrash against his hands, fighting to get free. If I can get free, I can make him see.

"Tristan," I choke, and he turns his head. His skin is bunched around his eyes, stress lines branching out from his forehead. "Stop. Please."

He shakes his head, his jaw tight. "I have to make the difficult decisions, Sienna. I'm so sorry, sweetheart. Next time—,"

But I'm shaking my head. A sob rattles up my chest, then another. Tristan turns away from me. "For fuck's sake," he says hoarsely. "Get over here!"

A door bangs in the distance. Tristan's lips tighten. "Fine."

He looks back down at me. "Sienna. *Stay.*"

It's not a request. It's a bark. An *alpha* bark.

My body locks into place, refusing to follow my silent screams to move, as Tristan sits up. He reaches for the syringe, his eyes meeting mine as he picks up my arm, pressing into my skin. "I'm sorry," he says grimly. "I have to."

My mouth shapes the words even as I feel the sting of the needle. I don't move, locked into place by Tristan's bark.

*No, you didn't.*

The medication takes effect quickly. Tristan keeps his eyes averted as the fire in my abdomen is replaced by languid, drowsy tiredness. I force out the words I need to say, before my eyes close.

*"Never forgive you."*

## 51
# GRAY

I sit in silence, staring at the wall of stars.

Sienna lies limply in my arms, just as still and silent as she was three days ago. My fingers rise again, following the familiar motion as they press against her neck.

Her pulse flutters weakly under my fingers.

It's a little stronger than it was yesterday.

Soon, we'll find out how much she hates us.

There's movement by the door and my hackles raise, relaxing when Logan walks in. His eyes move straight to Sienna as he crosses the space, sinking down next to me and handing over an open bottle of water. I take it gratefully, sucking down the majority with my free hand before I pass it back and he sets it aside.

Our silent vigil lasts for a few minutes before he stirs. "I'm desperate for her to wake up," he mutters. "But I'm dreading it, too."

I know how he feels. I don't respond, only nodding.

"Tristan wants to come in."

My head jerks to look at him. "He's not coming anywhere near her."

It was Logan and I who lifted her and carried her gently from the cold, concrete shed. Us who bathed her, washing the stink of the oil away from her skin and trying to keep our eyes averted as much as possible before we settled in here to keep watch. Jax reappeared a few hours later, his knuckles red and bleeding as he slipped down the wall opposite, his eyes on Sienna and his head bowed.

All of us in silent vigil. All of us, except for Tristan.

He only tried once. Once was all it took for Jax to grab him by the throat, Tristan not even fighting it as he let Jax do what he needed to do. Like he knew exactly how much he deserved it. He took one look at Sienna before he walked out, his lip and eye swelling up.

"She's going to leave us," Logan murmurs. "Soul Bonded or not. How could she not?"

*How could she stay with us now?*

"I know." I smooth her hair back, making the most of the final peaceful moments I'll ever get with our Soul Bonded. Lo touches my arm, and I pass her over to him, the movement natural after three days of the three of us taking it in turns to hold her.

We won't let her lay on the floor alone again.

Regret is ice cold in my veins, keeping me frozen in place as I revisit each encounter. God, the things I would have done differently given the choice.

Life doesn't come with a rewind button. If it did, I'd spend every waking moment making sure my Soul Bonded knew exactly how much she was wanted. Cherishing and adoring her, making it my life's work to make her *happy*. And with Logan by my side, we could all have been happy. Truly, deliriously happy.

But our cards have been dealt. All we can do now is live with the choices we've made.

Even when they taste bitter on my tongue.

Jax pads in, his arms already held out for Sienna. Logan gives her up without complaint, and we watch as he sinks down against the opposite wall, murmuring something too soft to hear. Occasionally, we'll hear a note, a handful of scattered words. Our vigil has been silent, for the most part, Logan and I lost in our regret.

But Jax hasn't stopped singing.

The low thrum of his voice cuts off abruptly, and I look up.

Sienna stirs weakly in Jax's arms, and Logan and I both scramble across the room, dropping to our knees beside Jax. My heartbeat pounds in my ears, my mouth dry as her eyes crack open.

"Shortcake," Jax murmurs, smoothing her hair back. "It's alright."

Those blue eyes open a little wider, her pupils expanding to swallow up the blue depths with darkness. She rolls her head to the side, her body convulsing as she dry-heaves.

"Get the water," I snap to Logan. Jax rubs her back as I push the hair back from her face, keeping it out of the way of the bile she expels. There's nothing in her stomach to bring up, the retching contractions of her body painful to watch. She's even thinner now than she was a week ago, a wraith compared to the vibrant omega we saw at our Bonding Ceremony.

Her hands reach up, weakly pushing at my arm, so I scoot back to give her space. My fingers itch to take her back from Jax, to curl her into me now that she's so familiar in my arms, but I clench my fists.

Logan wordlessly passes her a bottle of water as she struggles to sit up. My heart cracks when she hesitates, her eyes flicking between the bottle and us.

"Here," I say carefully, leaning forward. I show her the unbroken seal before I crack the bottle open and hand it back. She glugs it down with both hands in greedy gulps until the plastic crackles under her grip.

"What day is it?" Her quiet whisper echoes in the room.

"Thursday. It's been three days." Jax lifts his hand, but she flinches away from him, looking around her. Her breathing quickens as she pushes off Jax's lap, backing away from us. Her knees pull up in front of her as she wraps her arms around them, her back to the wall.

The shaking grows, slowly building until she's nearly vibrating.

"Sienna." Jax's growl is tortured. When he moves towards her, she holds up a shaking hand.

"Stop."

"I'm sorry," I whisper. "We're sorry, Sienna. We're so sorry. Tristan… we didn't agree with it."

Her eyes fix on me, unwavering and filled with so much fucking sorrow. "But you didn't do anything to stop it."

My throat feels thick. "No. We didn't."

She's still shaking, but her eyes are dry as she looks past us. "And here we are."

Logan leans towards her, like he can't help himself. "What can we get you? Do you want some more water? You'll be hungry, we can—,"

"Nothing." Sienna's voice is full of emotion as she picks herself up from the ground, her shaking limbs agonizingly slow as she uses the wall to pull herself up. "I want *nothing* from you."

She takes a single, wobbling step before her legs collapse underneath her. We dive forward, all of us freezing at her pained whine.

"Get away," she whispers, her face white. "Get *away*!"

The ache in my chest flares to a burning pain as she struggles to her hands and knees.

"Sienna," Jax pleads. "Let us help you."

She looks up at him. "Like you helped me? I *begged* you, Jax. When I needed you, I begged you. And you walked away from me like I was nothing."

She stays on her hands and knees, heartbreakingly fragile as she makes her way to the door before she pauses.

"I would rather crawl," she says quietly, not looking back, "than trust you to help me ever again."

I swear my heart caves in. Collapses in on itself like a building coming down, as I watch the girl we were supposed to protect crawl on her hands and knees to get away from us.

And we let her go.

## 52
# SIENNA

I need to get out of here.
I need to get away.

Away from *them*, from their sad faces and pathetic apologies.

If only my body would get the fucking memo. I'm weak as a newborn kitten, at my most vulnerable when I need to be the strongest I've ever been.

To face the reality that *this*, whatever this weird, twisted relationship between me and the Cohens is... I can't do it anymore.

I've just about made it to the stairs, my arms shaking with exertion, when my muscles lock up, a familiar scent invading my nose. The flinch is instinctive, the urge to cover myself, to hide.

"Sienna," a low voice says. Determinedly, I stay focused on one shuffle at a time, pushing myself forward. I only pause when my eyes fall across bare feet.

I squeeze them shut. "Get out of my way, Tristan."

"We need to talk." His usually commanding voice is the barest whisper, full of remorse, but I don't care to hear it. I don't want to hear anything from him.

There is *nothing* he can say to me. Not one single thing that could justify his actions.

I shake my head. "I have nothing to say to you. Please move."

A hand touches my chin, and I flinch, throwing myself backwards in a sudden desperate scramble. "Don't touch me!"

"I'm sorry," he says frantically. "I was trying to do the right thing. I couldn't think straight, and we'd just found you in that shed, and all I could think about was that you didn't want us for your heat. I had to make sure that happened."

My head lifts up, my eyes finally landing on his. He looks like shit, several days of stubble across his jawline, dark circles under his eyes and his usually pristine hair everywhere. There's a deep split in his lip, and I *hate* that I notice that, that I want to know what happened. I push the urge down, locking it away and throwing away the key.

"You didn't *have* to do anything," I say slowly. "You promised me a choice, and when I made it, you took it away. When I said no, you held me down and used your bark to keep me there so you could put me to sleep. I said *no*."

He drops his head. "I know. I panicked."

"Well, that's not fucking good enough for me. Stay away from me, Tristan. I mean it. Get off the stairs so I can go upstairs."

"You can barely move," he protests. "Let me carry you."

"Whose damn fault is that?" I snap. "Put your hands anywhere near me and I swear I'll bite them off."

He leans forward, a hint of dominance entering his tone. "Sienna."

I rear my head back. Agony spears my chest, yet another direct hit. "Don't you *dare*, Tristan Cohen. Don't you dare try that shit with me again."

Tristan blanches. "That's not – I wasn't going to do that."

"Well, I don't trust you. And the only person responsible for that is you. Now move."

He stands up slowly, but his lips firm as he takes a step towards me. "Hate me if you want to," he mutters. "God knows I hate myself. But you can hate me when you're upstairs and comfortable."

I try to push him away, but he lifts me like I'm a feather. The whine rolls up my throat, even as I feel the urge to sink into him, to breathe him in. "Put me down."

He holds me close as he makes his way up the stairs. "No."

"I hate you," I gasp. The burning behind my eyes starts to trickle down my cheeks, the emotion I've been keeping locked in since I woke up spilling over. "I hate you. I hate you. I hate you."

"I know," he growls. He kicks open the door to my room, standing in front of my bed. His hands tighten where they hold me, my shuddering sobs filling the room. "Tell me what I can do to put this right, Sienna. Please."

I have to force myself to breathe through the pain in my stomach, my chest, the burning all over my body. But my heart, that's the most painful of all. Like Tristan's taken a knife and slashed it straight through every hope and dream I ever had for my mating.

"You can put me down," I finally say quietly. "And leave."

His voice shakes. "I don't want to let you go."

I stiffen. "Then use your bark, Tristan. Make me stay with you. Like a little puppet."

He flinches. Then he sets me gently, so damn gently, on the bed, his hands grazing mine as he pulls them away.

"I'll make this right," he says softly. "I swear it, Sienna."

I move around, painfully slow as I lay down on my side and give him my back. "It will never be the same," I say tiredly. "Never, Tristan."

He doesn't respond, but the door closes a few moments later.

My vision blurs as I stare at the wall, the dam inside me breaking as I cry. For the choices we've made. The pain in my heart. And the future we could have had.

It lies in ashes and ruins. I can't see a way forward, but we'll need to find one, if I want to stay alive.

But there's one thing I'm completely certain about. They will never be mine, not completely. They have shown me that over and over again, and I'm finally listening.

And I will *never* be theirs.

## 53
# TRISTAN

My back rests against the door, listening to Sienna's broken sobs. It feels like there's a sinkhole in my chest, growing bigger by the second. Swallowing everything inside me up until all that's left is darkness.

I've made so many bad choices in the last few weeks that I don't even know what's left.

Movement thumps to my left, the sound of footsteps. I stay where I am as Jax comes into view, his battered knuckles clenching as he sees me.

"Get the fuck away from her door," he growls.

He's careful to keep his voice down as he advances on me, squaring up to my chest. Where once I might have given it back, I don't have the energy right now. All of my focus is in the room behind us.

I meet his familiar eyes. The gap between my pack and I has widened into a chasm, all of us clinging to different sides. I don't know how to fix it.

I didn't want this.

But it's where we are, regardless.

"She's exhausted," I mutter. "She needs to rest."

Jax pulls back, his face a mask of disbelief. "Are you seriously gonna fucking lecture me on her wellbeing? Fuck off with that, Tristan. Give her some fucking space."

"I am." I take a step towards the stairs, pausing for long enough that Jax loses his patience, shoving me forwards. My shoulders tense, but I swallow down the urge to bite back as I make my way slowly down the stairs. I keep my eyes down as I pass Gray and Logan, both of them hovering in the hallway, the few steps to reach my office feeling like an eternity.

As I settle behind my desk, the piles of paperwork draw my gaze. Working my ass off every day for the last five years hasn't gotten me anywhere. My pack hates me, my father is disappointed, and my Soul Bonded…

My mate thinks I'm an abuser.

I used my bark on her. Held her down, forced medication into her that she didn't want.

That's exactly what I am.

The paperwork fills the air like a blizzard as I sweep it away from me, my breathing ragged and broken as I hit the wood of the table, over and over again, until it cracks beneath my hand. My hands fit underneath and I flip it with savage satisfaction, the wood creaking and a leg breaking off as it tips onto its side.

My knees collapse underneath me, my face in my hands. Sienna's broken, pale face is seared into my brain, and it takes me a minute to realize that my cheeks are wet beneath my palms.

I can't do this.

I can't lose control like this. Not when there's so much still on the line.

It takes longer than I'd like, but slowly, I scrub my face clean. My desk slides back into position, the paperwork cleared up and placed back where it was. As I'm setting the last lot back into place, my cell rings.

"Tristan Cohen." My voice sounds raw, and I cough into my fist as a voice rings in my ear.

"Mr. Cohen. This is Councilor Hayward. I have been trying to reach Sienna Michaels for several days. And you, for that matter."

My back straightens. "Sienna is resting. After her heat. We have all been... busy. Apologies, Councilor."

"I see." Ollena sounds suspicious. "And all went well?"

I hesitate for a second, before I close my eyes and pray that Sienna will forgive me. In the grand scheme of things, this is minimal. "Perfectly well. I'll ask her to call you."

Or I'll pass the message on.

"I'm glad to hear it, Mr. Cohen. In that case, I am setting your final Mating Ceremony for this Saturday. Does that sound achievable?"

The timer is suddenly very, very real. The countdown settles like a choker around my neck. "Yes," I croak, my eyes sliding closed. "Thank you, Councilor."

My Soul Bonded is refusing to look at me or touch me, and my pack can't be around me without snarling. A Mating Ceremony in two days... I have no idea how we'll get over that line. But we need these ridiculous fucking Trials to be over, to put this shit with Erikkson to bed so we can focus on Sienna.

I send a brief message to Jax.

*Mating Ceremony Saturday. Please tell Sienna. I confirmed to Ollena Hayward that the third Trial was completely successful.*

His reply takes a few minutes, the bubbles that indicate typing popping up before stopping and starting again.

I don't expect him to barge into my office a few moments later. "Jax."

Gray and Logan follow him in, their arms crossed as they spread out, all facing me down with equally firm expressions.

"We're not calling Erikkson out at the ceremony," Jax says firmly. "Sienna deserves at least one public event where she's not humiliated on our account. We won't do it, Tristan."

"Agreed."

Jax takes another breath but pauses. "So, a normal ceremony?"

I nod, my eyes on the door. "As much as we can, given the circumstances."

"Circumstances we're in because of you," Jax snarls. "Good. I'll see you then."

He stamps out, leaving me with Gray and Logan. Both of them avoid my eyes.

I sigh. "Anything else that you need to say?"

Gray's face tightens. "What are we going to do about Erikkson?"

My head starts to pound. "We'll take it all with us. As soon as the ceremony is over, we do it then. Keep Sienna with us. And we tell them everything."

Logan nods. "And now? What do we tell Sienna?"

The pounding increases. "Nothing. She's already exhausted. I don't want to add to her stress by telling her Erikkson is planning to sell her off."

Just the words feel vile in my mouth, wrong on my tongue. "It won't come to that. I won't let it."

"There's one more thing," Grayson growls. "Alicia. I want that bitch to pay for what she's done to Sienna."

My fists clench on my desk. "I want that too, Gray. But we can't tip them off. Two more days, and they both go down for what they've done."

And he'll have to fight me to get to Alicia first, for what she did to my Soul Bonded.

They both walk out, leaving me to stew over how we're going to get through a fucking Mating Ceremony, how I'm going to get Sienna to forgive me, patch my pack back together.

My hands shake as I reach for the whiskey.

Just one glass.

## 54
## SIENNA

The room is still dark, but I can see tendrils of morning light poking through the slight gap in the curtains. I stare at it accusingly from my position, curled up in the corner of my bedroom where I've stayed for the last two days.

I couldn't cope with the bed. Too empty. So I pulled off the bedding and made my own little nest in the corner of the room, one free of anything relating to the Cohen pack.

I haven't spoken to them. Haven't been downstairs, haven't exposed myself to any more of the chaos that this damn pack is intent on bringing into every aspect of my life. They haven't pushed it, although I trip over Jax every time I go to the bathroom. He's kept a vigil outside my door, soft patches of song coming through the cracks that make my heart hurt every time I hear them.

The pain in my stomach is reaching nuclear levels, but at this point, I can't bring myself to care. I can't bring myself to care much about anything.

Today is my Mating Ceremony. The Trials will be over, the rest of our lives stretching out ahead of us.

A road of pain and broken promises littering the path like glittering shards of glass.

Every part of my body hurts when I force myself upright. I have to get ready.

Who knows what excitement today will bring.

I walk through the motions slowly. First, the bathroom. I step over Jax, his light snores filling the hallway where he's slumped next to my door. I close the bathroom door. Do my business. Run the shower. Clean my teeth. Wash my hair slowly. Check on my still healing leg, the stitches slowly dissolving into vicious shiny red skin.

Avoid looking in the mirror at all costs. I don't want to see the evidence of the last four weeks, and what it's done to my body.

I know I look different. I can feel it.

I'm not the same omega that walked into her Bonding Ceremony with hopes and dreams.

Now, I'm something else. Something a little bit broken.

But today, I'm going *home*.

I've made up my mind. Maybe we'll work things out, but I can't do that in the same house as them, breathing in their scents, tortured by their closeness. I'm in pain regardless. I'll take my old bedroom, my family, and we'll see what happens after that. If they'll fight for me.

My dad promised me my home would always be there. And I'm taking him up on it, as soon as the Mating Ceremony is complete.

When I open the bathroom door, I flinch at the sight of Logan, his hands filled with a long bag. He spins to me, the edge of the bag brushing over Jax's legs where he's slumped over.

"Sienna," he whispers. "I just… I wanted to give you this."

He holds out the bag, but I just stare at it. "What is it?"

His cheeks darken. "Just a dress. I realized you might not have one, and… you deserve something nice to wear."

Because that's all I'm good for. Pretty clothes and trinkets. Not for anything real.

My lips tighten, but I take the bag regardless. I can't go to my

Mating Ceremony in jeans, and there's no way in hell I'm putting my other dress back on.

"Thanks."

Logan rocks back on his heels, his face desperate. "Are you... how are you feeling? Can we talk?"

Shaking my head, I brush past him, ignoring the flare in my chest as our arms brush against each other. "I don't want to talk."

"That's okay," he rushes out. "If you change your mind, I'm here."

Nodding, I close the door on his hopeful face.

It doesn't take me long to get ready. Without any make-up, without my mama and Jess fussing and clucking around me, I'm making do with what I have. When I unzip the bag, the smallest jab hits me in the chest.

Because this dress is everything I would have wanted for my Mating Ceremony.

The lace is delicate, silver beading trailing down a delicate boned bodice in a curling pattern, before flaring out into a long, tulle skirt.

It's a princess dress. In the palest, softest shade of pink.

It takes a minute for me to move and pull it on, trying to ignore the stabbing at my heart when it hangs a little loose. It feels like I'm wasting away, like soon there'll be nothing left of me at all.

When I try to reach the back, I hit a snag.

Lips tightening, I move to the doorway, pulling the door open. "Jax."

He bolts upright, his eyes widening. "Shortcake. You look—,"

"I need my buttons done up," I blurt. I don't want to hear any pretty words from them. They don't mean anything.

Turning, I hold my breath as his fingers dance across my skin, doing up the hooks with ease. When he's finished, he leans into me for a moment, his breath ghosting over my ear. "You look beautiful, Bonded."

EVELYN FLOOD

My throat closes up as I step away from him, my door closing softly.

I wait, sitting on the bed as the house wakes up around me, footsteps padding up and down outside my room, the murmur of hushed voices. They always pause outside.

When the knock comes, I'm ready.

Gray is waiting on the other side of the door, his face pale and shadowed.

"Sienna," he breathes. He doesn't look down, his eyes on my face. "Are you okay? You haven't eaten anything."

"I'm fine. Is it time to go?"

He hesitates, ready to push the issue, but I move past him, descending the stairs. I'm more than ready for the Trials to be over. I'll do whatever it takes to get me there.

Including facing the alpha with mismatched eyes waiting at the bottom of the stairs.

He swallows as I move towards him. "Sienna."

"Tristan." Sweeping past, I move to the door. "Did you find me transport?"

It's the only thing I've asked for. I can't sit in a car with them. I need to brace myself, to gather my thoughts, and to do that I need space.

Tristan nods, although I can see the reluctance in his gaze. "You know we'd – we'd like it if you came with us. But there's a driver outside, if you want it."

"I do want it." My sharp tone rings out as I pull the door open. "I'll see you there?"

I hate that there's the smallest questioning tone in my voice, the way it rises at the end giving light to my final vulnerability.

"Of course," he swears. He takes a step towards me, but I turn away. "Good."

I make my way down the steps and across the gravel, ignoring the way it cuts into my feet. A man is standing next to a blacked out, long car, and I walk over to him. "You're taking me to the Ceremony?"

To his credit, he only nods. "I am. My name's Mal. I'm Jax's bandmate."

I peer at him a little more closely, vaguely recognizing him from the night Jessalyn and I went to see Haven's End. God, it feels like an eternity ago.

Jessalyn. I get to see Jess today.

Spurred on, I go to pull the door open, but a strong hand beats me to it as I'm engulfed in a misty scent. "Shortcake. Leaving without saying goodbye?"

My heart jumps, but I keep my voice level as I turn to face Jax. "Well, you weren't downstairs when I arrived. I thought you were busy."

He's a dark god in his tuxedo, the pale pink tie on his crisp white shirt a perfect match for my gown. "Never too busy for you."

When he holds out a hand, I take it hesitantly, allowing him to support me as I get into the backseat of the car. Jax gathers up the trail of my gown, tucking it in next to me, before he ducks down and presses a firm kiss to my forehead.

"One more day, shortcake," he promises. His voice shakes. "And it's all over."

I'm left to wonder what he means when the door shuts, Mal getting into the driver's seat. He asks me if I'm okay before pulling off, my eyes drawn to the four alphas standing on the steps, watching me go. Tristan is the last to turn around, his eyes still following the car as we pull out of the gate.

It's a good forty minutes to get to the Omega Hub, more than enough time for me to stew over Jax's words and work myself up into panic before I shove it back down again. By the time we pull up, Ollena is already waiting. And my numb mask is back in place.

"Thank you," I say quietly to Mal, and he nods at me. "My pleasure."

He doesn't wish me a happy mating or reference the pack at all. I wonder what Jax has told him.

Ollena sizes me up, her lips thinning until they're almost bloodless as I climb out of the car. "Sienna. You look... different."

"New diet," I say flatly. "My pack will be here soon."

She hesitates. "Very well."

I follow her into the same room I sat in four weeks ago with my dad, that room where the naïve, hopeful Sienna asked innocent questions about the Bonding Trials and waited to meet her alphas. I settle into the armchair without asking, waiting for Ollena to speak.

It takes her a minute.

"I'll admit," she confesses, placing her folder on the small table to her left, "that I don't quite know where to begin with this ceremony, Sienna."

I smooth down my dress. "I know that it's all been a little... unorthodox. But I'm here. My pack is on their way. We're very much ready to continue on with our lives."

Whatever the hell that looks like.

Ollena purses her lips. "I'm going to be honest. Quite brutally so, but I believe it would serve us best for this discussion."

She leans forward. "You look terrible, Sienna. You are clearly malnourished, you have lost a significant amount of weight, and there is bruising on your left arm."

Jerking, I look down. I'd forgotten about the deep purple splotches, now turning a nasty shade of green.

"Leftovers from my heat. It was very... active."

If you count being thrown onto concrete and dragged down a gravel path active. Good job my dress covers my legs. She'd probably pass out.

The pain in my stomach pulses as she sighs. "I don't know what's going on here, but it's out of my hands, since you refused to withdraw when I offered it. But I hope you know... you can talk to me. I appreciate that I am part of the Council, but my duty will always be first and foremost to the omegas in my care. And that includes you, Sienna. Bonded or not."

A lump appears in my throat. "Thank you. But that's not necessary."

She nods, her eyes dropping to my bruises one more time before she stands. "In that case, let us head out. As you may know, this is a closed ceremony, only open to family and friends."

Thank God. I think a second public event might be the thing that tips me completely over the edge. As it is, there's a numbness in my chest as I follow Ollena. If it wasn't for the pain, I'd worry about keeping my balance. But the pain keeps me sharp, focused on putting one foot in front of the other until I'm standing back where it all started, back in the circle, staring down the aisle at where the Cohens and I had our first, disastrous meeting.

They're not here yet, but it doesn't matter. My eyes are firmly focused on my family, and my throat burns as I force back tears. My eyes move over them, my mother and father, Jess, Elise.

They're all here. All of them looking at me, horror on their faces. Even Elise.

Have I changed that much?

"I'm going to fucking kill them," Jessalyn snarls, her voice ringing out across the hushed gathering. She jumps up, but mama grabs her arm, tugging her down and her lips moving frantically. I can see her wet cheeks, and my heart clenches.

I didn't mean to put them through this. My eyes lock with my dad. He looks furious, but the lines on his face smooth as he catches my eye. He pats his chest and holds his hand out, a silent reminder of the promise he made.

I can't look at him. My eyes move across the aisle, to where the Council members and people I'm assuming are related to my pack are sitting. I recognise the Council leader, Tristan's father. His face is dark as he looks at me, an apology in his eyes. Next to him, Tristan's mother is pale, her lips drawn in as her eyes skate down to land on my bruises.

Can't look at them either. My eyes move to the end of the aisle, waiting for my alphas to appear. They should be here any second.

I wait.

And I wait.

Until the murmuring grows a little louder, worry and concern filling the air. Ollena moves over to me, her face tight. "Sienna. Are you – are you certain they're coming?"

For the first time, fear enters my chest, my heartbeat starting to race. "They're coming. They promised."

My voice sounds desperate, and Ollena nods. "I see. Then we'll wait."

But the minutes tick on, and there's no sign of them. I hold my breath until my chest burns, staring at the doors ahead of me.

When they creak open, my whole body relaxes. They're here. They didn't break their promise.

Except it's not Tristan, Jax, Logan or Gray who steps out onto the aisle. Who walks towards me, a cruel smirk on that painted mouth.

Alicia Erikkson stalks towards me, her face set in false sympathy.

My muscles turn to stone. No.

They wouldn't do this to me.

They *wouldn't*.

My conversation with Gray and Logan filters through the panic in my mind.

She wanted us to Deny you.

This isn't happening. I watch in a daze as Jessalyn jumps back up from her seat, this time my mama right behind her as they head directly for Alicia. I watch the heated argument, Tristan's father and Councilor Erikkson getting up from their seats, Ollena storming down to them, her face turning back around to mine. Paling.

I grip the skirt of the dress Logan had made for me, lifting it as I make my way with careful steps towards Alicia. My hand lands gently on my mother's shoulder, moving her aside as she berates the beta who stands there with victory on her face.

I wet my lips. "Alicia."

"Little omega," she croons. "I'm so sorry to be the bearer of bad news, darling. But Tristan asked me to give you this."

She pulls an envelope from her bag and hands it to me. Everyone around us falls silent as I turn it over, the Cohen crest in crystal clarity holding the contents closed.

My fingers shake as I lift it, the wax cracking as it comes away from the paper.

The note is short, to the point. Clinical, even.

> *The Cohen pack declines to attend the Mating Ceremony.*
> *We have decided that Sienna Michaels is to be Denied.*
> *Our decision is final and binding by law.*
> *Tristan Cohen*

I look up slowly, the paper crumpling in my hand as I stare at Alicia's face. She raises an eyebrow. "Well? Don't keep us all in suspense."

Rather than answer her, I turn, pressing the envelope into Ollena's hands.

I don't feel my knees hit the floor. I don't feel anything except the blinding pain that rips through my insides, searing me from the inside out. I can't breathe for the agony, can't focus on Jessalyn's face as she lands in front of me, the tears in her eyes as she grabs my face, pressing our foreheads together.

"Not happening," she sobs. "They're not doing this to you, Sienna. I won't let them. I won't let them."

Everything is chaos, everyone shouting around me. My parents are both shouting, my mother angrier than I've ever heard her, my sister crying as she crawls into the chaos next to me, her arms wrapping around me.

My heart breaks that little bit more. I didn't know there was anything left to break.

*Elise.*

"Enough!" someone yells. Jessalyn clings to my hand, swearing at whoever tries to move her away. I feel my dad's hand on my shoulder, gently sliding under my arms, lifting me to my feet.

"Courage, sweetheart," he murmurs. "We're going to sort this out."

But my eyes are still drawn to those doors. "They wouldn't do this," I croak. "They wouldn't, dad."

He doesn't say anything, his silent censure clear. He doesn't understand.

I'm lowered into a chair, my mother and father coming to stand on either side of me, Jess behind me as we face the Council.

"An immediate vote," Ollena hisses. "It's well within our power to do so. This is unconscionable!"

"But it is the law," a dry voice interjects. "And for the law to change, Ollena, we require a unanimous vote."

Everyone turns to stare at the speaker.

"Justice Milo." Tristan's father steps forward. He looks at me with an apology in his eyes, and I look away, back to the doors.

They will come. I can *feel* it.

"Surely a majority vote will be more than sufficient," he pushes. "Given the urgency of this situation?"

The Councilor shakes his head. His gray hair is cropped close, his pale eyes grim as they skate across me. "The law is the law, David. It must be unanimous."

Tristan's father sighs. "Fine. This should be sorted reasonably enough. I move to abolish the Denied by-law from the governing laws of Navarre. The motion should be removed from the Bonding Trials process effective immediately. Ollena?"

"Seconded." Ollena's voice is crisp and confident. Tristan's dad nods.

"Elio?" The Health Councilor tries to smile at me, but his brows are too deeply drawn together for him to pull it off. "Agreed."

"I also agree," Councilor Cohen motions to the Justice Councilor. "Milo?"

He hesitates, long enough for Ollena to lose her patience. "Milo, be reasonable!"

He holds up a hand. "The law is the law, even when it is harsh. However, I am not so outdated that I cannot see when a law needs to be repealed. I agree."

My dad squeezes my shoulder, my mom letting out a shuddering sound of relief. Everything still feels hazy, most of my focus still on the doors.

"Erikkson." There's a hesitating note to Tristan's dad's voice, one that makes me finally focus on what's happening in front of me. Because Councilor Erikkson is Alicia's father.

He smiles, a slow, creeping smile that moves across his face like shadows. "As Milo said, the law is the law. However, I'm afraid that I cannot agree with his sentiments. Are we to change every law, every time it doesn't suit one individual? I do not agree."

Ollena steps forward. "Adam," she pleads. "Please."

He purses his lips. "My decision is final."

Tristan's dad looks at me one more time, before he closes his eyes. "The vote is not unanimous. Motion rejected."

Motion rejected.

*I am Denied.*

My shoulders start to shake as I look up at my parents. "Mama? Dad?"

Ollena steps in front of me. "I request a closed Council session to debate the matter further."

Justice Milo looks uncomfortable. "You know that we cannot do that, Ollena. I am truly sorry. But the vote must stand."

"This isn't right," Ollena looks around wildly. "I will not stand for this!"

"Then it is lucky that you are not the one in charge of our laws, Ollena." Councilor Erikkson stands up. His face is full of false sympathy as he takes a step towards me, my parents closing ranks as they move in front of me.

"You," my father says, his voice shaking, "are not taking my daughter anywhere."

Jessalyn leans down while they argue, her breath ghosting my ear. "Get ready, Si. We're going to run. We'll hide somewhere, make a plan."

Her desperation makes my throat ache. I can't run. I can barely even walk, thanks to the pain coursing through me.

"Enough of this," Erikkson snaps. The doors open, a number of Justice officers spilling into the room. My body starts to shake as they move up the aisle, boots crunching over the petals.

"What the hell is this?" Councilor Cohen asks, aghast. "Erikkson!"

"I expected some resistance," Erikkson says. "So I asked some of our Justice force to be on standby, in case they were needed." He tilts his head. "It looks to me like they are."

"Touch her, and I'll kill you," Jessalyn threatens. My hands touch her back as she moves in front of me, touching my mother, my father.

"Stop." The numbness is stealing over the pain, giving me the strength to push to my feet. "Stop this."

I force my eyes away from the doors. They're not coming.

They chose to keep their secrets, to protect Gray and Logan, over me. And as my eyes brush over Alicia, I make my own choice.

"I'll go." My words are quiet, unheard over the shouting that's erupted again.

"I said I'll go!"

My shout finally gets their attention, my parents swinging around to look at me with matching expressions of horror.

"Sienna," my dad says, his voice shaking. "I can fix this."

I shake my head, looking around at the Justice officers. "No, you can't, Dad. And that's okay."

My dad's face crumples, tears spilling down his cheeks. "Sienna."

I push myself forward, wrapping my arms around him. His tears wet my neck, and I wipe them away as I move back.

"A new start, Dad," I whisper. "Don't think of it as an ending."

My mother lets out a single sob. "You're not going anywhere, Sienna. Sit down."

"No, mama." I do the same, wrapping my arms around her and breathing her in, the familiar scent. "Not this time. I have to go."

She shakes under my grip, and I release her to my dad. Jessalyn steps forward.

"I'm going with you," she says firmly. "Nobody can stop me."

I shake my head. "I need you to stay with my parents, Jess. With Elise."

Elise burrows into my side. "You can't go."

Jessalyn tries to pry her away, but Elise clings to me. "You can't go!"

The tears start to come, and I blindly unwrap my sister's arms, peeling her off and pushing her towards Jess. "Love you, 'Lise."

Even Ollena is crying as she steps up to me. "Sienna – I'm so sorry—,"

I hold up my hand. "Not your fault. You didn't make the laws, Ollena."

Ignoring everyone else, I take a few steps forward towards the Justice officers. One of them, stern and expressionless in a blue tunic marked with their emblem, steps out of the line.

"Sienna Michaels," he says abruptly. "As a Denied omega, you are hereby banished from Navarre."

I don't feel anything as he continues.

"You will be escorted across the wall into Herrith. You will take no belongings, and no help will be offered. You are forbidden from entering Navarre again. Do you understand?"

I force my head down. "I understand."

When he takes my arm, I hear shouts behind me. My father is screaming at the Councilors, my mother joining him. Some of the officers move past me, and I glance back as the beta in the tunic starts to pull me away.

My father reaches for me desperately, even as officers push

him back. "Sienna!"

The tears burst out, my breath gasping as I blindly follow the lead of the man pulling me. The doors close behind us, my last glimpse of my family swallowed up.

I try to pull myself together, to make a plan, as I'm pulled through more doorways until the sun hits my face. We're close to the wall, right at the edge of the city, and it looms above me, pale sandstone as tall as an apartment building as they push me forward.

"I can walk," I insist, but they keep hold of me, not responding as we march on.

Ahead of me, giant gates start to slide open, revealing the dark green of the forest on the other side. Panic seizes my limbs. I just need a minute to breathe, to pull myself together.

To say goodbye.

But they keep marching, dragging me forwards until my feet move from warm stone to the cool, damp earth of the forest floor. Sun breaks through the trees in long spears as I'm pushed through the gates of Navarre.

I wait for the ceremony, the pomp.

But there's nothing. As I turn around, the gates are already closing behind me. I make a last, desperate attempt to run, to get through even though I know they'll only push me back.

But it's no use. The gates close anyway, in terrifying finality as the boom sounds through the air.

I hit the wood a moment too late.

I'm locked out of my home.

I sink down to my knees, my breathing shuddering as I fold over the pain consuming me, the separation from my Soul Bonded threatening to tear me in two.

I have lost everything. I have nothing left. And I have no idea what to do now.

Desperate.

Abandoned.

*Denied.*

# DENIED PLAYLIST (IN ORDER)

Find it on Spotify

Breakaway – Avril Lavigne
Bad Things – Jace Everett
Naked – James Arthur
I Don't Wanna See You with Her – Maria Mena
Made to Love You – Dan Owen
PSYCHO – Anne-Marie, Aitch
Million Reasons – Lady Gaga
Say Something – A Great Big World, Christina Aguilera
Look What You Made Me Do – Taylor Swift
Face in the Crowd – Freya Ridings
Jar of Hearts – Christina Perri
Some Kind of Heaven – Sleeping at Last
Boy – Little Mix
Before You Go – Lewis Capaldi
Exile – Taylor Swift, Bon Iver
Believer – Imagine Dragons
Run – Nicola Scherzinger

# A NOTE FROM EVELYN

How are you feeling right now?

I know. I'm SORRY.

Sienna's story continues in the conclusion to the Bonding Trials duet, Devoted.

If you'd like to keep up with the latest news and updates on my releases, or come and discuss all things Bonding Trials related/shout at me for emotional damage caused by my books, come and hang out in my Facebook group, The Evelyn Flood Collective.

If you enjoyed this book, please consider leaving a review on Goodreads or Amazon! Reviews are so, so important for indie authors to help us keep doing what we love.

Thank you!

Evie x

## OTHER BOOKS BY EVELYN FLOOD

### THE OMEGA WAR

Omega Found

Omega Lost

Omega Fallen

## STALK ME!

Newsletter: https://mailchi.mp/449ab054db99/evelynflood
Goodreads: https://www.goodreads.com/evelynflood
Bookbub: https://www.bookbub.com/profile/evelyn-flood
TikTok: https://www.tiktok.com/@evelynfloodauthor
Instagram: https://www.instagram.com/evelynfloodauthor/
Facebook: https://www.facebook.com/groups/evelynflood/

Printed in Great Britain
by Amazon